SO-ADM-456

"Dan Harde ... y about a romance novel into a warm and witty tale of finding love in some very unexpected places. Ingeniously devised and deftly plotted, it unfolds on a richly evoked Central California Coast of vineyards and cattle ranches, in a small town full of charming characters. As the lovers stumble over each other and themselves, this book-with-in-book offers another kind of happy outcome—a reader's delight in being swept away by a good story." —Steven Winn, former Arts and Culture Critic of the *San Francisco Chronicle* and author of *Come Back, Como: Winning the Heart of a Reluctant Dog*

"*Rancho de Amor* by Dan Harder presents many satisfying surprises as his characters strive for success in both life and love. Vulnerable yet strong, they come alive on the pages. This is a wonderful book—and one I expect could make a terrific film!" —Susan Terris, *Familiar Tense*

"This mash-up of literary whodunit, romance, and fish-out-of-water caper defies genres, as Harder whisks us from Manhattan to cowboy country and back again; I'm very happy to have gone along for the ride." —Deborah Bishop, *Hello Midnight, An Insomniac's Literary Bedside Companion*

"Romance, roadkill, and wicked wit—" —Yves Fey, *Floats the Dark Shadow*

"It's a Romance and all, but it's got a good bit of us in there, too." —Brad Lundberg, cattleman/former manager of the Cojo/Jalama Ranches

"Harder masterfully peels back the layers of the rarified publishing world to reveal its—and his—romantic heart." —Susan Vogel, Publisher: Pince-Nez Press, author of *Becoming Pablo O'Higgins*

# RANCHO DE Amor

## BY DAN HARDER

WEST
MARGIN
PRESS

Library of Congress Cataloging-in-Publication Data

Names: Harder, Dan, author.
Title: Rancho de Amor / by Dan Harder.
Description: [Berkeley] : West Margin Press, [2020] | Summary: "In a last-ditch effort to save a New York publishing house facing imminent closure, editor Catherine Doyle travels across the country to the small town of Sisquoc, California, in search of the famous Loretta de Bonnair, an elderly recluse and breakout author of the bestselling self-published romance novel that has the nation in a fervor. Instead, she runs into nothing but dead ends with a handsome cowboy who she's not sure if she should trust"—Provided by publisher.
Identifiers: LCCN 2020014580 (print) | LCCN 2020014581 (ebook) | ISBN 9781513264301 (paperback) | ISBN 9781513264318 (hardback) | ISBN 9781513264325 (ebook)
Subjects: GSAFD: Love stories.
Classification: LCC PS3608.A72528 R36 2020 (print) | LCC PS3608.A72528 (ebook) | DDC 813/.6—dc23
LC record available at https://lccn.loc.gov/2020014580
LC ebook record available at https://lccn.loc.gov/2020014581

Proudly distributed by Ingram Publisher Services.

LSI2020

Published by West Margin Press

WEST
MARGIN
PRESS
WestMarginPress.com

WEST MARGIN PRESS
Publishing Director: Jennifer Newens
Marketing Manager: Angela Zbornik
Project Specialist: Gabrielle Maudiere
Editor: Olivia Ngai
Design & Production: Rachel Lopez Metzger

How could I *not* have written a good romance
while living with and loving you, my ever-inspiring Ora?

# CHAPTER 1

At 6:17 on a cold November morning, Catherine Doyle finally gave up on trying to sleep and decided to confront the situation. She rolled out of bed, wrapped herself in a robe, and sat down at her desk. She was resolved—the relationship was never going to get better, so, instead of letting things stumble toward the inevitable, she would end it with one fell swoop—or, as it were, one irrefutable e-mail. She clicked "compose," typed an address, coughed twice, sniffed once, and began:

> Dear Ralph,
> Love is supposed to be a moving experience, but so is falling off a cliff. Before we hit the ground, I think we should open our parachutes and find something that...

She stopped, searched for what that "something" should be, then shook her head. As a book editor, Catherine was obsessively careful about how things were written, which was one of the reasons she wasn't a writer. She loved to read and, as an editor, help others to improve their writing, but the sloppiness that came with spontaneous creation made her uncomfortable. Reading her own writing was like walking into an art gallery where half of the paintings were hanging crooked on the wall. And she definitely didn't want crooked here. Nothing too angry, nothing too kind, nothing too clever— something simple, clear, and final.

She started over:

> Dear Ralph,
> Last Friday, you said that you felt cramped in serious relationships. Unfortunately, that is exactly what I want: a serious relationship. So, let's amicably call it quits and

5

move on in different directions—without agony, regret,
or endless discussion. Be well in whatever you do,
wherever you do it.
Sincerely,
Catherine

She reread what she'd written, and, satisfied with its clear and terse finality, she sat there for a few seconds in the blue glow of her monitor to let the moment and its implications settle in. Then, slowly and deliberately, Catherine hit the "send" button.

She closed her e-mail, got up, leaned on her desk in a confrontational pose, and announced into the surrounding darkness, "I like how I live and where I live, and I don't need anybody else to make it better."

As if to soften the edges of her declaration, her cat, Emily, gently brushed against her leg.

"Correction"—Catherine kneeled down and tickled Emily's chin—"I don't need anybody but you."

How much of this Emily understood was debatable, but she knew enough to purr.

# Chapter 2

Having gotten up earlier than usual, Catherine was able to take a long, cathartic shower. (She added a few tears to the water down the drain.) After fixing herself half a toasted bagel with jam, she fed her endlessly hungry cat, then strode briskly into a crisp Monday morning toward her favorite supplier of strong caffeine—Bleecker Street Brews.

On the way, she passed one of the few remaining bookstores in the neighborhood. The bookstore owner changed the display in the window every Sunday afternoon, a routine that made walking past this window a whimsical delight on Mondays.

Typically, five to ten different books would be choreographed in a frozen dance of clever commercial seduction—propped on boxes, dangling from strings, lounging on colorful, eye-catching posters. Last week's display had been well timed to attract a New York audience. It was an invitation to fantasize an "escape" from the imminent onslaught of sleet and snow. Decorated with coconuts, palm fronds, beach towels, and insistently sunny dust jackets, the display inspired the bundled pedestrian to imagine Costa Rica, visualize Casablanca, conjure Havana, consider Santa Barbara. Prominent in the middle of the window had been a handmade sign with the existential tease, *You are where your mind takes you. Save yourself $2,000 and fly a book to someplace warm!*

As she walked past the window this morning, Catherine saw that the escapist theme of the previous week had been replaced by an even more strident appeal to escapist fantasy. One book and one book only was on display—the new and wildly popular romance *Rancho de Amor.* Everything in the window had been color coordinated with the loud pink cover of this book. Pink, the frill-trimmed backdrop; pink, the cloth that wrapped the shelves and boxes on which the pink book sat; pink, the cascade of hearts tied

7

to a series of pink strings. Word on the street was that the author, an aging recluse living somewhere in the middle of nowhere out West, had won some sort of prize for *Rancho de Amor*—her very first book—and now, less than a month after publication, it was on its way to becoming the bestselling romance novel in years.

The large and largely unexpected popularity of this book was even evident in Bleecker Street Brews. Catherine counted four people reading it, two of them while dabbing their eyes with napkins. It was good to see people reading, but Catherine couldn't help wishing that more of them would be reading and reacting as passionately to the books that she and her company published, books that she and her coworkers proudly described as "serious new literature," books that she and her coworkers were having an increasingly hard time selling.

The personal repercussions of this fact hit her in the face the moment she walked into work. No sooner had she exchanged pleasantries with Ali, the Banter House Books receptionist, than Ali told her that the boss wanted to see her—first thing.

"Oh..." Catherine nervously said. She loved and was loved at her work, though she knew that more than half the staff at the company had recently been laid off. Would she be next...?

"Don't look so worried," Ali assured her. "Vito would sooner fire himself than fire you. I'll bet he just wants to share his latest scheme."

"You're probably right. Vito should never be allowed to have a weekend off, or we'll have to find him some all-consuming hobby so he doesn't have time to fret and fantasize."

"Something like exotic stamp collecting," Ali suggested.

"Or marathon race training."

"Or, better still"—Ali flashed a wicked grin—"BASE jumping."

"Perfect. No time for scheming, just screaming."

As Ali laughed, Catherine turned and walked to the large, messy office of Vito Di Luca-Bellingham, the president and CEO of Banter House Books, Inc.

# CHAPTER 3

Please—close the door and have a seat," Vito said when Catherine walked in. "I don't want everybody to hear this."

Catherine softly closed the door, gave a quick, nervous pat to a rebellious strand of hair, and took a seat in front of her boss, the maniacally energetic, if not always focused, Vito. In her seven years at Banter House Books, she and Vito had had their ups and downs. The highest point had been four years before, when one of their authors garnered a Pulitzer, another won a National Book Award, and yet another had her book adapted into a film—a book Catherine had been responsible for bringing to Banter House.

The low point had come two years later when Catherine had invited her best friend, Rachel, to meet her newly single boss for dinner. Her good intentions had resulted in a four-night stand of legendary and mutual disappointment. The relationship had begun inauspiciously well. How could they have been so lucky to have found someone so right and essentially right under their noses? What was so right on the first night quickly turned into what was so wrong on the next three nights. The affair had begun with passionate possibility and ended in passionate disputes about everything.

Rivaling this failed effort at matchmaking, however, was the presently slow but seemingly inevitable collapse of Banter House. Admittedly, the possible demise of the company had less to do with Vito's stewardship than with the rapid changes to the book industry as a whole, though Vito was not the best person to navigate such choppy bibliographic seas. He was a scrappy businessman who liked brassy blonds (he'd married and divorced two of them), fast cars (he'd wrecked three of them), and driving hard bargains. Instead of inheriting a publishing house, he should have inherited a chain of distressed hotels. He was far better suited to haggling over the price of shampoo and pillowcases than discussing line breaks and metaphors

9

with temperamental poets. And yet, he did his best to stay the course Grandfather Bellingham had set: "Banter House Books—the publishing company with a heart, a soul, and a discriminating mind," as the company mission statement put it.

For a disconcerting few moments after Catherine had taken her seat, Vito said nothing but looked at her as if measuring her for some impossible mission. Then, from under a pile of papers on his desk, he slowly extracted a copy of a big pink book and held it up for her to see.

"Oh, Vito, not you too..."

He looked perplexed.

"Have you joined New York's collective sentimental swoon over that book?"

"I swoon at the sales numbers for this unknown author's first book." Vito leaned forward and placed the book at the edge of his desk in front of Catherine. "Do you know anything about her?"

"Other than that she is ridiculously popular, no." She picked up the book with a slight frown and gave it a quick glance. "Why?" she asked, then put the book back down as if it were contagious.

"Over the weekend, I was thinking and... well, if we could just find this author and sign her for the publication of pretty much anything she's ever written—poetry, old love letters, even her shopping lists—we could make enough money to keep Banter House afloat for another year or two. And maybe things will have changed for the better in our part of the industry by then. She's the hottest ticket right now, and she's definitely worth pursuing."

"She's a romance writer, Vito, and Banter House has never, ever published a modern romance writer."

"Yes, and Banter House has also never been in such a financial fix before. Have you even read this book?"

"Why would I?"

"Because it might actually be good—or at least half-decent. We know it's incredibly popular."

"And since when has popularity ever been a measure of literary value?"

"Shakespeare hasn't done too badly in the popularity department."

"The man's got name recognition," Catherine tossed back with an impish grin.

Vito reached across his desk and patted the big pink book. "And so does this woman, Loretta de Bonnair."

"But... what would publishing a schmaltzy romance writer do to *our* name recognition? Instead of being known as a publisher on the cutting edge of literature, we'll become just another publisher playing it safe on the dull edge."

"I don't know," Vito mused. "If you push hard enough, even the dull edge can do some cutting. And anyway, we won't have a name to worry about if we're not in business any longer." He stared at her, then smiled broadly.

"So," she asked tentatively, "how should we do this, or at least *try* to do this?"

"We first have to find her, which probably won't be easy. Seems *no one's* found her yet. We know her name, we know she won some contest for older unpublished authors, and she apparently lives in or near the tiny town of Sisquoc, California, but she's got no address, no phone number, no social media connections. My guess is that she's dead and *Rancho de Amor* was published posthumously, or she is one of those wealthy recluses who is embarrassed by all of the public hubbub, or she's living so far out in the woods that the Pony Express hasn't delivered the news of her success to her yet. Whatever is keeping her from being found by anyone makes it possible for us to jump in and maybe get to her first—unless, of course, she *is* dead. Though even then, maybe we could find her desk and see if there isn't an undiscovered manuscript or three in a drawer just waiting to see the light of day."

"But if everybody in publishing is hoping she'll give them a call, how can we hope to compete with companies that can offer her huge advances?"

"Her books will sell no matter who publishes them now, and with the kinds of sales she generates, she won't need to insist on a fat advance. No, what she's going to want is respectability and a legacy she can proudly leave to the grandkids. We all know she can't get that from Blushing Dove Press, and she can't get that with pretty much any other big publisher, but she *can* get that from Banter. All we have to do is ride out West, find her hidden ranch or, for all we know, her condemned double-wide, and convince her we're the ticket to enduring respectability."

"We?" Catherine asked with a hint of concern.

"Well, someone who can relate to an elderly woman who writes romances and convince her that she should care about her literary legacy."

Now more than slightly concerned, Catherine asked, "In other words, you want *me* to ride out there and lasso Loretta...?"

"Look"—he sighed—"I realize I should probably go myself. I am the owner of the company and all, but... well, do you really think I would be the best person to inspire an aging female writer of romances with thoughts of respectability?"

"Ahhh, well..."

"Don't answer that. Face it, you'd have a much better chance of relating to Loretta de Bonnair and convincing her that Banter House will give her the kind of reputation she wants and deserves."

"I'm not so sure about that. I'm not even an acquisitions editor."

"That's just a title. You're the best *editor* I've got."

Catherine sighed, looked down and slowly shook her head, then looked at Vito and asked almost plaintively, "Would I have to be gone for long? Emily doesn't like it when I'm gone for more than a night, and even then, she's not happy."

"I'm sorry to hear it."

"And I really don't like California. The one time I was there, the most memorable thing about it was the sunburn I got—in January!"

"I'm sorry to hear that too. We'll get you some sunscreen this time."

"Oh, don't patronize me, Vito. If it's the only way to save the company and all the people who work for it, I, well, of course I'll go. I've got to say though, this isn't what an editor usually does."

"Not usually, no, but this operation needs your intelligent touch. I'll give you a good, if not lavish, expense account, so find yourself a nice place to stay—"

"In downtown Sis-cum-bah, population thirty-seven," Catherine interjected snidely.

Vito ignored the remark and continued, "You won't need to be away for more than a couple, maybe three, days. And I'll be there, at least virtually, backing you up all the way." Then he leaned toward her and asked, "What d'ya say, kiddo?"

"I don't know, Vito. To be honest, I don't really like romance novels. None of that gushy stuff works for me. To me, diamonds are just overpriced pebbles, roses make me sneeze, and I hate pink. Really, Vito, I don't know what Loretta and I are going to talk about."

"Talk about something romantic. Tell her about your boyfriend."

"*That* is *not* a particularly good topic this morning."

"Ah... sorry. So you and Ralph are..." He raised his hands and made a gesture of someone breaking a baguette in two.

Catherine nodded.

Looking both embarrassed and desperate, he said in a low voice, "Honestly, you don't have to do this, Catherine, if you really don't want to."

"Yes, I do," she said with a resigned smile. "If it will help save one of the last truly adventurous publishing companies in America, of course I have to."

"You know we can't offer de Bonnair much of an advance," Vito admitted, "so we've got to offer her something most writers care more about than money: flattery. So, while you're reading *Rancho*, take notes on anything that's even half-decent about the book: a nice turn of phrase, an interesting transition, a good description of character or place... hell, just a well-placed comma—anything, anything at all we can use to butter up dear de Bonnair and convince her we're the only publisher that really understands her."

"You do know you're asking me to lie..."

"Maybe it won't be a complete lie. Ms. de Bonnair might actually surprise us. I'm going to start reading the book tonight, and, who knows, maybe it won't be so bad."

Catherine grimaced. "I'm not good with make-believe, but for the sake of Banter, I'll pretend to like her and her ridiculously pink book." She got up, lifted *Rancho de Amor* from Vito's bill-cluttered desk, gave him the kind of wave an astronaut might give before stepping into her space capsule, and walked out of his office. She considered removing the dust jacket to hide that irrepressibly pink cover, then thought better of it. If she was going to commit herself to this dubious expedition, better to commit boldly.

13

# CHAPTER 4

Skeptical about Vito's impulsive scheme but diligent in her efforts to play along, Catherine read the most recent review of *Rancho de Amor* in the *Washington Post*:

> By now, it is clear that no book since *Fifty Shades of Grey* has swept the country as completely as *Rancho de Amor*. It's a rip-roaring Western; it's a passionate ROMANCE in capital letters; it's a bigger-than-life drama that plays out on the formerly Spanish coast of California; and it's a grand literary success. Oh, Ms. de Bonnair, whoever you are, wherever you are, keep those books coming!

She looked up from her screen and argued with the air, "Well, of course Stacy Bornstein would write that. A novel like *Rancho de Amor* gives her the perfect excuse to be her most overblown self!"

True as that was, Ms. Bornstein wasn't wrong. No one could argue with the fact that Ms. de Bonnair's book had, indeed, had the most successful first four-week sales of any romance since *Fifty Shades of Grey*—if *Fifty Shades* could really be called a romance. It was also true that whoever and wherever the author might be was a mystery. Apparently, the only piece of tantalizing evidence was a letter signed by a woman named Loretta de Bonnair and postmarked from Sisquoc, California. And so, before she left work, Catherine booked a flight for early the next morning to LA and, finding that there were no regular hotels in the area, reserved a room at a quaint-sounding and reasonably priced B&B.

After an exhaustingly long cab ride home through rush-hour Manhattan traffic snarled by wind and rain, Catherine took off her coat, shook the water onto her landing, then opened her door to the strident yowl of her cat. "Hello, my spoiled little beast. I'm sorry I'm a little late. Business—weird, weird business... so let's get you a treat then see if your favorite buddy is available to pamper you for a couple of days."

Although Catherine had a wide net of supportive friends, they tended to be better at caring for the passionate and profound than the practical. Long conversations well into the night about boyfriends imminent or just past were easier to manage than opening cans of cat food and cleaning kitty litter boxes. And so, Catherine called her father and asked if he would mind looking after Emily "...just for a couple of days. I've got to go out to LA on a very last-minute business trip."

"I wouldn't mind at all," Jonathan Doyle reassured his daughter. "Emily and I get along *purrrfectly*. I pamper her and she pretends to like me, so I pamper her some more, and she pretends to like me even more."

"So that's why she was two pounds heavier when I came back from Maine last August, and I'd only been gone for four days."

"She may have been a bit heavier, but she was happy," her father replied in a self-satisfied tone.

Catherine's father was a stately widower of sixty-four who dressed in bowtie and tweeds and owned an antiquarian bookstore in Midtown. He specialized in naval architecture, exotic sea life, and erotic memoirs—all chosen for practical bookselling purposes. His personal preference in literature, however, was the modern spy novel. He loved equivocal situations where good and bad were simply different degrees of gray, but where those differences were always potentially deadly.

"So why is Vito sending you out to California?" he asked.

"A brief little suicide mission. He wants me to go out to some tiny town outside of LA, find Loretta de Bonnair, and sign her with Banter."

"I hate to ask, but... who is Loretta Debonair?"

"Really, Dad, you're in the book business and you haven't heard of Loretta de Bonnair yet?"

"I'm in the antiquarian book business. Has she written an old and rare book?"

"No, though I hear she's pretty old and rare herself. She wrote *Rancho de Amor*."

Humorously horrified, her father exclaimed, "That ubiquitous pink book?!"

"Yup. And I'm supposed to find her and bring her into the Banter House stable of important modern authors."

"A romance writer at Banter? This *is* a suicide mission. Isn't Vito concerned about Banter's reputation?"

"Not very. He's more concerned about our plummeting sales. If I can find this heralded hermit and convince her that Banter will confer upon her a better reputation than the other romance publishers can ever hope to offer, maybe we can stay in business a little longer, but what that will do to *our* reputation is not something I want to think about."

"I must say, *Rancho de Amor* is a stunningly bad title in a seductive sort of way. And her name, Loretta Debonair or whatever it is, *has* to be a pseudonym."

"Pseudonym, pseudo-literature, and my pseudo-mission is to find her. Nobody even knows exactly where she lives. I don't think anyone in the book business has even met her."

"Really? Well, well, such mysterious details *are* intriguing. You say she lives in some small town and no one knows her?"

"They say she lives on a ranch outside of a tiny town. She's undoubtedly well known to cows and buzzards but unknown to everyone else. You know, it wouldn't be so bad if I hadn't just broken up with Ralph, but the idea of having to read a sappy romance novel and schmooze with its author about 'love' is the last thing I want to do right now."

"I'm sorry things didn't work out for you and Ralph. He seemed like a promising chap."

"He wasn't," Catherine replied like a slammed door.

"Well... then you should try to make your trip to the middle of nowhere as much of an adventure as you can. It is the Wild West, after all."

"All I want is to get back to the Mild East as soon as I can. Thanks for taking care of Emily. Knowing she'll be fine is a big relief."

"We'll have a grand old time. And whatever happens, text me and let me know how you're getting on. I might even do some sleuthing on the Internet and see what I can find out about this Loretta person."

"That would be great, Dad. Love you, and see you soon."

She started to pack but realized quickly that she had no idea how she should dress for this odd adventure. The only thing she knew for sure was that she was going West—*way* West—into sartorial circumstances she was not prepared for. What did one wear in weather potentially ranging from cold and wet downpours to heat waves when meeting an aging female romance writer who may just also be a cattle rancher? This whole crazy escapade was twisting her well out of both her comfort zone and her closet.

As she held up a series of disappointing choices before a mirror in her bedroom, she realized that the challenge was less that she didn't have anything to fit the occasion but that *she* didn't fit the occasion. Catherine was a twenty-eight-year-old woman with long dark hair, large brown eyes, full lips, a pretty face, and a shapely figure, although at that moment of self-conscious cataloging, she wasn't so sure about any of it: her bones seemed a little too large, her hair seemed a little too wild, her skin seemed a little too pale, her eyes a little too round, her cheeks a little too wide. After confronting these exaggerated defects in the mirror, she moved on to other, more obvious reasons that she was the wrong woman for this job.

For one, she didn't like romance novels, Western or otherwise, and, with the exception of books by Austen and the Brontë sisters, she never read them. To her, they offered little more than a collection of unrealistic characters pirouetting through unrealistic plots toward unavoidably happy endings. And yet, she was now expected to flatter a writer of this sort of romantic froth and get her to sign a book contract with a publishing company known for its discriminating taste.

And then there was California. The most memorable part of her one and only trip to the Golden State was the sunburn she'd cooked into her skin while sitting at an outside café with fellow book editors— *in the middle of winter*. And she wasn't just going to California; she was expected to find someone somewhere in cowboy country. Had she been a six-year-old boy, this might have been a dream adventure, but Catherine found nothing particularly interesting, attractive, or compelling about either cows or the men and women who pushed them around.

The most annoying thought, however, was that this really wasn't her job. She wasn't an *acquisitions* editor, she was a *copy* editor who much preferred working with improving contract-settled manuscripts than searching for that tiny shiny needle in the immense haystack of mediocre prose. In short, had the mission she'd been given not been so vitally important to her job, to the job of her many and much-loved coworkers, and to the very survival of Banter House Books, she wouldn't have agreed to her boss's request that she fly out to California and look for a reclusive romance writer in some isolated cow pasture.

But she *had* said yes, and now she could do nothing but pack a few marginally acceptable pieces of clothing, her toiletries, a small container of Dramamine, two phone chargers (she invariably lost at least one wherever she went), and four books—the biggest and pinkest being a copy of *Rancho de Amor*. She would do what she told Vito she would do. And anyway, she briefly reflected, whatever it was, it was going to be different, which meant it would push Ralph and her own romantic disappointments out of her mind for a few days. With that thought in mind and her bag ready to grab before the crack of dawn the next morning, she rushed out to join a handful of friends at their monthly book group.

# CHAPTER 5

Catherine wriggled out of her wet coat and announced while walking into Rachel's Upper West Side flat, "Sorry I'm late, and I'll have to leave early, but at least I made it."

Arriving late to book group was intriguing enough, but to arrive late and say you'd have to leave early? Questions from the assembled group were inevitable:

"Where are you going?"

"Why?"

"And with whom?"

Methodically, Catherine replied, "California for a couple of days, for business, and alone. I've got to go out to the middle of nowhere and find an aging romance writer my boss desperately wants to publish."

Catherine took her place on a pillow on the floor. Even if a chair had been empty, she'd have taken the floor in order to be closer to Rachel's untiringly friendly chocolate lab, Coco. As Catherine settled on the pillow and scratched Coco's back, Rachel brought her up to speed with where they were in the discussion of this month's book, Vivian Gornick's *The End of the Novel of Love*. "We've just landed on the line that 'Love comes as something of an anti-climax,' and I was saying that the problem, as I see it, is that love, in literature, doesn't really move or challenge us these days, and that's because we don't *allow* love to move and challenge us in our real lives."

This was a comment to which everyone had something to add in quick, enthusiastic succession:

"Because we've read too much."

"Dreamed too much."

"Seen too much."

"Done too much."

"We're jaded and tired of the whole friggin' thing."

"Except as a sentimental memory."

"And that's Gornick's point, I think."

"The *anti*climax."

"Metaphorically."

"And sometimes literally, if that's all there is to love."

"Yes."

"Which it isn't, even when it looks like it is."

"Which is why, well..." Catherine paused to gather her thoughts before wading into the subject. "I don't know... I just think we need to let ourselves want *more* out of love."

"Which makes it less easy to find..."

"But less easy to forget."

"Like it was in the good old days."

"Which weren't particularly *good* for women."

"You got that, girl, though in fiction, at least, the men were *so* much more interesting."

"Ah, Rochester. Where are you now?"

"Dead."

"Before he even had a chance to be alive!"

"But such a good fantasy."

"Where are the Brontës when we need 'em?"

"Dead."

"And instead, what do we get today?"

"Loretta de Bonnair!"

"And her big pink book."

"*Rancho de Amor.*"

To which Catherine replied with an innocent, task-focused question, "But, if anyone's read it, what do you think of the writing?"

No one answered. Although her book group friends were easy and honest in their conversations about most things, to admit that any of them had read—and maybe even liked—a popular romance was taking candor a bit too far.

"Have *you* read it?" asked three voices in jagged unison.

"Not yet, no, but... Loretta de Bonnair's the author I'm supposed to track down in California."

There was a general expression of sympathy and well wishing, after which the conversation slid quickly sideways to other subjects, specifically to the new Vietnamese-Italian restaurant in the Flatiron called Pho and Fettuccini, the new incomprehensible exhibit at the Guggenheim, improbable heroes in the movies, unsung heroines in real life, and George Clooney—would you have married him if you could? Blessedly, no more was said about *Rancho de Amor*.

After a break for nibbles and drinks, the conversation returned to the book of the month. Though present only in print, Ms. Gornick inspired an energetic discussion. Catherine was able to stay for most of the rest of the discussion but had to leave while the group debated one final question: why is a novel about love not taken as seriously as a novel about war? As she stood up to leave, Rachel offered a provocative answer. "Because we're so much more afraid of love than of death. We have to trivialize it to handle it."

Catherine smiled broadly and said, "I'm not sure I agree, but I'm not sure I disagree either. I'm sorry I can't stay and wrestle with it, but I've got to catch an early morning flight to LA."

"Don't stay out there too long, honey," Rachel cautioned. "You've got to be back for the year-end party. I'm going to Zabar's to get a monumental nosh, but you make the best hummus in the world, so, if you could..."

"Absolutely. Love to."

"And let us know how it's going, or at least how it went out West."

"When I get back from the land of barbed wire, mindless violence, and swaggering cowboys, I'll text you the gory details." Catherine gave a quick wave from the door and was gone.

# CHAPTER 6

How Ms. de Bonnair had become such a phenomenon was itself a mystery. Not only was this author a complete unknown, but the details of the contract she had signed with Blushing Dove Press were equally unknown and seemingly unknowable. All that was known for sure were the terms of the prize she'd already won: five hundred dollars and publication of two thousand hardbound copies of the book. Since its original publication, however, another seven hundred thousand copies of the book had been printed and sold. With a few good reviews, some splashy PR, and a lot of Internet buzz, *Rancho de Amor* had quickly become a phenomenal moneymaker for Blushing Dove.

But was Loretta getting any of that money? Had she renegotiated her original deal? The rumor was that Blushing Dove got it all, and Loretta, instead of receiving the hundreds of thousands of dollars she would have received had she been paid royalties, was given nothing more than the five-hundred-dollar prize money. This was just conjecture, however, and wishful conjecture on the part of any publisher interested in giving Ms. de Bonnair a better deal on her next sure-to-be-successful book. Predictably, Blushing Dove was quiet about everything including any details about where she might live and what deals they might or might not have with her. But their silence was, itself, adding to everyone's interest. Why would a publisher want to keep its best publicity tool in a drawer? No book tours, no Oprah, no NPR? Something was up.

The only way to find out what was going on would be to go out to California and find Ms. de Bonnair, if she could be found, and talk to her directly. If conditions were right, a new deal for a new book with a new publisher might just be possible. With the first phenomenal sales numbers having just been cited in *Publishers Weekly*, there was plenty of motivation to find her, though it seemed that no one had yet put boots, or heels, on the cow pies of California in a calculated effort to do just that. Vito's hope was that they would be the first to traipse through pastures and poke around barns, and Catherine was his designated and intrepid detective.

Although she was far from sure she'd ever meet the woman, Catherine planned to read Ms. de Bonnair's book quickly, though completely, before whatever meeting might possibly occur. To that end, she pulled her copy of *Rancho de Amor* out of her bag at the Newark Airport the next morning and prepared to dive into its shallow depths. She had arrived at the airport with enough time to start reading, but before she'd even finished the first page, it was announced that her flight to Los Angeles was going to be indefinitely delayed for unspecified reasons (rumor at the terminal was that it was a TSA issue of some sort). In order to arrive in little Sisquoc in time to claim her room at the local B&B, she would need to put together a series of short-hop flights. It wasn't a difficult task, but it did disrupt her reading plans. She would spend more time taking off, landing, and dashing from one gate to the next in Cincinnati, Denver, Albuquerque, and finally LA than quietly reading at thirty thousand feet.

Because everyone on her initial flight had to scramble to find other ways to Los Angeles, a number of her original Newark companions remained companions throughout. This gave her a chance from time to time to watch and wonder: who were they, and why were they going to LA? That muscular sixty-year-old in a tight T-shirt and ponytailed gray hair (he owned, she was sure, a skateboard factory in Los Angeles); that young, tall, bespectacled Black man carrying an elegant briefcase (a recent Harvard law school grad on his way to join a West Coast case); that well-tanned Eurasian woman with the Louise Brooks haircut and oversized jewelry (a hairstylist for a reality TV show); and that twenty-something woman with thick russet-colored hair wearing a tight skirt and carrying a small pink suitcase and matching carry-on (she *had* to be a rising editor at a New York–based fashion magazine on her way to Hollywood to secure a photo shoot with the celebrity of the day).

The other common companion she noticed in every airport and on every flight was the big pink book she had in her hand. To her, it seemed that every third person was reading it, and everyone reading it seemed to be moved by the experience. Some dabbed their eyes with tissues, some looked up with dreamy expressions, others would suddenly look shocked and shake their heads with profound concern for something they'd just read.

Before Catherine had gotten very far into the book, these theatrical expressions seemed ridiculous. But by the end of her hop to Denver, Catherine, though much less demonstrative than most of her sniffling neighbors, began to understand their reactions. *Rancho de Amor* wasn't half as bad as she'd hoped it would be. In fact, it was more than half-decent.

But why? she wondered as she stared out the window while flying across the brown tones of the Mojave Desert.

It certainly wasn't the thematic depth and breadth, although Ms. de Bonnair did wander into some intriguing, even controversial topics—like the conflict between private property and public concerns, and the disastrous conflicts between Anglo, Hispanic, and Native cultures.

Nor was it the depth of character, although the main character, Isabella Guerrero, was, if not a particularly complex character, at least a character with interesting complications, and the man she loved was, for an erstwhile pirate, surprisingly appealing.

And it wasn't even the plot, although that plot had more enjoyable twists and turns than a country lane in the Berkshires. De Bonnair kept her readers busy with the exciting, if improbable, exploits of an honorable pirate, a dishonorable general, a kindly though compromised priest, and a beautiful, dutiful daughter in love with a man she was forbidden to see.

No, what caught her attention and held it was the tone of the narrator, a sort of jaunty, almost athletic intelligence, nimble but sure-footed with lines and insights that surprised her and which, for professional reasons, she would occasionally circle:

> Wanting not only to *be* but to *look* like the man who held another man's life in his hands, the newly appointed local magistrate, Don Domingues, tugged at the lapels of his borrowed robes and tried, unsuccessfully, to pull them together over his irreducible girth. The former magistrate, whose robes these had been, was a much smaller man, and the far more capacious robes Domingues had ordered from

Madrid six months before had yet to arrive.

Giving up on distinguished appearance, Domingues leaned over the bar heavily and addressed the defendant in a supercilious tone, "And how do you plead... *Sir?*"

"Guilty of everything but malicious intent. I shot a man who'd shot at me—and he died. I ordered my men to ransack the Orlando house for any valuables we could sell for provisions. I am a traitor to Spain and a confrere of those who fight for an independent Mexico. And I am guilty of loving someone who is forbidden to love me. I am yours to do with as you will, Your Lordship... *Sir.*" To this, the audience in the overcrowded gallery reacted with a mix of jeers and cheers, gasps of disbelief, revulsion, pity, and even a tear or two.

The forbidden one, however, did not cry. She had done more than enough of that already. Stoically, she sat unmoved, though her heart and mind were racing.

That the first few chapters of de Bonnair's romance were written with fairly engaging, even compelling prose came as a relief. To do her job, Catherine would have to meet the author of this book. Now she wouldn't have to lie about liking at least parts of the first third of the book. She even thought that she might end up liking the aging hermit who had written it.

But she would have to find this talented hermit first, and that part of the process was not beginning well. She finally got into LA at four in the afternoon, a good five hours later than she'd expected to get there. And then there was the issue of getting out of Los Angeles. Catherine didn't do much driving in New York, and when she did, she was a cautious conductor, at least until she got comfortable and forgot that she should be cautious. The San Diego Freeway has rarely inspired comfort. Initially her greatest concern was why, when all the signs said that the speed limit was sixty-five, everyone in the slow lane was traveling at seventy-five miles per hour. She couldn't even guess how fast the maniacs in the left lanes were going. Everyone was forced to race whether they wanted to or not. The one good thing about this was that she could now make up for lost time in her pursuit of Loretta de Bonnair.

# CHAPTER 7

An hour later and approaching signs for Newport Beach, however, Catherine began to wonder if she were actually hurtling in the right direction. Before leaving New York, she'd Googled directions to Sisquoc. It was somewhere to the north of LA. But as she sped down the 405 she saw that Newport Beach was to her right, which meant that the Pacific Ocean was to her right, which meant that she was—and had been for over an hour—going south. She pulled off the freeway to ask for directions. To her dismay, she discovered that, indeed, she'd driven an hour and fifteen minutes toward San Diego and, if taken by a sudden urge to continue much further, Patagonia.

She took a deep breath, girded herself for the race back north, and pulled back onto the freeway going in the opposite direction, discovering that her concern about excessive speed was no longer an issue. Traveling north on the 405 at 5:15 p.m. was anything but "rushed." From Newport Beach up to and through Santa Barbara, Catherine moved more like an 8 a.m. taxi on Broadway than a driver on a West Coast autobahn. From LAX to Sisquoc, her trip should have taken two and a half hours. Instead, it took close to five hours. When she finally reached Santa Barbara, she needed to take a highway up and over some mountains and down to Sisquoc at the east end of the Santa Ynez Valley. At first, this highway seemed like an extension of the freeway—two lanes each way, divided, relatively straight, and well lit, but it soon narrowed to one lane going each way, became incredibly steep and curvy, lost its lane divider, and went dark. At about this time, Catherine also began to see warning signs: *DEER CROSSING, STEEP GRADE, FALLING ROCKS, CATTLE ON ROAD*, and at the crest, right after a sign pointing to Chumash Cave Road, she drove past another sign where the only words of which she could read while whizzing past were *WARNING! MOUNTAIN LIONS IN...*

From the crest, the drive down into the night-dark valley wasn't without its challenges as well. She had to swerve to avoid a skunk and, a mile later, had to swerve to avoid a raccoon. She saw that other drivers had not been so careful, or the animals so lucky. Before getting to Sisquoc, she counted at least seven animals, including a deer, mangled and dead on the side of the road.

Catherine was relieved finally to turn off the dark highway and into the town of Sisquoc, where her room at Violet's Bed and Breakfast would presumably be waiting. Not only was it described on the Internet as "the cutest darn place for a cozy bed and a good cup of coffee West of the Rockies," but all of the rooms were meticulously decorated to recall various details of famous romantic novels including the Flame and the Flower Room, the Pride and Prejudice Room, and the Outlander Room. Unfortunately, this "cutest darn place" with the book-inspired rooms required guests to check in before 10 p.m. When Catherine arrived at 10:17, she found the front door locked. Far too tired to want to go anywhere else, Catherine insistently rang the bell until a large woman in a purple robe glided through the dark and opened the door. Neither scowling nor smiling, she said in a calm voice, "You must be Catherine from New York, and you're a bit late."

"I'm sorry. I... well, I got lost."

"I understand," said the woman in the robe, "I really do, but I just gave the last room to another woman from New York."

"Oh," Catherine said and paused briefly, wanting to contest what she knew was incontestable. Knowing it was both fruitless and impolite to fight, she asked simply, "Do you know if there is anything else available in the area?"

The woman sighed, stared at a very dejected and very tired Catherine, and said, "In a real pinch, we occasionally offer my husband's workroom in the back, and seeing that the NRA convention in Buellton has filled all the hotels in the area, this is probably one of those occasions. I must say, the room does have one of the best beds in the house. We call it the Lazarus Room."

"Is that the title of a novel? I hate to say it, but I've never heard of it."

"No, dear. Our newest room is the Rancho de Amor Room. Lazarus is, well, just a joke between me and my husband."

"You have a Rancho de Amor Room, as in...?"

27

"The novel. Yes. By Loretta de Bonnair. She's our newest local celebrity." Violet beamed.

"I'm sorry I didn't reserve that one, although I guess I'd have lost that one too, arriving as late as I am."

"Yes, you would have lost it, if you'd been lucky enough to reserve it in the first place. We started to advertise it two weeks ago, and it's now reserved six months in advance," Violet said with pride.

"So, you say the Lazarus Room has a very nice bed?" Catherine asked with resigned interest.

"Yes, certainly one of the most comfortable, and the bathroom's right across the hall."

"It's dark, it's late, I don't know where I am, so Lazarus and its comfortable bed sound very good to me right now. Why, by the way, is it called 'Lazarus'?"

"Like I said, it's a little joke. You'll see when you walk in. So come, come... and let's get you settled."

"That would be great, though before I get too settled, I'd really like to eat something. Is there any place open where I can get a salad or something?"

"In this town at this hour, I think you'll have better luck with something other than a salad. I sometimes have leftovers from the little things I bake for evening snacks, but tonight, all of my lavender shortbreads were devoured. Not a one left. We have a very pleasant single man staying here tonight, but men, particularly if not accompanied by a woman, tend eat everything in sight—even if they're not hungry."

Although not sure this observation was right, Catherine nodded politely in assent.

"About the only place open at this hour is the Black Barn, which is not probably the best place for a single young woman from out of town, but it does have what some people call food. Save plenty of room for breakfast though. It's at least as famous as our book-inspired beds."

Catherine took the room, sight unseen, and Violet Smith, as she introduced herself, offered her a little discount. "Your room is a bit less romantic but certainly more curious than my other rooms. And it's very convenient. As I said, the bathroom is right across the hallway."

Catherine took the key Violet proffered, thanked her, moved her two bags into the plush common room, then went out in search of something edible "other than a salad."

The Black Barn was four blocks away, not far at all, except that this little town either couldn't afford or, for whatever reason, didn't want to light its streets. But for a few anemic porch lights on a few houses, nothing lit her way until she rounded the corner onto Cota Road, the main street in town, and the light from the Black Barn burst into view like a luminescent blood blister. Its lurid red lights did not look very inviting, but this was clearly the only place still open where one might get a meal.

As she was about to walk up the steps to the Black Barn, the saloon doors were suddenly flung open by a tall man in a cowboy hat.

An unexpected act of gallantry?

Hardly.

The man was in the process of leaving the Black Barn as quickly as he could—backward. Catherine stared, open-mouthed, as he tumbled down the three stairs and onto the street.

There had been a slight "altercation," a barroom brawl, more precisely, and this unfortunate customer was on his way out, having been propelled by a well-placed punch. With a grunt, he slowly got up, dusted himself off, picked up his hat, and started back up the steps. Noticing Catherine, his eyes widened as he quickly glanced from head to toe, then, after giving his jaw a rub, he smiled and said, "Pardon, ma'am. We're just having a little bit of fun inside. The food's good too, if you're in the mood for some local beef." He smiled again, winced, and this time gallantly opened the doors for her.

Catherine stood there for a moment, unable to respond. Mindless violence and swaggering cowboys indeed, but with two of the most penetrating blue-gray eyes she'd ever seen set in a tan, handsome face. Momentarily stunned in more ways than one, Catherine paused, cleared her throat, and lied politely, "No, thank you. I... I've already eaten."

"What a shame. Well then, maybe tomorrow. Have a good night." With that, the man dove back into the restaurant. Loud cheers exploded from the Black Barn as Catherine pivoted then walked toward the only other significant light in the distance—a gas station with a convenience store.

# CHAPTER 8

With a mushy banana, a Baby Ruth, and a Diet Coke in hand, Catherine walked back from the convenience store to Violet's Bed and Breakfast. Instead of going straight to her room, she turned the light on in the common room, sat down on an overstuffed divan, and spread her sumptuous meal on a low antique table.

Violet seemed to have let her name guide most of her aesthetic decisions. Violet, or its close approximation, was the predominant color of the rug, the walls above the wainscoting, the shades on the lamps, the upholstery of the chairs and the divan on which Catherine now sat, and even the doilies on which she had placed her food and drink.

After devouring the banana and candy bar (she was hungrier than she'd thought), Catherine went up to a large bookshelf to peruse the collection. Looking at someone's books was usually the first thing Catherine did whenever she entered a room, if, of course, the room had any books. It was a sort of silent, preliminary conversation with the person whose books were on display. To scan the shelves was to get answers to a whole host of introductory questions: Who are your heroes? What do you dream of doing or being? What's bugging you these days and what is your political inclination? Catherine's second biggest complaint about the e-book phenomenon, after, of course, its chastening effect on her part of the publishing industry, was that it hid all of this personal information away from view. Most books were on bookshelves because someone wanted to read them, not show them, and in that sense they were more revealing of a person's taste, predilections, even obsessions. The bookshelves in Violet's B&B displayed their owner's unabashed obsession with hardbound abandon. Even from a distance, Catherine could see what genre was the most popular. Romances in red, purple, or pink dust jackets filled the shelves, with such titles as *Impossible Paradise*, *Miss Understood*,

*The Flame and the Flower*, and numerous well-read copies of *Rancho de Amor*.

Whether or not Loretta de Bonnair actually lived in the area, she was clearly popular at Violet's place. And why not, Catherine asked herself. Ms. de Bonnair allowed various locals to bask in the glory of geographic association, and Violet was indulging in this to benign excess. While staring at the spine of de Bonnair's garishly pink book, Catherine couldn't help admiring the author. After all, she'd really *done* something in her life. She'd written a better-than-half-decent book. Maybe they'd end up sitting on a warm porch sipping tea and talking about Jane Austen if she could ever find her. That was the overwhelming challenge: finding Loretta de Bonnair. At this thought, Catherine heaved a sigh, swallowed the last swig of her Diet Coke, turned off the light, and went in search of something a little easier to find—her room.

Carrying her book bag over her left shoulder and dragging her suitcase with her right hand, she couldn't avoid brushing or bumping every door on her way down the narrow hallway. When she finally got to the door, she turned the key, pushed, looked inside, and stifled a scream.

"Lazarus" all of a sudden made sense.

Stamp collecting and birdwatching aren't terribly exciting hobbies, but neither are they particularly frightening. The hobby of taxidermy, however, is in a different category. And Ezekiel Smith, husband of Violet Smith, was interested in a particular aspect of the hobby: fresh roadkill which he liked to freeze in attitudes of vicious aggression or terrified flight. Had Catherine thought she could easily find a different room in a different establishment, she would have left right then and there, but it was too late and she was too exhausted to be looking for an alternative in an area she knew nothing about. She accepted Lazarus as her room of last resort.

Catherine slowly turned around and took in the décor of her unique accommodations. Hawks, crows, and ravens hung from thin wires—their wings fully spread, their talons extended, frozen in the moment just before they grabbed some hapless prey. Coyotes, possums, raccoons, squirrels, field mice, two deer, a bobcat, and a mountain lion leered, lunged, or cowered in every corner of the room. There were only two surfaces in the room that were free of any fierce or frightening specimens: an incongruous chest freezer against a side wall and a surprisingly large and attractive bed against another wall. It was to this island of comfort that she turned for some measure of shelter. She lifted her suitcase onto the foot of the bed and aligned it to provide at least psychological protection from the stuffed creatures lined up along the opposite wall.

When she got into bed, she quickly closed her eyes, sure that she would soon be asleep, and sure that she didn't want to glance at any of the creatures glaring at her from the shadows. Unfortunately, exhausted as she was, she did not fall immediately to sleep. Various aspects of the day replayed themselves in her mind—the four flights, the realization she'd driven for over an hour in the wrong direction, and the unsettling image of a handsome blue-eyed cowboy landing at her feet after being violently expelled from the only restaurant in town.

Worse than these upsetting recollections was the fact that, tired as she was, she just couldn't keep her eyes shut. Every minute or two, she would squint through one eye at the beasts surrounding her bed. She knew they were all dead and couldn't possibly move, but... she did want to keep an eye on them just in case. After about half an hour of bouncing back and forth between the unpleasant things in her head and the unpleasant things surrounding her, she gave up on the idea of sleep, sat up, and confronted the morbid menagerie.

Staring at this display, she went from disgust to pity and eventually to an odd sort of recognition. As she gazed at an aloof little weasel, the face of Ralph Kuzac, her most recent romantic failure, seemed to grow out of and into its shape. It was a surprisingly good fit. She quickly glanced at another animal to see what would happen. It didn't take long for the face of a fat, crafty, and blessedly dead raccoon to become the countenance of the emotional kleptomaniac Peter Amadole—a man she'd dated seven months before. She surrendered to this transformative indulgence, and soon she was looking from one taxidermic portrait to the next: Gene Schmidt was a frightened squirrel; Shane McGregor, an indifferent feral pig; Josh Levinson was the flesh-tearing hawk; and the three Bobs she'd dated years before became, in turn, a fence-sitting crow, an aggressively confused possum, and a skunk. No wonder she was increasingly disheartened by dating. She was finding that books were usually better than boyfriends and a lot easier to put down when they weren't.

As she lay there reviewing this rogues' gallery of her ill-fated love life in the faces of various stuffed animals, she let herself sink into an all-too-familiar feeling. She wanted to blame others for her failures but, as always, ended up blaming herself. She'd already begun to realize that there was something inevitable—frighteningly inevitable—about the shape of her relationships. Curious though cautious, she would wade in a little ways and assess the risks before taking the plunge. Thus far, she'd only really plunged once, and, luckily, because the water hadn't been very deep, she'd been able to drag herself to safety quickly enough. Her safe, sane, and settled expectations wouldn't let her plunge past concern and into passion's most dangerous and desirable depths.

Some of it was because, between the ages of nineteen and twenty-two, she'd focused her attentions on her mother, terminally ill with breast cancer. During and for a while after this ordeal, she didn't have the emotional reserve to indulge any other passions.

Some of it was because she thought too much. It's not that she didn't feel things, and sometimes felt them very deeply, but she tended not to feel her way through things but to *think* her way through things.

And some of it was because of her demanding expectations— high hopes built on high standards that were not easily met. The result was that though Catherine had been in love before, she had never *fallen* in love and lost herself in its passionate yearning, confusion, and delight. At that moment, alone in a strange bed in a strange town late at night, surrounded by a ghoulish reminder of her romantic disappointments, the prospects of wading into anything romantic seemed very unappealing.

Eventually, Catherine drifted into a sleep troubled by a dream. In it, she was driving down a dark country lane, lost, while various small animals held up road signs that seemed to lead her deeper and deeper into darkness. Just as a huge black bear loomed up out of the darkness and started to run at her swerving car with a stop sign dripping with blood, she woke up with a start. Someone—or something—was opening the door to her room. Terrified, she pulled the covers up to her eyes and squinted at the door as a large raccoon began to glide sideways into the room. She gasped, the raccoon froze in midair, and a gloved hand reached out and flipped on the light.

Ezekiel Smith was home from the evening's hunt with a bit of fresh roadkill. He was carrying his newest project into his workroom, intending to place it in the chest freezer. The next day, he would take it out to gut and dry. Violet had not informed her husband, however, that someone would be sleeping in Lazarus.

"Oh... Oh," Ezekiel stammered, "I, um, I didn't know anybody was in here tonight. My wife didn't tell me and, um, well, it's not often anyone's in here, except for my, well, my stiff little friends."

"Violet said it was the only room left. I'm sorry, I didn't realize it was also your..." Catherine trailed off, still breathless with surprise.

"No, no, I'm sorry. I'll just wrap up my new friend and put him... well, put him in the freezer. Sorry for the... the, ah, surprise." So stuttering, Ezekiel quickly wrapped the racoon in one of the plastic bags next to the freezer, gently put the wrapped package in the chest, and backed out of the room. With a quiet click of the door, he was gone.

Catherine slipped back onto her pillow and lay there blinking at the ceiling for a while. Realizing that her dreams, unpleasant as they might continue to be, were easier to take than her present reality, she closed her eyes and willed herself into oblivion.

# Chapter 9

The next morning, Catherine kept her eyes closed until she was prepared to see what she knew she would see by the dawn's eerie light. She reminded herself that those creatures that would be staring at her were all quite dead. They couldn't hurt her, and so she opened her eyes slowly to confront the macabre scene. Blinking the sleep out of her eyes, she looked around the room. Instead of being either frightened or offended, she became more and more sad as she looked at the animals in the sunlight. "Poor things," she thought, "just trying to get home with a bit of food for the kids, and *whack*, just like that, they're a furry lump on a road."

She got up, slowly, to look at each one of the motionless creatures. It certainly was a strange hobby and one she couldn't imagine doing herself, but there was something almost noble about it; instead of becoming red stains on a road, these unfortunate few at least were given a chance at another life in the minds of those who saw them. Fierce or frightened, there they were—lifelike and moving to the imagination. The most beautiful one was the hawk descending, talons extended, toward some close but invisible victim. The most pathetic, however, was a little field mouse not far from the hawk, its head cocked, an eye in the air, and a tiny paw reaching either to grasp something forever out of reach or defend itself from an eternally imminent disaster. Catherine imagined that in a parallel universe, this hawk and this mouse might have been in the same postures and about to collide, not with a car but with one another. The whole display made her feel as if she'd just stepped into some PBS nature program, and she wasn't altogether comfortable there. It was one thing to watch this sort of natural interaction on television in a warm apartment in the middle of Manhattan. It was a very different thing to see it in feathers and fur and frozen fear six feet away.

Catherine turned back to her suitcase to gather her toiletries and clothes. Why, she wondered, would anyone want to live in a place where all these small natural disasters were happening all the time right out in the open? She retreated across the hall to a warm, though rather dark, shower. The violet color scheme of the common room was also the color scheme of the bathroom. Instead of bright white or something close to it, the bathroom tiles were a somber shade of purple. Ditto the color of the floor, the painted trim, the sink, and the toilet. Although it was unique and did create a certain mood, Catherine found herself wishing that the proprietor's name had been a shade brighter—Amber, say. Or better still, Blanche.

This violet theme, however, reached its pinnacle at the breakfast table. Not only were the tablecloths and flowers purple, but the scones, the scrambled eggs, and the butter were various shades of the same color. Even the proprietress herself was holding forth at the head of the breakfast table draped in her own name. The lemon-yellow dress she was wearing heightened the effect of the dark purple scarf she had wrapped once, ceremonially, around her neck and which hung down in front like a deacon's stole.

"Here's one of my New York girls," she said brightly, pausing the story she was telling to the five guests already seated at the table. "Arrived late but up early. Admirable." She then turned more fully to face Catherine and said, "I hear my husband and his new raccoon gave you quite a surprise last night. I hope it wasn't too unsettling."

"No, no. I got over it quickly enough, thank you."

"The bed was comfortable, I trust? We put an especially good bed in there to make up for the curious decor. The name Lazarus does seem to fit, doesn't it?"

"Yes, though I couldn't have guessed why until I walked in."

"Ah," said Violet with a gentle shake of the head, "what can you do but laugh when you've got a husband whose hobby is... well, what it is? Oh," she added as she saw Catherine staring at the numerous violet options on the buffet table, "and be sure to take one of our boysenberry scones—it's a specialty of the house—and come join us. I was just telling our guests about something I'd heard concerning our local celebrity author, Ms. de Bonnair. We are *so* lucky to have her here in our midst."

"She's actually the reason I'm here," Catherine said as she sat down with her plate of purple eggs, purple jam, and purple scone. "Do you know her?"

"No, but I do know more about her than most."

"You can say that again," said a giddy young woman wearing one of the two Universal Studios T-shirts at the table, the other one being worn by her young male companion. "Bill and I are staying in the Rancho de Amor Room and it is *just* like the book—every little detail."

"It's our new honeymoon suite—" Violet started to explain.

"We wanted that one," the T-shirted woman interrupted almost breathlessly, " 'cause Bill and I just got married about a year ago, and it is *sooo* cute and cozy."

"Yes," said Violet, surfing on her patron's youthful exuberance, "we decorated it to look exactly like the room where Isabella and John finally spent their first night as husband and wife."

"Excuse me," asked a middle-aged man in a Norwegian sweater seated next to Catherine, "but who are Isabelle and John?"

With a condescending smile, Violet explained, "It's Isabella—with an 'a'—and John, and the two of them are the almost star-crossed lovers in Loretta de Bonnair's now famous novel, *Rancho de Amor*. And Loretta is the author we've been talking about."

"Oh," said the man with a nod. He looked confused and very much out of place.

"So do you know where Ms. de Bonnair lives?" Catherine asked.

"Wouldn't we all like to know that..." Violet said, wistfully.

"Yes," Catherine replied, "though my interest is purely business."

"Really?" Violet asked on the verge of incredulity. She was used to breathless fans interested in gossip or autographs. "Well, I suppose it was bound to happen. When an author sells a lot of books, it must be good for a lot of people's business."

"I'm hoping, actually, to make it good for both hers and ours," Catherine said. "You wouldn't at least know how I could contact her? Phone number, e-mail, a contact person?"

"No, dear. I just know the book. And the good news is, though it may be wishful thinking, I hear she's very busy on her next one. I can't wait to read it. Unfortunately"—Violet sighed—"no one's been able to get this busy author on the schedule of our FORC event this weekend."

"A *fork* event this weekend?" asked the man in the Norwegian sweater who was still trying to catch up with some part of the conversation.

"F-O-R-C," Violet replied with a jolly smile, "the Fans of Romance Convention. And it's happening right here in our town. With the publication of *Rancho de Amor*, little Sisquoc is definitely on the map of romance."

"So I imagine someone in town knows how to contact Ms. de Bonnair," Catherine wondered aloud, "even if just to hear that she's too busy to come to the convention."

"Yes, somebody probably does, but I don't know who that is. I've never met anyone who's actually met her, or at least met the person who would admit that she was Loretta de Bonnair."

"So she could be somebody else," suggested Bill, surprised at his own realization.

"You mean, could she have another name?" Violet clarified. "Yes, it's definitely possible."

"Which means she *could* be anyone," Catherine said.

"Yes." Violet nodded. "Indeed."

"Well," said the man in the Norwegian sweater, "about all I know for sure is that I'm not Loretta D. Boner and that I've gotta get going. Loved the food. And those cakes you made for snacks last night, I could've eaten all of 'em."

"I think you did," Violet noted politely.

"Hmm, yeah, maybe I did. They were real good."

"Yes, well," Violet said with a smile, "that's what they're there for." She shot Catherine an apologetic glance before turning back to the man. "Have a good day. I hope your visits to the vineyards are productive. Just leave the key in the box by the front door, please. And do come back for another stay sometime."

"Yes, and I'll even look for that book you're all talking about, *Ranch: A Day More*."

"*Rancho de Amor*," Violet gently corrected him. "You'll love it. I'd tell you to go to our local bookstore to pick one up, but the young man who runs it never carries enough copies of her book. He likes modern poetry and things like that, and he's not a real fan of romance. We could really use another bookstore in the area."

At the close of this pronouncement, the sweatered man left, and

Violet turned to Catherine. "Speaking of things we need, did you at least find something suitable to eat in town last night?"

"I went by the Black Barn, but I never got inside. Just as I was about to walk in, some guy came flying out the door backward. There was apparently a fight, which was bad enough, but when the man got up, he went back inside, apparently to fight some more—and he looked happy about it! It wasn't exactly the kind of entertainment I was looking for, but I did go to the convenience store and got all I needed."

Violet sighed loudly. "Loretta de Bonnair lifts our local reputation and the Black Barn drags it down. There are, however, plenty of nice, quiet places to eat in the next town over, Tres Robles. It's just a few miles up the road. Oh, and since you reserved a room for two nights," Violet said, remembering the details of her business, "I might have another room for you tonight. It would get you out of my husband's zoo."

"I admit, his zoo was a little hard to get used to in the beginning, but to be honest, I like the bed and there's a cute little mouse in his collection that I'm growing fond of, so I may as well stay put—that is, if your husband doesn't mind?"

Violet chuckled then said, "Oh, not at all. He'd be pleased that you're fond of at least one of his dead friends."

Not knowing what to say to this last remark, Catherine smiled crookedly and went back to her purple eggs. What an odd relationship this couple had: one was a fan of romance literature, and the other was fascinated with roadkill taxidermy. How, she wondered, did they make it work? Was the trick to find someone completely different from yourself? Catherine quickly rejected this idea. It might work for others, but it wouldn't work for her. Between bites of a violet scone, Catherine sighed. No, she felt that for the right man to be The Right Man, he'd need to embrace pretty much everything she embraced—ideals, ideas, attitudes, and activities. Romance and roadkill were just too different. And yet... it certainly seemed to work for Violet and Ezekiel. But of course it would have to, she concluded as she took a final gulp of her purpled orange juice; there were too few people in little Sisquoc to be choosy about ideal partners.

# CHAPTER 10

After breakfast, Catherine walked back to the hub of town, Cota Road, where she'd gone in search of food the night before. It looked a good deal more inviting than it had in the dark. It was, in fact, a charming little main street dressed up in Western style. There was a newly built but vintage-looking boardwalk on one side of the street, and except for a couple of awkwardly out-of-place modern structures, the rest of the buildings looked authentically old and Western, down to the false fronts that rose above the rooflines and would have been the perfect hiding places for outlaws had this been the set for a Western movie.

It was, however, a little early for the outlaws. In fact, it was a little early for pretty much anyone that Wednesday morning. With the exception of a café and a large feed store at one end of the street and the gas station at the other end, everything was closed for business, including the local bookstore Violet had mentioned at breakfast. A bookstore had seemed like a good place to start a search for a local writer. What author could resist stopping by every once in a while to see how her book was selling? But Catherine and any sales-concerned author would have to wait an hour for the bookstore to open.

With a sigh, Catherine decided to take a walk out of town. She had time to kill, it was a brilliant, sunny day, and she was, after all, in "de Bonnair country." It might be a good idea to see what that country looked like.

Although Catherine had been born, raised, and still lived in Manhattan, she had certainly experienced "country" before. Every summer from the ages of eight to sixteen, she had visited her aunt on the coast of Maine. It was a chance for all her cousins on her maternal side to gather, get into a little harmless trouble, and experience something other than the hot, congested cities in which they all

40

normally lived. In high school, she'd gone to a music camp in Upstate New York (she'd played the violin with promise but little purpose).

These places were definitely "in the country," although the country back East seemed different from the country out West. Back East, she loved to walk along the rough and rocky shore of Maine where, however wild and remote it seemed to be, there was always a house nearby. She also loved walking along some leaf-strewn path in the quiet woods of Upstate New York. There, she could be isolated and alone, but she knew that if she walked far enough—that is to say, about twenty minutes in any direction—she'd find a farm or town or road. Looking down the road ahead of her, she saw nothing but fields and then hills and then a chain of mountains capped with snow, with an insistently bright sun rising slowly above them. It was undeniably beautiful, but it was all a little overwhelmingly vast.

As she walked out of town and into the big beyond, she wasn't really worried or nervous, just slightly more aware of her surroundings than usual. She didn't know what she might run into. And so, when something wriggled deeper into the brush next to her feet, she jumped back a foot or two—just in case. And a few minutes later when a hawk, unmoving and unseen on a fence post, burst into flight as she passed, she instinctively ducked, put her hands over her head, and ran a few feet into the road. Realizing that the further she walked from town, the more likely she'd think that every rustle in the brush was a rattlesnake and every movement in the trees was a mountain lion or a bear, she decided to abandon her solitary stroll and walk back to the well-known wilds of human society.

Moments after turning around, a pickup truck rumbled to a stop on the opposite side of the road. One of the two dusty dandies leering at her from under their cowboy hats yelled, "Can we give you a ride to heaven, little lady?"

Catherine instinctively looked around, sure that such a rude, brash question had to have been directed at someone else. When she realized they were shouting at her, she crisply replied, "No, thanks."

"Well, then how 'bout takin' a ride just back to town? No need to walk when you got two good-lookin' guys willin' to give you a ride..."

"I'm fine," she tossed over her shoulder as she quickened her pace. Behind her, she heard the two idiots cackle as they roared off with a dirt-spitting scratch.

Catherine was relieved to walk back into the relatively civil confines of town. And between the time she'd walked out of Sisquoc and the time she walked back in, most of the businesses had opened.

As she walked toward the bookstore, she passed the office of the *Sisquoc Patriot*, the local paper. It was open, and, after a moment's thought, she realized it might be a decent place to look for leads. Surely a celebrity with as much national notoriety as Loretta de Bonnair would be well known and covered by her local paper. Accompanied by the noisy jingle of a small bell attached to the door, Catherine walked in and saw a portly man in a cowboy hat seated at a very large desk at the center of the back wall, a large sign, *TED POMBO, EDITOR-IN-CHIEF*, prominent on the wall above his head. He was staring absently at something above the door that Catherine had just walked through. Slowly, he lowered his gaze to Catherine and raised an eyebrow as if to say, *You just interrupted me, so whatever you have to say had better be good.* It was, however, a thin, mousy woman sitting at a small desk to his left who was first to speak. "What can we do for you?"

"I'm... well, I'm trying to locate Loretta de Bonnair," Catherine replied, turning to the woman.

Although this woman fulfilled four important functions at the paper—she was the sports and entertainment writer, the accountant, the receptionist, and the wife of the editor-in-chief—she looked worried about carrying the responsibility of answering this particular query and turned to her husband, who responded gruffly, "Got something bad to say about her?"

"Ah, no. I'm out here from New York on business, book business."

"Well then, we can't help you. When you come up with a good angle on something new that de Bonnair's done wrong, you come on back and talk to us."

"Something 'new' that she's done wrong? Has Ms. de Bonnair already done something wrong?"

"She wrote that damn book, didn't she? That ain't bad enough?"

"Well... I guess that depends on what you think of the book."

"Not much."

"You're in rarefied company these days," Catherine said with a hint of a smile.

"And proud of it. She's a left-leaning, tree-hugging noise-maker who's getting way too much press for my liking. If you're here to help Loretta de Bonnair, you're on your own. Have a good stay, but don't stay too long."

Catherine paused, nodded slowly, and turned to go back out the door she'd just entered. She looked up and saw what the portly man had, presumably, been staring at when she walked in: a large picture of the actor Charlton Heston, smiling broadly and holding up a large rifle at an NRA convention. "Thank you," she said, briefly looking back over her shoulder. "And don't worry—I haven't seen much that would make me want to stay." She walked out the door and closed it with a snap. As she walked away, she heard the little bell ring with a sharp metallic hiss.

She checked the time on her phone: 9:50. The bookstore would probably be open by now. When she got to the door, however, she saw that she'd still have to wait another ten minutes. She looked around and saw a public bench conveniently placed across the street where no one would ever think to sit, in the direct sunlight against the blank, uniquely non-Western-styled wall of the Sisquoc public utilities building. It was, however, perfectly placed for anyone who wanted to watch the comings and goings at the bookstore across the street, which was exactly what Catherine wanted to do. It was also a good place from which to watch the midmorning crowds of Sisquoc.

The crowds on Cota Road hardly rivaled the crowds on Fifth Avenue, but there were enough people passing to keep her amused. One of the first things she noticed was that more than half the people wore cowboy boots. On her walk into the country earlier that morning, she had seen a few cattle in the distance, but she was seeing far more cowboy boots in town than she'd seen cows outside of town. It also appeared that half the people who walked past her had spent no more than a hundred dollars on all their clothes while the other half had spent at least five times that just on their shoes.

One young man especially caught her eye as he walked along the sidewalk on the other side of the street. He was definitely of the "under $100" variety, though that had not seriously cramped his style. He had dark, wavy hair that he wore long and brushed back from his forehead and ears. As he strolled down the sidewalk, his hair undulated like a thick, dark wave. His arms, legs, and body were long and slender. Had he been a woman, he'd have been perfect runway material; his jeans were tight, and his T-shirt seemed almost to float around his slender form. Instead of cowboy boots, he wore laceless black canvas shoes, modest but modern. It wasn't so much his physical features, however, but the brooding, intelligent, almost otherworldly look on his face that held her eye. And best of all, he stopped at the door to the bookstore, took out some keys, and opened the door. The Shelf-Discovery Bookstore was now open.

She waited a few minutes on her bench to give him some time to arrange himself and the store for the day, and then, anxious to find out both what he might know about the elusive Loretta de Bonnair and who this comfortingly familiar apparition might be, she strolled into the bookstore.

The young man who had just opened the shop was not visible when Catherine walked in—probably in the storeroom turning on lights, she thought—so she walked up to the nearest display of modern fiction, her favorite section, and started to browse through the titles, happy to see that many were Banter House books. Her glance was stopped by a catchy title she didn't recognize: *Getting to No*. Intrigued, she pulled it from the shelf and started to read a page in the middle. This was her thirty-second way to test a new title. If the writing in the middle of a book was dull and listless, she wouldn't waste her time reading any more of it.

She'd read three pages of a book that didn't seem to be as catchy as its title when the long-haired bookstore clerk walked over and, in a soft, deep voice, asked if she would like any help finding anything.

"I, well, I'm not actually looking for a book—though I do love books," she added hastily. "But right now, I'm looking for someone."

"Ahhh, aren't we all?" replied the clerk with a languid smile.

She returned his smile and after the slightest pause said, "Yes. I'm looking for Loretta de Bonnair." As his eyes widened with surprise, she added, "Not for me personally. For my company. I'm an editor in New York."

"An editor. Interesting. Who are you with?"

"Banter," she said with quiet pride. His eyes widened again with surprise, but this time, Catherine added nothing. His reaction was that of someone who knew the reputation of Banter House in the world of books.

"The real thing," he replied, impressed. "I knew you didn't look like the typical romance novel enthusiast."

"You're right. We're hoping that I can meet her and convince her to publish something with us. It would elevate her reputation… and help us financially. The problem is, I have to find her to be able to offer her anything. And she doesn't seem to want to be found. I was thinking someone in the bookstore might be able to help me since she is apparently one of your local celebrities."

With a grin, the young man replied, "It's not often a bookstore clerk gets to come to the aid of a beautiful damsel in distress, but this is one of those rare occasions."

"So, do you actually know her?" Catherine asked anxiously.

"Me, personally? No. But I'm sure if she *is* local, I can find her."

"That would be great."

"How much time do I have?"

"If you could do it by yesterday, that would be wonderful, though if you need another day or two, that'd be okay."

"I'm on it. I must say, I haven't heard that she's come into the store since she's become famous, and I don't recall ever having heard her name around here before she was famous. Still, I suspect she's using an assumed name. Loretta de Bonnair—that sort of syllabic scramble *has* to be a nom de plume, don't you think?"

"Possibly, yes… possibly," Catherine agreed.

"What if I make a list of all our old female regulars? She is supposed to be older, isn't she?"

"That's what they say."

"Good. That'll narrow it down a bit. And I'll make another list of the regulars who like romances and see where they intersect. It'll likely be a slow day, and this'll give me something interesting to do."

"That would be wonderful." Catherine smiled; this guy was definitely on the right track.

"But once I've got this list of probable suspects, I have to get that list to you. And one of the best, and most enjoyable, ways to do that would be to discuss, probe, and explore the possibilities over a glass of something later, if you'd like…" he suggested with a soft, inquisitive look.

"I would like," she said, then extended her hand. "I'm Catherine Doyle."

"Devon de Vries, at your service," he said, taking her hand and bowing his head ever so slightly. "Can I text you when I've got an idea? Then maybe we can get together and compare notes."

"Absolutely."

They exchanged numbers, and then she bought the book she was holding. She always liked to buy something, even just a little something, from any independent bookstore she visited. They served a civic purpose that she wanted to support with her business. Furthermore, the clerk of this particular bookstore had kindly volunteered to help her, and who knew where and to what such help might lead? All of this was certainly worth the price of a book.

# Chapter 11

No matter how clever and considerate this bookstore gallant might prove to be, however, Catherine wasn't going to put all her faith in his noble efforts. And even if Devon were able to identify one of his bookstore customers as the one and only de Bonnair, she'd still need to get Ms. de Bonnair's address, phone number, e-mail, or social media details. Her work wouldn't even begin until she could make contact with the author, and simply knowing that the novelist might occasionally buy books in Sisquoc didn't get Catherine a whole lot closer to that.

Outside the doors of the Shelf-Discovery Bookstore, she looked down the three blocks of Cota Road. To her right and down the street, she saw the bank and the police station. To her left, on her side of the street, she saw a large feed store across from the Black Barn. A feed store had not been on her original list of places she thought she should visit, but she realized it should have been. If Loretta de Bonnair lived on a ranch of some sort, surely someone at a feed store would have heard of her and maybe even delivered whatever such places delivered to her ranch. It was certainly worth a try.

No sooner had she walked onto the parking lot than a small, tan man in a huge cowboy hat throttled back the engine of his forklift, gave her a big grin, and said loudly, "Howdy."

Catherine assumed that the proper response to this folksy salutation was a "Howdy" of her own, but she just couldn't push herself to say it. She knew she would have sounded incredibly affected, and so she simply smiled and nodded.

The man leaned down toward her and asked, "What can I do you for?"

"Do you happen to know a Loretta de Bonnair?"

"Heard of, I think, but never met. You want to go inside with that one," and he nodded toward the side door of the store.

Not ten feet into the store, Catherine heard a female voice hail her from a side aisle. "Howdy. Can we help you?"

Catherine turned and saw a young woman in a cowboy hat arranging the new inventory of halters and bridles in a display. Her blond hair was pulled back into a long ponytail that looked particularly fitting for the job she was doing.

"I'm trying to find someone who might know the author Loretta de Bonnair, where she lives, or how I could contact her. She apparently lives on a ranch around here and probably buys her"—not sure what the right word was, Catherine plugged in the universal placeholder and went on—"ranch *things* in your store."

"Ooh, that's an interesting couple of questions. Personally, I loved *Rancho de Amor*, but I can't say that too loud around here. I never met her though. You should talk to my boss at the counter."

"Oh. Okay. Thanks." With a nod, Catherine headed to the counter.

She took her place behind a tall, broad-shouldered man in a cowboy hat and very muddy boots. He smelled like a combination of sweet grasses, pungent dung, and aftershave. Catherine took a couple of steps back and listened to the conversation between this odiferous rancher and the thin, middle-aged, leather-tan woman behind the counter.

"Now, Betty, you know you're the only woman I flirt with in town."

"Sam, I'm not even the only woman you flirt with in this store."

"Well..." Sam said with a slow drawl, "you're the only one I'm serious about. I'm just waitin' for you to dump that good-for-nothin' horse trainer of a husband you got. Twenty years of a perfect marriage is long enough for anyone, don't ya think?"

The woman laughed, then said, "We gotta get you started on a perfect marriage of your own. You got a pack of fine-lookin' girls runnin' after you in this town."

"Well, they can just keep runnin'. I slow down for a dance or two every now and then, but talking to the breeze and listenin' to the moon is all the serious company I need."

"That's what you say, but I don't much believe it."

"Like I say, if you weren't already married, things'd be different. My timin' was off..."

"Yeah, by about twenty years."

"Yeah, well, what can you do?" He shrugged. "I gotta run. We're about outa burgers and bacon, so me and the boys are gonna shoot us a month's worth of meat this afternoon. You want me to save you a couple of rib-eyes?"

"We just slaughtered a steer of our own before Thanksgiving. We got plenty of steak for a while, thanks all the same."

"All righty then. Say hello to that lucky husband o' yours." He backed up slightly, picked up the ninety-pound bag of feed he'd just bought, and tossed it over his shoulder. "I'll see you in a couple, Betty." Then he backed straight into Catherine.

Instantly, she fell backward onto a pile of bagged fertilizer.

"Oh my Lord," said the man as he spun around and looked at Catherine seated, awkwardly, on a bag of manure. "I'm so sorry. I didn't see you there."

As the man leaned down to help her, she looked up and was struck by how very blue, very intense, and very familiar those eyes were. This was the man who had tumbled out the doors of the Black Barn the night before.

"Boy, I really knocked you scallywag. You all right?" he asked, extending a hand to her.

Without taking his hand, Catherine pushed herself back onto her feet and said, "I'm fine, thank you. It was a soft landing."

"Lucky none of those bags broke, eh?"

She glanced back and saw exactly what had made it so soft. "Yes," she said, chuckling slightly. "Very."

"Well, I've done enough damage here. I think I'd best be movin' along. See you, Betty," he said over his shoulder, then he turned back to Catherine. "This wasn't the way I wanted it to happen, but I can now honestly say that I've knocked a very pretty lady off her feet."

"I doubt I'm the first you've knocked over, though I'm probably the first you've knocked onto a pile of... well..." She raised an eyebrow in mock concern.

"I don't think I made a very good first impression last night, and I'm sure I'm not making a very good second impression. I do hope I get a chance to make a third."

"I'm here on business for another day or two, then I'm back to New York, so I doubt we'll have a chance to find out."

He opened his mouth, paused, then said with quiet sincerity, "I do believe that would be a shame." He looked in her eyes for a moment, then smiled, nodded, and walked out.

A bit shaken and confused by the whole event, Catherine took a deep breath, patted down an errant wave in her hair, and stepped up to the counter. Betty smiled, shook her head, and said, both to herself and to Catherine, "He's quite a character, and he seems to have an eye for you."

"It seems he's got an eye for most women," Catherine replied.

"True enough, but I've never seen him blush while talking to one."

Catherine simply hummed noncommittally in response. She didn't know what to say about this or anything else she'd seen of this pungent, pugnacious, and perplexing farmhand with the deep blue eyes.

"What can I do for you?" Betty asked.

"I'm trying to find someone who probably lives around here and maybe uses the... the things you sell."

"Most of our 'things' are used by horses and cows, but I'll see what I can do if it's a person you want. Who is it?"

"She's an author who supposedly has a ranch around here and goes by the name of Loretta de Bonnair."

"Loretta de Bonnair, huh?" the woman asked with an angry edge. "You and everybody else is looking for that gal these days. Good luck."

"So you don't know who she is?"

"No idea. Wish I did though. I'd give her a piece of my mind all right."

Again, here was that same angry response that Ted Pombo, editor of the local paper, had made. Catherine asked, "Why?"

"The things she writes in that book of hers. She ain't no friend of ours in this neighborhood. She talks about environmentalism and socialism—and from what I hear, that ain't the half of it. No, there are a whole lotta ranchers around here who would like to have a word or two with her."

"Is that what her book's all about?" Catherine asked as innocently as she could. Despite the fact that she'd already read over a third of the book and had not found it overwhelmed by those incidental motifs, she didn't want to debate this woman; she just wanted her help.

"Well, most of it, I guess, is about some lovey-dovey stuff between a Mexican gal and a white guy, but she gets into that other stuff too. I haven't read it myself—that sorta mush don't interest me much. But I got a worker here who did read it, and he marked up all the dirty parts—and I'm not talking about where they take off their clothes. I'm talking about where she basically says that raising broccoli is better for the world than raising good beef cattle. You think anybody around here is gonna go for that?"

"No, probably not. But does anybody around here know who this controversial woman is? She's an older woman who apparently lives on a ranch. Can you think of anyone like that?"

"An older woman who maybe has a coupla horses? I can think of a good coupla dozen. There's a lot of rich retirees up from LA who own a few horses and keep them on manicured ranchettes around here. But if she's runnin' cattle, that'll mean a bigger operation and I don't think she'd be buying her own feed. She'd get some young ranch hand to do that. I'll bet you though, that whole ranch thing is as fake as her name. In fact, I'll bet she don't even live around here at all. With her ideas, I'll bet you she lives up there in San Francisco."

"Oh, no... I hope not," Catherine said, shocked by the idea. "God, that'll make her impossible to find. But it is an interesting idea. I suppose I should thank you, though it'd be terrible if you were right."

"Guess I should stop while I'm behind, unless there's something else I can help you with which we might actually have."

"Not right now, no, but the next time I need some hay, this'll be the place I come. Thanks."

"Y'all have a good day. And good luck with your looking. If you find her, tell her to stop by for a chat. We'd love to set her straight."

With a polite nod, Catherine said, "Will do," and walked out of the feed store.

The thought that Loretta might not live anywhere in the area was not at all what she'd hoped to hear. With a sickening feeling, Catherine realized that, for all she knew, Loretta de Bonnair could be her downstairs neighbor in New York.

What she needed was some positive identification from someone who either knew her personally or needed to know her professionally. With no clue about who might be personally connected to this woman locally, Catherine decided to turn to those who had a professional need to know who and where she was: the Sisquoc police, the men and women whose job it was to protect and serve. Someone as well known as Ms. de Bonnair would definitely need protection, if not service.

As she walked into the police station three doors up the street from the feed store, she saw a large, broad-faced man look up from his desk and raise an inquisitive eyebrow.

"Hello," Catherine began quietly.

The man nodded politely and raised both eyebrows in silent encouragement.

"I'm a"—Catherine paused, then quickly pivoted and said— "a freelance journalist from the *New York Times* out here to write a piece on one of your celebrated citizens."

"Yeah? Which one today?" he said in a voice that was half-bored and half-annoyed.

"Loretta de Bonnair."

The officer set his jaw and lowered his eyelids. "What do you want to know?"

"You know who she is, of course?" Catherine asked as guilelessly as she could.

"Not that I want to, but she's a little hard to avoid."

"So you do know her personally."

"I know *of* her personally."

"And where she lives?"

"Can't tell you that."

"Oh," said Catherine, seemingly pained, "I suppose you've got to keep it secret."

"No. She's keeping it secret. I have no idea where she lives."

"Really? And with the Fans of Romance Convention here this weekend, with all sorts of people doing all sorts of things to find her, the police don't even know where she is?"

"As long as those fans of romance don't steal cars, burn down a barn, or start sleepin' in the streets, we don't much care what they do or who they want to meet. If they start to bother her, she'll call us and tell us where she lives, then we'll go out and help her. But until then, finding her is a problem for her fans, not for us. Seriously, lady, I'd love to help you, but I can't. I don't know who the hell she is, and if I did, I'd do her a big favor and ask her if she'd ever thought of moving, say, to LA where her neighbors might appreciate her more."

"You mean people around here don't like her very much?"

"I can't speak for everybody. I'm sure she's got a few local fans. I hear that gal at the B and B actually has a room she rents all decorated like something out of one of her books."

"You mean Violet?"

"Yep, I mean Violet. Nice gal, though her and her husband are a little... off center. She's into the romance thing in a big way, and he goes out looking for roadkill late at night, stuffs 'em, then gives them as presents."

"Yes, I've seen his collection."

"Lucky girl."

"Mm..." Catherine intoned tepidly. "I'd be luckier, though, if you had any way to help me find out who Ms. de Bonnair is and where she lives. It's really an important story."

"I'm sure it is... to you. But I honestly don't know who she is, where she is, or even who might know all that other than Violet and her husband. Now, if you don't mind, I've got to get back to the reports from last night," he said, picking up a short stack of papers and quickly flipping through them. "A stolen truck, a domestic dispute that looks like it got a little noisy, some cattle rustling out on one of the coast ranches, and a fender bender between some old Hollywood star in a Rolls-Royce and some teenage girl driving her mom's old Honda... and it looks like the star wants to sue the girl. None of it's as exciting as a romance novel, but it's what I've gotta deal with."

"Well, thanks anyway. It was a long shot, I guess."

As Catherine turned to go, the officer tossed out a final idea.

"Here's another thought for you, and who knows, maybe it'll help. This whole de Bonnair thing seems made up to me, like a name one of those Hollywood people would think up. We got plenty of them living around here. You might ask one of them if she isn't Loretta herself. Those writers'll try anything."

It was yet another possibility, and, like the others, led her potentially further from finding the well-hidden Loretta de Bonnair. Catherine stopped just outside the door to the Sisquoc police station and realized it was time to take a break and regroup. She was clearly going nowhere fast.

# Chapter 12

After ordering a latte and a turkey sandwich at the Saddle Up for a Cup Café, Catherine walked out to the inescapably sunny patio to eat her lunch and lick her wounds.

She thought that maybe she should call someone—Vito, Rachel, her father—but what would she say? That she hadn't found her author yet and was increasingly concerned that everything she thought she knew about Loretta was wrong and that she wasn't even living in the area any longer—if she'd ever lived there? Catherine needed to commiserate with someone, but that would be admitting, if not defeat, at least serious disappointment, which was something she never liked to share. It wasn't anyone else's problem, and it wasn't anybody else's business.

Abandoning the idea, she pulled out a list of places she thought she should visit and made notes about the places she had already seen: *Newspaper—zilch and the editor hates her; Police—nothing—and the cop dislikes her; Bookstore—no lead yet, but intelligent and cute clerk will help and is sure he can find her.* Below her list, she added: *Feed store—zero, and more animosity for Loretta. Literally knocked onto a pile of manure by some cowboy.* And below that, a final note: *Walked out of town—vast space, fields, mountains, beautiful and uncomfortable. Obnoxious locals in cowboy hats.*

After finishing her latte and lunch, she put away her notes and started off to the one bank in town. Catherine was sure that Loretta, not being of the generation that lived half of its life and did most of its banking online, would have gone into the bank from time to time and been known even before she'd become famous.

A young teller greeted her with a huge smile and what seemed to be the required local salutation, "Howdy." He wore a perfectly pressed and tightly buttoned blue cowboy shirt with a matching blue cowboy hat. The hat seemed to be some sort of company uniform, as everyone behind the counter wore identical cowboy hats in a shade of blue that just happened to match the color of the ubiquitous company logo.

"Hello," Catherine replied.

"And how can I help your banking today?" the teller asked energetically.

"I don't actually have a bank account here."

"Oh, I'm sorry. Would you like to open one? We have a great new product for first-time customers, a no-fee, interest-bearing, three-in-one flex account with a—"

"Thank you, but no. I live in New York and I'm only here on business."

With a salesperson's indifference to resistance, he continued, "Well, we do have a wonderful business account that comes with—"

"I'm sorry, but I don't want a bank account. I would just like to know if a particular woman has an account here."

"Oh, you're doing a little celebrity hunting?"

"Not really. No. This is strictly business. Can you tell me whether the famous Loretta de Bonnair does her banking at your fine establishment?"

"Loretta de Bonnair—that's who you want to know about?"

"Yes, that's exactly who I'd like to know about. Have you ever met her?"

"Well, I met somebody a couple of weeks ago who *said* she was Loretta de Bonnair."

"Really?" Catherine replied, both excited and impatient to hear more.

"A woman came in saying she was Ms. de Bonnair and tried to cash a two-thousand-dollar check from Loretta to herself. She looked the part—an old woman with her own book under her arm, a cane, a very pink dress, lots of makeup. The problem was, her gray hair didn't quite cover all the blond underneath. And when 'Loretta' started to argue, loudly, with a teller who told her she needed to have an account here to cash her check, the manager called the police. Old Loretta all of a sudden dropped her cane and her old woman voice, cursed a couple of times, and ran out the door. She hasn't been back since." The teller shrugged and gave a crooked smile. "Unfortunately, that's as close to Loretta de Bonnair as I've ever been. Sorry."

"That was a nice little story, but a fake Loretta's not going to do me much good. So the *real* Loretta de Bonnair doesn't have a bank account here?"

"Even if she did, I couldn't tell you. We can't just tell people those kinds of things."

"No, no, I suppose you can't." She sighed. "Though you kinda did with that funny little story. I've gotta say, whoever de Bonnair is, she's certainly the focus of a lot of odd attention."

She walked out of the bank thoroughly discouraged. She decided not to ask anyone else where someone who didn't want to be found might be. Instead, she decided to try the one place where Ms. de Bonnair's name would have been marked on all sorts of things, if she were actually anywhere around Sisquoc. Though undoubtedly not rivaling the amount of online mail addressed to Blushing Dove Press, the physical amount of fan mail coming to her through the local post office would have made her name an inescapable presence, and if that mail was delivered anyplace, that place had to be the place Catherine wanted to find.

When she walked in, three people were silently standing in line while one person was talking loudly at the counter. The man at the counter, a tall, thin, disheveled fellow in his mid-sixties, was trying to buy one of the commemorative American Flags stamps. Unfortunately, they came in a set of four, and he only wanted one of them.

"But I don't want the Continental Colors flag, the Betsy Ross flag, or the original Star-Spangled Banner flag, I only want the Gadsden flag—the yellow one with the 'Don't Tread on Me' on it."

"But, sir," said the harried postal worker whose hair, done up in a tight bun before work, was now beginning to unravel at the edges, "it's a commemorative set and only comes in a set of four stamps that are all attached."

"So detach them."

"We can't do that."

"You don't know how to?"

"Yes, sir, I do, but we're not supposed to."

"Give them to me and I'll take them apart."

"If you buy the whole set, you can do whatever you want with them."

"This is ridiculous. The government is forcing me to pay for something I don't want so I can get something I do want."

"I'm sorry, but that's just the way it is."

"That's the way it is *these days*," he declared, "but it wasn't always like that."

As he turned and stormed out, he tried to slam the door to punctuate his righteous ire, but the door was hydraulically controlled. The more he pushed, the more resistance the door gave to being shut. After a couple of grunts, he gave up and walked to his car. The door, no longer being forced, slowly and quietly closed on its own.

The three other customers, though far less vociferous, nonetheless had complicated issues: picking up mail without proper ID after a long vacation, trying to send something by certified mail to Madagascar, trying to send a frozen trout to a cousin in Iowa. Seventeen minutes after walking in and after the postal worker had finally dealt with all these issues, Catherine walked up and asked if she knew—or knew of—Loretta de Bonnair.

"I know her book, and I love it. Are you interested in sending a copy to someone?"

"No, I'm frankly interested in meeting the author for business, but I have no idea where she lives. I don't expect you can tell me that, but can you at least tell me if she lives anywhere around here?"

"There are a lot of people who think she does."

"Are they wrong?"

"Not necessarily, but without an exact address, we can't deliver anything. See back there?" The woman pointed to a large mail tub with a mound of mostly white and pink envelopes rising above it—a candy-colored mountain of undeliverable mail. "All for her. We get about fifty new ones every day. If you can find her and get us her complete address, we'd really appreciate it."

"No one's come in to claim any of it?"

"Well, there's a cowboy living around here who tried one day to convince us he was working for her, but, charming as he was, we can't let anybody have anybody else's mail, and Loretta de Bonnair hasn't shown up yet to claim her own mail."

"So, what you're saying is that no one has the right address for Ms. de Bonnair—not her fans, not her lawyers, not even the IRS?"

"I don't know about her lawyer or the IRS, but I can tell you that a whole lot of her fans don't know her exact address."

"Funny, it's written in the flap copy of her book that she might live somewhere outside of Sisquoc, California, but..." Catherine exhaled, exasperated, and just shook her head.

"She might," said the postal clerk, "but she hasn't bothered to tell many people where that somewhere is."

"Which could mean she doesn't live anywhere around here at all."

"It could," the clerk replied matter-of-factly. "Still, if you get back far enough into those mountains, there are all sorts of people who haven't been found—and don't want to be found."

"But... she's famous."

"Yeah, but would you want to read and answer all of that?" said the postal worker with a nod toward the mound of pink and white mail.

Not having a good answer, Catherine thanked the woman and left her to the next set of complex postal issues.

# Chapter 13

Dead—yes, she must be dead; what else could it be, Catherine thought as she walked out of the post office and onto Cota Road. And if Ms. de Bonnair were dead, she certainly wouldn't be writing anything new, though she might have left a few fine manuscripts behind. But would anyone know this, and who would that "anyone" be? A husband with a different last name who was a rancher and who never liked the fact that his wife wrote "those darn mushy books"? A husband who then destroyed her piles of unpublished but well-written manuscripts when she'd died, and who, from grief or guilt, died himself a week later?

Catherine smirked, looked up, and saw the Shelf-Discovery Bookstore down the street. Should she go in and tell Devon all she had—and hadn't—discovered, or should she leave some intriguing distance between them for the time being? It was a tricky situation; she'd need to show enough interest to sustain his interest, but it might look as if she were a little *too* interested in his interest. And anyway, she reflected, she might be seeing him that evening. He had said that they might get together later to compare notes... Best to let him make the first significant move and, for now, concentrate on making that list of possible Lorettas.

Abruptly, she turned around and went back to the Saddle Up Café, there to continue reading and taking notes on the entertaining—if improbable—events that both attracted Isabella Guerrero and John Powell to one another and kept them painfully apart. It was a strange way to spend an afternoon, in part because she was reading what she had not wanted to read, and yet she found herself enjoying it far more than she wanted to admit.

When she walked out of the Saddle Up at closing time and into the chill of early evening, she decided that instead of taking Violet's advice to drive over to Tres Robles for a decent dinner, she'd stay closer to "home." For one, it was getting dark, and she wasn't anxious to look for anything new in an area she knew nothing about. And then there was Devon, who had said they might get together "later." She felt it was a good idea to stay put, which left the Black Barn. It was not a place she wanted to spend time in, but it was the one and only restaurant in town, and though she was certain that Loretta wouldn't want to hang out there (why would she?), various rancher types did, and one of them might, by chance, know something about Ms. de Bonnair and her ranch.

As she got to the top of the stairs and was about to push through the saloon doors, she was met by a chorus of hoots and hollers. It sounded like a sports bar during the Super Bowl. She paused—this wasn't the atmosphere she wanted, but there really wasn't much alternative. She pushed through the doors and saw that the raucous sporting event wasn't on TV but right there at a table. A man loudly counted, "One, two, three..." and two men seated facing each other with their hands tensely clasped together began to arm wrestle. As Catherine set a course toward a group of empty booths as far away from this testosteral turbulence as possible, most of the cheering men surrounding the wrestlers looked up and approvingly watched her progress. So did the arm-wrestling man who was now facing her. Out of the corner of her eye, she saw him look up and watch her as she walked by. As she passed, she glanced down and... there were those intense, unsettlingly blue eyes looking at her again.

He blinked, looked as surprised as she felt, and, momentarily distracted, relaxed his grip. The other man quickly took advantage of it, and, with a growl and a sneer, he reversed his own imminent loss and victoriously slammed Sam's arm down on the table. Instantly, all of the other distracted men turned back to the contest and began to hoot, holler, and howl again. As she walked away, Catherine heard one man say, "That's how to beat Sam, all right. Dangle a pretty girl in front of his nose." There was laughter and more hooting from which Catherine retreated quickly.

No sooner had she slid into a distant corner booth than a middle-aged waitress with the name tag reading *Charlene* came up, tossed a menu on her table, and said in a rush, "Howdy, darlin'. You expecting anyone else?"

"Ah, no. I'm here alone."

"Well, you won't be for long. But before you're dealing with trouble in a cowboy hat, I'll be back and get your order. We run outa the seafood special about ten minutes ago, so if that's what you had a hankerin' for, better find somethin' else."

"That's okay. I'm in the mood for a steak."

"Got plenty of those, dear, pretty much any way you want it cooked. You want anything to drink? Wine, beer, Coke?"

Catherine paused to consider. "Well, maybe I'll have some wine."

"White or red?"

"Red."

"Cheap or pricey?"

"Cheap and local, if you have anything local."

"The local's the pricey stuff."

"Is it good?"

"Me, I drink beer before dinner and bourbon after, but they say it's good, particularly the peeno."

"Fine. I'll try it."

"You got it." Charlene rushed off.

Catherine turned her attention to the oily, plastic-covered menu. As her host at the B&B had hinted, the fare wasn't impressively healthy. It featured lots of beef (said to be local); a few chicken dishes (not said to be local); a seafood special (no longer available); boiled carrots; boiled broccoli; boiled, mashed, fried, or baked potatoes; an iceberg wedge salad; and six different kinds of pie for dessert.

"Your wine'll be up in just a minute," Charlene said as she swept back up to Catherine's table with a glass of ice water and an order pad at the ready.

"The flank steak, well done," said Catherine, "and a salad, please. You only have the wedge, right?"

"Yep."

"Well then, I'll have it with... with the ranch dressing." Although she usually ordered blue cheese, she decided to go with something nominally regional.

"Coming up," said Charlene, and she bustled off to another table with her order pad.

After taking a sip of water, she turned her attention to the surrounding decor. On the wall above her booth was some sort of framed collection. At first, it looked like an army of pale beetles—

dead and not very carefully aligned behind glass. It was the strangest and least attractive display of insects she'd ever seen. The hand-printed description of the contents read, *All of these was taken from the Cojo Ranch between 1934 and 1936. Diamondbacks and regular rattlesnakes.* Shocked, Catherine stood up and examined the display more closely. They definitely weren't insects. They were, instead, a collection of some ninety-three rattles from snakes found on the Cojo Ranch, wherever that was. Unnerved, she sat back down as far from the wall as she could.

Almost afraid of what she'd see next, Catherine glanced around the restaurant and bar. The first thing her glance landed on was the arm-wrestling cowboy with the blue eyes. It was bad enough that her glance unintentionally landed on him, but even worse was that he was, at that very moment, looking at her. Both looked away quickly. She was determined not to look in that direction again. He was an unnerving presence that would best be ignored. So she turned her gaze to the back of the bar and as far from the blue-eyed man as she could.

The crowd in the bar was almost exclusively male, and all the men wore either cowboy hats or baseball caps with team insignias or tractor company logos. On the walls behind the bar were posters of prize-winning cattle—huge, preslaughter pieces of meat that had won renown for their owners as a result of their beefy bulk. She wasn't impressed. In fact, she now wanted to get out of there as soon as possible, and so, while waiting for her food, she decided to go up to the bartender—a tall, beefy specimen himself—and ask about Loretta de Bonnair. After all, if what little anyone knew about her were true, she was, or had been, a rancher of some sort. Maybe she had liked or, if she were still alive, still liked to come into town from time to time for a beer and a little arm wrestling.

When Catherine got to the bar, there was no room for her to sidle up and discreetly chat with the bartender, and it was to him, alone, that she wanted to speak. Not only was he drinking less than pretty much anyone else in the place, but as the person who was paid to serve drinks and listen to bar talk, he was most likely to have heard something about the mysterious Loretta. Quietly, Catherine stood and waited for two men to get their drinks and go back to the pool table. While she stood there trying to look both confident and inconspicuous, a fifty-something man in a cowboy hat caught her eye and smiled. "Howdy. What are you drinkin'?"

"Water," Catherine replied dryly.

"Well, hell, that's cheap enough even for me. Can I get you a double?"

"That's a generous offer, but I've already got a glass at my table. I just want to ask the bartender something."

"He's too young to know half the stuff he should. Maybe I can help. I'm Tim," he said, offering his hand.

Catherine perfunctorily shook his hand and had the momentary feeling she was shaking hands with a turtle, the skin being so rough and calloused. "Well, Tim, maybe you *can* help. You have, maybe, heard of Loretta de Bonnair?"

"Oh-ho-ho," the man chuckled without humor, "don't get me started on that one. I know plenty about her, and there ain't much I like."

"I'm not sure I like her either, but I would like to meet her. If you knew how I could get in touch with her..." Catherine smiled encouragingly.

"If I did, I'd get in touch right here and now and give her a piece of my mind's what I'd do. What's a pretty city girl like you doin' lookin' for her? You need some love advice?" he asked with an inviting laugh.

"No," Catherine responded with polite and terse clarity. "It's business, pure and simple."

"Business, huh? I ain't so sure business is simple, and I know it's almost never pure."

"That may be, but that's all I'm interested in, thanks," and she turned to get the attention of the bartender.

Although he was a good fifteen feet away, he noticed this new and attractive customer, turned his head, and raised his eyebrows expectantly.

"Can I talk with you a moment?" she asked.

The bartender put a hand to his ear.

Catherine raised her voice and enunciated, "May I talk with you a moment?"

He nodded, handed a couple of beers to a waiting patron, then walked over to her. "Yes, you *may* talk to me a moment," he said, playfully echoing her formal tone. "What can I do for you?"

"It's about Loretta de Bonnair. Do you know her?"

"I know *of* her."

"Well, that's a good start. Do you know how to get in touch with her?"

"I've never had to."

He was not an easy man to interview. "Okay, but if you or someone else needed to, would you know how to contact her?"

"Hey, Walt," yelled someone at the other end of the bar, "stop trying to pick up that cute tourista and get us some brews."

Walt turned and shouted down the bar, "A little respect for the needs of our new customer, please. Cop a swig from somebody else's beer, and I'll be right with you, George." Then he turned back, stared at Catherine for a moment, and asked, "You working with that other gal?"

Confused, Catherine asked, "What other gal?"

"The life of the party at the table over there," and with a quick nod, he indicated a table in a dark corner behind the pool table. Sitting with three men was a woman in a very pink cowboy hat. Catherine squinted to get a better look. All of a sudden, her eyes widened. Under the hat Catherine recognized the thick, russet hair and the pert profile of the woman she'd seen at the Newark, Albuquerque, and LA airports, the one she had been sure worked for a New York fashion magazine. That guess now looked very wrong. Here she was in a tiny town in the middle of nowhere, laughing and flirting with the locals. She seemed very much at home.

"That woman in the pink hat?" Catherine asked.

The bartender nodded.

"No. Why?"

"She was up here just before you came in asking the same questions and getting the same answers."

"Really..." Catherine exhaled and then asked with more than a hint of concern, "Did she say... well, did she say who she worked for?"

"As far as I could tell, seems she works for some book company in New York."

"No!"

"Well, if you know better than me, you go with that. I'm just tellin' you what I heard."

More quietly now, Catherine repeated, "No..." and she started to laugh. Then, refocusing on Walt, she said, "Well, whatever she does, we are definitely *not* working together. In fact, just between you and me, I suspect it may be the opposite."

"A little rivalry for Loretta's attentions, hmm? I'm sure Ms. de Bonnair will be flattered."

"If anybody can ever find her."

"Yeah, well," Walt said raising his eyebrows, "I'll see what I can do. What do you want to tell her?"

"You actually think you can contact her?"

Walt paused, pursed his lips, then said, "Pretty sure. A bartender's got lots of contacts."

"Well, if you can talk to her, tell her I have an offer—an attractive offer."

A very drunk young man in a brown cowboy hat raised his wobbly head from the bar and, as his hat slipped off and fell to the floor, he turned toward Catherine and said, slurring, "You got a attrackive offer? I'm allears and I'm all yers... Name's Sean an..."

Walt interrupted and said with gentle command, "Go back to sleep, Sean. Unless you are owning up to bein' Loretta de Bonnair, it ain't any of your business."

"You callin' me Loredda?!"

"Sean... no one would *ever* call you Loretta. Now go back to sleep, or go home. One of the two."

"O-kay, I'll gobaktozleeb..." he said, and with that, he put his head back on his hands and returned to bleary-beery dreamland.

"I'll do what I can for you," Walt said. "But just to let you know, that gal's got an offer too."

"Well, that may be," she said, glancing at her newly discovered rival, "but I suspect I can top it, one way or the other."

"Loretta's one lucky woman. I'll let her know... if I can get to her."

"I'm Catherine Doyle with Banter House Books," Catherine said as she handed him her business card. "I'm staying at Violet's Bed and Breakfast—but only for another day or two. If you could possibly run into her sooner rather than later and have her call, that would be really great for her and for me."

"I'll sure do what I can as fast as I can." He smiled and gave a nod.

65

"Can I come back tomorrow and check in, just in case?"

"Absolutely. I'm always here and at your service. In the meantime, can I get you a drink?"

"No, thanks. I have a glass of wine coming to the table." With a nod of her own and a smile, she leaned down, picked up Sean's fallen cowboy hat, and placed it on the counter next to his snoring head. She then returned to her seat and discovered that her glass of wine, along with her dinner, had arrived in her absence. As she settled in, she gave another quick glance at the woman in the pink hat. It's not as if Catherine needed any more incentive to find Loretta, but the prospect of losing to this russet-haired rival added another nudge.

# CHAPTER 14

After pouring a few more rounds of drinks for a handful of customers, Walt took advantage of a temporary lull and motioned for one of the cowboys sitting at a table to join him outside.

When the man got outside, Walt turned to him and said, "We got two young ladies looking for Loretta in there. Both of 'em are workin' for publishing companies in New York and they're here to offer Loretta some money, and it sounds like *good* money, Sam. Real good."

"Oh really..." said Sam, raising an eyebrow. "They working together?"

"Nope, though they're both staying at Violet's crazy B and B."

"The perfect place for a couple of book people. Is one of 'em that cutie in the short skirt at Jeff and Danny's table makin' 'em all feel special?"

"Yep. Short skirt, tight top. A real player."

Sam nodded. "And the other one is the gal who was just up at the bar?"

"Yep. Kinda formal-like."

"Kinda," Sam said, looking down and nodding. "Though maybe also..." he said trailing off inconclusively. He took a breath, looked back up at Walt and said, resolutely, "Well, well—'Loretta' will have to hear what these two attractive young ladies are offering."

"Uh-huh. And if 'Loretta' is smart, she'll play one against the other and push up those offers."

"Yes," Sam said while letting a cascade of possibilities tumble through his mind, "and nobody's gotta know what's really goin' on. I think our good friend Loretta is finally getting smart. Let's have some fun, my friend."

So saying, Sam nodded, Walt winked, and they both walked back into the bar.

Sam sauntered up to the woman in the pink cowboy hat and short skirt. She was at the bar ordering drinks for herself and her new best friends. Quietly, he said, "I hear you'd like to talk to Loretta de Bonnair." She shot Sam a quick, inquisitive look. "I can help you out, if you'd like," Sam continued, "but we need to keep it quiet. Why don't you buy your drinks then find some excuse to meet me at one of those empty tables in the back of the restaurant."

The woman cocked her head, stared at him a moment, then smiled—satisfied and seductive. "All right. I'll be right there after I deliver these drinks."

Sam put a finger to his pursed lips and winked.

"Got it," she said with a nod. "I can keep a secret."

"I bet you can," said Sam with an appreciative chuckle. Whatever was going on with these two young, good-looking ladies from New York, Sam saw various opportunities, and he intended to serve whatever interests he could.

He then walked over to Catherine's table. She was engrossed in reading the back of the menu on which the history of the Black Barn was printed—a history rich with gruesome gunfights and visits by Hollywood celebrities. Sam had to clear his throat to get her attention.

"Oh," she said as she looked up, did a double take, and blinked. There he was with those damn blue eyes looking at her again. "I guess it's a good thing I'm already sitting down."

Sam smiled and replied almost shyly, "Prob'ly so. Sorry about that last time we met, or collided."

Catherine raised an eyebrow and said, both wary and curious, "No harm done, though I think I'll stay seated. Can I help you?"

"Not sure, though I'm absolutely sure I can help you."

"Oh, really?"

"You *are* looking for someone, right?"

"...Yes," she said. He was certainly an arresting presence, but Catherine had no desire to play games with this bar-fighting flirt. He was handsome, young, and vigorous, yes—but if he could read much more than a road sign, she'd have been impressed. He'd spilled out of the Black Barn the night before because of a barroom brawl, and then he'd gone back in for more with a smile on his face. This was the man who, while chatting up the woman at the counter of the feed store with tales of seduction and slaughter, had backed her smack onto a bag of manure. And he'd just been noisily arm wrestling in a restaurant as she walked in. He was exactly what Catherine didn't like about the mythic West: brash and mindless violence in cowboy boots and hat.

"The bartender tells me that..." he began to explain, but before he could give whatever excuse he was likely to give, Catherine's phone jingled with an incoming text. "Um... just a moment," she said as she took her phone out of her purse and read: Got a very good idea about de Bonnair. Surprisingly close to home. Should we meet tonight and discuss? She smiled, looked up at this disquieting cowboy and said, "Excuse me, but I've got to send a quick text. Can I..."

"Take your time. I'll be sitting over there." Sam motioned then walked to an empty table nearby.

As he turned, Catherine briefly saw how broad his shoulders were, how slow and lanky his gait was, how his boots were clean and stitched with an attractive design, and how, instead of a trace of farm in the air, there was only a hint of aftershave. Whatever else there was about him, he did clean up nicely. She was only vaguely aware of all of this, however, since she had more important—and promising—things to think about. She looked down at her phone and texted, Yes, can't wait. Where/when? She put her phone down and anxiously waited for a response.

Twenty-six seconds later, she had one. Everything except Black Barn is closed and Black Barn is disgusting. So my place, your place, or a dark parking lot of the sort Hitchcock would've liked?

She laughed, then considered her options. If her place at Violet's B&B hadn't included a nosy woman in purple and a room full of dead animals, it would have been preferable, but, under the circumstances, she chose the only other viable alternative. Despite the cinematic attractions of a dark and isolated parking lot, she texted, Your place. Where is it?

Devon quickly responded. Go east to Happy Canyon. I'm at 1608, ten minutes out of town in a little pocket of civilization. Easy to find. In an hour or so?

Catherine immediately replied. Yes, thank you! Slowly, meditatively, she slipped her phone back into her purse, took a very satisfied breath, and sat there and considered: though sooner than she'd have liked after the collapse of her last relationship, here was a new and promising possibility. He read books, had a nice sense of humor, and that flowing hair of his... After a few moments of indulgent, if vague, reflection, she shook herself back to the present and reluctantly got up to find out what in the world this booted and blue-eyed bother would claim he could do for her.

# CHAPTER 15

She didn't sit when she got to his table but, instead, stood some distance away and said, "I'm sorry, you were telling me you could help me find someone?"

"I'm pretty darn sure I can," he said with an excessively friendly smile.

"And who do you think I'm looking for?"

"I hear you're looking for Loretta de Bonnair."

Blinking with surprise, Catherine said, "That's exactly who I'm looking for. You know her?"

"Yes, but because both she and I don't like gossip and publicity, I ask you not to talk about any of this to anyone—at all."

"Oh," said Catherine, wary though intrigued, "okay." This man didn't just say he knew *of* Loretta de Bonnair; he said he knew her.

Just then, the woman with the russet hair and pink hat walked up. "Am I interrupting anything?" she asked coyly.

"No, no. Have a seat, both of you," Sam said, spreading his arms in a gesture of expansive invitation.

Not sure about any of this, Catherine slowly sat in the chair furthest from Sam while the other woman quickly sat in the chair nearest to him.

"I wanted to talk to both of you together because both of you coincidentally—and serendipitously—are in the same business and lookin' for the same person." Catherine and the other woman darted each other quick glances as Sam continued. "I'm also sure both of you, like I, want what's best for that good friend of mine, Loretta de Bonnair, am I right?"

"Absolutely," replied Miss Pink Hat with excessive conviction.

"Yes," Catherine replied, her response falling somewhere between an answer and a question.

"Loretta, as you may know, is... well, not really sick, but very old

71

and very frail. She also hates publicity—any sort of publicity, which, these days, is difficult to avoid. She really, *really* hates seeing and having to communicate with other people, particularly all of those crazy, gushing fans she's got all of a sudden."

"Yes," said the russet-haired woman, "I feel for her. It must be a real strain."

Catherine said nothing.

"Well, yes it is," Sam said, "and that's why she's asked me, a friend and fellow rancher, to be her 'agent' so that I can take care of all of that messy business and publicity stuff and let her concentrate on what she does best: write her books. So you see, if you two gals have anything to say to her, you're gonna wanta say it to me."

"That would be wonderful. You are so kind to do this for her," said Miss Pink Hat.

"Ah, yeah, perhaps, but," Catherine asked, "how do I know you are, as you say, her friend and 'agent'?"

Sam looked at Catherine and, with a hint of a smile, said, "Do I look like a guy who'd read romance novels just for fun?"

"Ah... no, you don't," Catherine replied.

"But I know that book of hers real well. Ask me anything you like about it."

"I do have a question, but not about the book. I was in the post office this afternoon where there's a stack of mail for her. Don't you think her 'agent' would have tried to pick that up and brought it to her?"

"Well, yeah, and I tried, but I don't exactly look like Loretta, and she's too—well, like I say, frail to come herself, and, well—"

Catherine jumped in again. "You couldn't just put her in a taxi or car or truck or whatever you drive out here and get someone at the post office to come out and confirm her identity and intentions?"

"A good idea... and I've even suggested that to her myself, but if you could see poor, crippled Loretta these days, a veritable wisp of what she used to be, hardly able to move, and too vain to be seen in her current state. For such a frail thing though, she's fiercely proud. You don't move Loretta de Bonnair—she moves you."

"I didn't know it was true in her life too," said the other woman with breathy admiration, "but it is definitely true of her fiction. *Rancho de Amor* is *so* moving."

Sam started to grin, then quickly stifled it. In a businesslike tone, he continued, "Yes, it is a fine book for a—well, for a romance."

Though still far from convinced that this man was telling the truth, Catherine realized that there might very well be a real Loretta de Bonnair somewhere who was very old and very frail and maybe even close to death. Her skepticism momentarily softened by concern, she asked, "Does she at least have what she needs? Health care, human company, financial resources? I hear she only got a small amount of prize money for her book, and if she's so frail, how can she run a ranch or farm or whatever?"

"She actually declined the five hundred dollars," Miss Pink Hat asserted clearly, "saying she was secure enough financially."

"Yes," Sam added after a moment's hesitation, "she is comfortable enough financially, but I know she feels kinda undervalued. And y'all know the book business better'n me." He looked first at the russet-haired woman, then, while shaking his head sadly, at Catherine. "Ain't nobody lookin' to spend much money on anything these days. Maybe I shouldn't say this, but you two young ladies are the first to make it out to this far-flung corner of the civilized world, and you come with serious interest in Loretta's new work. What's buzzing around here most of the time are fans who sigh too much and reporters who want to pick at her for a free story, and frankly she don't like any of it. It interrupts her writerly ways."

"The poor thing," said the other woman with broad sympathy. "I'm sure my offer will cheer her up though."

"I'm sure both of your offers will cheer her up," said Sam looking first at her then settling his gaze on Catherine. He squinted slightly as if either confused or curious. She blinked and looked away. The whole situation made her very uncomfortable.

The woman in the pink hat quickly pulled his attention back by loudly announcing, "I'm Sharie Blanchard," as she thrust a business card and her chest at him, "with Blushing Dove Press, the company that originally published *Rancho de Amor* and launched Loretta in the first place. Without us, no one would know her at all. But we now think we can launch her even further and with a very nice advance for her new book."

Catherine coughed with surprise. "You're from Blushing Dove Press, and *you* don't know who she is or where she is?"

73

"Well, we know she's a wonderful writer—we saw that before anybody else—and we know she didn't want to be bothered, but, well, her popularity is just out of control, so we figured we can guide her through it to more success while making sure nobody else bothers her. She is, after all, our writer."

"Without a contract, she's anybody's writer," Catherine clarified pleasantly.

"So you're with Dove... Well, well... I'm Sam, Sam Wilson," he said taking Ms. Blanchard's card. Then he turned to Catherine. "And you, ma'am?"

"Catherine Doyle."

Sam extended his hand toward her, but she did not place a business card in it. Instead, she took his hand. Much like the hand of the man at the bar, it was work hardened and rough, but he presented it more gently. She did not, however, respond so gently, but gave his hand a quick, hardy squeeze. She wanted to leave no false impressions; she was there to meet Loretta de Bonnair and until this storytelling cowboy could produce her in the flesh and blood, he would get nothing more than a name and a handshake.

"Nice, finally, to know your name, Catherine." He smiled and quickly looked from one to the other of Catherine's dark brown eyes.

She blinked, looked down, and heard him say with an excessively twangy accent, "I gotta say, with a grip like that, ya oughta do some arm wrestlin' around here yerself. You might beat that guy who juz beat me."

"Is that one of Ms. de Bonnair's favorite pastimes too?" Catherine asked.

"She's a little frail for that these days, but I wouldn't be surprised if it had been. She's a pretty tough cookie—or used to be."

"She's not only a good writer—she sounds like an interesting person. I look forward to meeting her as soon as possible," Sharie remarked.

Sam took a breath and, in a serious, measured voice, said to the two women seated in front of him, "I'll talk to her and see how she'd like to proceed." He paused, then leaned forward with a relaxed smile. "Loretta's gonna be interested in both of you, so... why don't you tell me a little about yourselves." His smile broadened. "For example, what do you two big-city gals like to do?"

"On the tame side," Sharie began coyly, "I like to read Westerns and romances, dance the Texas two-step, and discover new, wonderful writers like Loretta de Bonnair."

"Sounds good, and maybe we'll get to the not-so-tame side later," Sam said, raising an inquisitive, approving eyebrow. Then he turned to Catherine and raised both eyebrows expectantly.

She wasn't going to be pushed by either this swaggering cowpoke or a russet-haired rival into some ridiculous flirting duel. Feeling as if she were answering a cringeworthy query at the end of a Miss America contest, she replied coolly, "On the wild side, I read Arctic adventures from a comfortable chair in my warm apartment in Manhattan, talk to Emily, my cat, and try to do the job I'm asked to do—which, right now, is to find Ms. de Bonnair and discuss the possibilities of publishing another book of hers—if she has one."

"Oh, yes, most definitely she has," Sam said.

"You've read it?"

"Just about finished it."

"And?" Catherine asked, hesitantly intrigued.

"I think it's even better than the first, a little better crafted, more probing, and ..." He paused to find the right word.

Catherine tilted her head in interest.

Sharie, concerned with Catherine's professional interest and Sam's apparent interest in her interest, quickly inserted a question of her own. "And what do you like to do, Mr. Sam Wilson?"

"Well, we don't have quite as many things goin' on around here as you gals do in New York City, but we like it like that. We're simple and pretty unsophisticated, but we do have our fun."

"I'll bet you do." Sharie winked, then she turned to Catherine and said, "So you're from New York too. What publishing house are you with? Is it one we might have heard of?"

"Banter House," she replied with understated confidence.

"Oh my," said Sharie with exaggerated admiration, "we should be honored. They publish Literature with a capital L—inspiringly depressing novels and incomprehensible poetry. This sudden interest in romance is an exciting departure from sophisticated doom and gloom."

"I'm so sorry that you see literature, with or without a capital letter, as little more than doom and gloom. You obviously haven't read very much of what we publish."

"Oh, I've read plenty, and what I've read recently is that your literature isn't selling so well, and that is sad. I guess that's why you're testing the waters of romance. Admit it, you're only interested in de Bonnair's books because of what you think her books can do for you. You're just trying to save a drowning company."

Catherine paused to consider her answer, then said, "I'm here to serve a company that has been at the center of the best publishing in America for a very long time, and I wouldn't be here if I didn't think this particular author were better than most of the authors most publishers of romance novels carelessly toss out to the public."

"That's all very noble, but honey, your hoity-toity part of the book industry is dead."

"Dead? To publish books that inspire people to think, to care, and to explore?"

"The proof's in the pudding, and how many books have you been 'pudding' out there recently?" Sharie said, laughing at her own pun as she squared her shoulders and leaned toward Catherine. "Word on the street is that your company's on the ropes financially."

"Then you're on the wrong street listening to the wrong people."

"The trades don't lie."

"They also don't know everything."

By this point in the conversation, their voices had become rather loud and distinct.

Sam, more amused than embarrassed, coughed conspicuously, then said, "Ladies, ladies, this is not Madison Square Garden here. This is a quiet, civilized town. We might do some arm wrestling or throw a friendly punch every once in a while, but to contend with such rhetorical animosity..." He shook his head in mock disdain while Catherine briefly glanced at him with surprise. She had not expected "rhetorical animosity" to come from his lips.

Many within earshot of this commotion were also surprised, but it had nothing to do with Sam's choice of words. What they were hearing was a unique twist on the idea of the barroom brawl. When, however, Sam reestablished order, all went back to their business talking, drinking, and laughing over which sounds Sam now said, "Why don't y'all meet me at the Saddle Up tomorrow, and we can talk—individually—about how we can help you and our frail friend, Loretta. I promise to pass along whatever you want me to tell Loretta and get back to you. And I want to thank both of you wonderful, spirited young ladies. It's so heartwarming that you want to do something good for that remarkable woman. A real book contract with royalties and all would be, well... transformative. So why don't you, Sharie, meet me at the Saddle Up, say, at about noon, and you, Kate—"

"Catherine," she corrected.

"Sorry. Catherine, why don't you come by at about one o'clock, if that'd be all right with you gals?"

"Yes," said Sharie.

Catherine simply nodded. The whole thing was utterly confounding. She didn't know what to think about Cowboy Sam, and she knew exactly what to think about Sharie. She felt pushed and pulled in all sorts of directions by hopes, concerns, competition, and confusion.

Sam stood up, closed his eyes, bowed slightly, and said as he re-opened his eyes, "I look forward to seeing both of you tomorrow."

The two women shot each other icy looks and got up. Sharie thanked Sam with a warm, earnest handshake while Catherine, unhappy that she had to perform any further obsequious tasks, thanked Sam with a quick handshake, then both women went back to their respective tables like boxers at the end of a messy, indecisive round.

Sam stood where he was for a few moments, then he pursed his lips, walked slowly to the bar, winked at Walt, and continued out the side door. He'd done enough talking for the night and was headed home for a think.

# CHAPTER 16

Loretta de Bonnair, the elusive, frail, and aging author of *Rancho de Amor*, had good reasons to shy away from the glare of her recent success. She'd written a book that had questioned a few sacred notions near and dear to some of her neighbors. Mind you, these notions and her questions were not overwhelmingly important to either Loretta or her book. Quite frankly, had the popularity of Loretta's book not put the small town of Sisquoc, California, in the cultural spotlight, none of the locals would have much cared about the occasional reproach, even if that book had been written by Sisquoc's very own mayor. The fact that *Rancho de Amor* had become enormously popular, however, had many of its readers thinking about the little things Loretta suggested might be wrong with the way the good people of Sisquoc, California, lived their lives; and to the good people who lived those lives in and around Sisquoc, this was more than a little annoying. Loretta could write whatever she liked as long as nobody, or close to nobody, read any of it. But Loretta and her big pink book had crossed the line when they'd both become famous. Hordes of outsiders now flocked to town and questioned all the things that Loretta had questioned, and even added a few questions of their own. This wasn't just wrong; it was a betrayal of friend, of neighbor, and of a fine way of life. It might not have been obvious to the people outside of town why she might want to keep her identity hidden, but everybody in town knew perfectly well why that would be, were she local.

And then there was the other reason Loretta wanted to keep a low profile. It was a reason both outsiders and insiders would have understood, had they known what it was. Ms. de Bonnair had become fabulously famous when her romance novel won the Blushing Dove Barbara Cartland Historical Romance Prize. In order to open publishing possibilities for women who feared that they had missed the boat, the conditions of the prize stipulated that the author be a woman, be over fifty years of age, and the novel be a historical romance. Unfortunately, only one of these three conditions had been met. *Rancho de Amor* was certainly historical, but Loretta de Bonnair was twenty eight years old and a man by the name of Sam Wilson. Had Sam's friend Walt not picked up a magazine someone had left behind in the bar, Loretta would never have been born. But he had, and one slow night at the Black Barn, he showed it to Sam. In it was an advertisement for a contest open to any previously unpublished female author who could write a compelling, dramatic love story set in the past. "You could do this, Sam," Walt said. "You change your name and no one would know. Lotta authors do it. It's called nom d'plum. And you already got that short story about the French pirate and that pretty Spanish gal. I'll bet if you ramped up the lovey-dovey, put in more stuff about history, and made it hurt, you could get yourself published and make a little money. Why the hell not?"

Indeed, thought Sam, as he drove back up to the Circle D that night, why the hell not...

Money wasn't his object. He didn't need it, and it wasn't very much anyway. Much more of a goad was the challenge to turn a decent, recently abandoned short story into a full-fledged novel, and to finish that by an arbitrary, though inspiring, contest date—which he did.

Complications began, however, when he discovered online that he, or the older woman he claimed to be, had won the prize. To put anyone who might be curious off the trail of his false claims, he immediately sent the following letter to Blushing Dove:

Dear Blushing Dove Press,
I am honored to have won your Barbara Cartland Historical Romance Award. I look forward to seeing my little effort in print soon. As for the cash prize, please keep it and consider donating it to a worthy charity. The book is yours completely to do with as you wish: reprint, translate, make into a movie, or do whatever people do with books these days (computers and all of that strange business). I am an old woman who lives on a large ranch way out West. I have all I need, and now, with the publication of my book, I have even more than

I need. Thank you, every one of you.
Sincerely,
Loretta de Bonnair

And that, he was sure, would be that. There was no return address, though the postmark was from Sisquoc, California. This information, along with what "Loretta" had written in her letter, was about all anyone knew and anybody needed to know about the woman who had penned what was now the bestselling romance novel, *Rancho de Amor*.

Anybody who'd known him when he was a rough, tough kid breaking horses, a few noses, and an occasional heart wouldn't have imagined that Sam Wilson would ever have become Loretta de Bonnair. He'd grown up doing physically demanding jobs on various local ranches and helping his father build barns, fences, and stables in the area. He was a country boy through and through. But Sam began to bust people's expectations of him as soon as he left town for college. Sam had been an indifferent student through high school, but when he got to college, he discovered that he enjoyed studying pretty much everything—and he was good at pretty much everything he studied. One of those hitherto unseen aptitudes was for writing. He even took a creative writing class in his third year, but after running into more pretense than practice, he dropped the course and replaced it with a class in botany. He was much happier learning about the genetic construction of plants than the literary deconstruction of everything.

His happiness and independence, however, came to a violent end two months later when he got a call from his fifteen-year-old sister. Sobbing, she told him that their parents had just been killed in a car accident. Sam immediately dropped out of college and returned home to take care of his younger sibling.

The first thing he had to do was to find a job. And so, he went to the offices of the local newspaper, the *Sisquoc Patriot*, and offered his budding literary talent cheap. They let him write a few test pieces about regional events, but when he'd tried his talents on a large feature about the difference between ownership and stewardship, Ted Pombo wrote him a pointed note of severance: *Talent is not enough. Perspective and predilection are more important, and your predilections tend toward the unpopular side in this part of the world. It's one thing to write about the "needs of nature," but it is a very different thing to question the rights of the rich who own that nature. Without the rich, we cannot afford to publish this paper. Wise up and call me in ten years.*

The only other thing Sam was both good at and loved doing was ranch-hand work. With his local writing career stymied, he took a job way up the valley on the Circle D Ranch. He would've been paid more had he taken a job at one of the fancy horse ranches closer to town for which his father had often worked as a contractor. Sam, however, felt more comfortable working a little further from sophisticated taste. And even more importantly, he wanted to keep his sister a little further from sophisticated temptations. He was, after all, both her parents now.

Quietly, steadily, and without complaint, he did what he had to do. He worked as a ranch hand, then as a cowboy, and eventually as the young foreman of the Circle D. And he took care of his sister. Had Sam not been there to ease her back to balance, it was anyone's guess whether she would have survived adolescence. She was bright, beautiful, headstrong, and not just slightly self-destructive. With an intuitive mixture of support for who she was and guidance toward what he thought she could become, Sam raised her, or, as he preferred to say, "helped her to become herself." And throughout it all, he continued to read whatever interested him and to write whatever moved him—stories, essays, random ideas, even the occasional poem—some of which he sent out, almost all of which were rejected, and all of which he put in an ever-increasing number of boxes in a closet.

As for love, that was something he kept at arm's length. Handsome, smart, hardworking, and charming, it didn't take him long to find female companionship, though whatever relationships he had tended to be over almost as soon as they began. He wasn't collecting lovers—although he'd had a good few. And it wasn't that he had commitment problems. Quite the opposite. After high school, he became a serious student, and when his formal education came to a premature and tragic end, he became a serious surrogate parent. And by the time that last responsibility was taken care of, he became by habit what he was by nature—outwardly lighthearted but inwardly serious and demanding. In short, he didn't care to waste his time developing relationships he didn't think could develop very far. And so, if he couldn't find what he really wanted to find, he would do what he really wanted to do, which was to manage a huge cattle ranch on the edge of a seemingly endless forest, write what he wanted to write, think what he wanted think, and listen to the music of the wind.

He knew very well that after he'd launched his sister into independence, he could have quit ranching and either gone back to school or gone to a city where he would have found less physically demanding work and more intellectual stimulation. But he didn't leave the country principally because he liked where he was and what he was doing. He didn't have to keep up with the neighbors because he didn't really have any. He didn't have to mow the lawn because the cattle did that for him. Because he wasn't surrounded by the demanding bustle of others and because he didn't watch much TV, listen to the radio often, or sit on the Internet for long, he didn't have to react to the distracting noises of a world he didn't particularly like or care about. He loved all of the time and quiet in which he could think and dream and read and write while comfortably surrounded by the inescapable closeness of nature— and the only thing he really missed was being able to share that experience with someone else.

It was a paradox he couldn't easily resolve, but with a lot of time to think about it, he had imagined a few attractive solutions. If, for example, he could find a good-looking large-animal veterinarian who played the fiddle as a hobby, listened to NPR for the news, and read *American Cattlemen* for fun; or better, if he could meet a former Spanish teacher and one-time exotic dancer who wanted the peace, quiet, and space to research and write the definitive history of the pre-Columbian Americas; or even better, if he could find an ex– beauty queen whose talents were horse jumping, translating Chinese poetry—her grandfather having been a minor, but important, Chinese poet—and caring for homeless autistic children, then he might just be willing to have someone else in his life, and they would, when they chose to talk, have a whole lot to talk about.

Sam knew it was all very improbable. Smart, independent, beautiful, gutsy, and kind—yes, it was a little much to ask for in one person, but that didn't keep him from his fantasies. And those fantasies had, if nothing else, prepared him to write *Rancho de Amor*. It had not been written with any serious intent, and it was not what most would call a serious book. Much of it, in fact, was tongue in cheek. But not all of it. Despite his intent, and without even realizing it, the romantic core of his book was very serious, which was one of the principal reasons it had become so successful. Whether he acknowledged it or not, Sam Wilson was profoundly romantic, and not so deeply hidden in his book were the honest yearnings and frustrations of someone who wanted to love and care for someone he hadn't yet met. *Rancho de Amor* was, in a sense, a love poem to an unknown lover.

# CHAPTER 17

What an idea, Catherine reflected as she walked out of the Black Barn. On her way back to Violet's where her car was parked, she alternately chuckled, snorted, and shook her head as she thought about all she'd just heard. Of all the people in Sisquoc, California, Sam Wilson was the *only* one who had direct contact with Loretta de Bonnair? *Impossible.* She punctuated that thought with a slammed car door.

The very presence of this cowboy had made her both annoyed and nervous right from the start, and those feelings only increased the more she saw of him. He was so much of what she *didn't* like—macho maleness proud of its physical prowess and seemingly in constant need of proving it. There was also his stated preference for people who were, as he'd described them, simple and unsophisticated, a preference that made him about as different from anyone she'd want to involve in her life as she could think of. Even more baffling and unnerving were the parts that didn't seem to fit. That he could even claim to be a close friend of a sophisticated writer was hard, very hard, to believe. And then there was the way he spoke and what he said—a confused and confusing mix of "shucks, ma'am" folksy and rhetorical precision. Clearly, he was at least street—or pasture—smart. He was also, obviously, playing some sort of game and promising more than he could possibly deliver. Access to Loretta de Bonnair? Did he really think she was so gullible? He was handsome—yes; physically strong—yes; charming—yes, but all of that in combination with everything else made him essentially a charismatic country thug. What did he want, really, and what was he willing to do to get it? As she started her rental car and accidentally over-revved the engine, she decided that she probably would not be meeting him the next day. About all Catherine knew for sure was that Sam Wilson was, at best, a shameless flirt, and the whole thing was a shameless way to get her to go out with him, which she had no intention of doing.

Devon, on the other hand, hadn't claimed that he, and he alone, could conjure Ms. de Bonnair out of thin air. He simply said that he had a good idea about who that stubbornly secretive author was and where she might be. He was, as well, a kindred spirit in the world of books, genuinely witty, and not just slightly handsome himself. Most compellingly, he made her feel comfortable, which was something that cowboy definitely did not.

Despite feeling much better dealing with Devon about the possible whereabouts of Loretta de Bonnair, she did not feel completely comfortable about driving into the dark in a strange place to meet a man she didn't really know, however much less unnerving he seemed to be than Cowboy Sam. To feel a bit safer, she decided to give Vito a quick call. She'd promised to text or call with frequent updates, and this would give her a chance to do that and to feel a little more protected as she drove into this nighttime adventure. At least someone in the world would know where she was going and why. So she looked down at her phone and called her boss—just as she drove past Happy Canyon Road.

"Hello?" softly croaked a groggy-voiced Vito.

"Hi, Vito. I thought I should probably give you an update, and, well—"

"What time is it?"

"Nine-thirty here, twelve-thirty there. Is this too late?"

"Late, but not too late." He took a loud breath to help wake up, then asked, "So, what's the good news?"

"The good news is that there's no bad news and I may be getting some good news in a couple of minutes. I'm driving out to, well, out to meet the guy who works in the local bookstore. His name is Devon de Vries, and he says he's figured out who and where Loretta is."

"That sounds promising, but why out of town? Is he bringing her to you in an unmarked paper bag?"

"I'm meeting him at his place."

"Out of town past midnight or whatever time it is out there? Sounds serious or foolish, or both."

"He is a nice guy."

"Uh-huh... and he knows lots about books, he writes some poetry, he's got nice hair, and he looks a little underfed."

"You don't know that."

"Oh yeah? How long have we known each other?"

"Okay, some of that may be true, but this meeting is strictly de Bonnair business. Nothing else."

"One of the reasons I wanted you to go out there is 'cause you're a lot gutsier than you think you are, though maybe you're being a little too gutsy right now. Out to the middle of nowhere to meet some guy you don't really know, who claims to have information you need, but he can't just tell you in a text?"

"He could, and I'm sure he would, if I'd asked him, but just in case things are weirder than I'm sure they are, that's the other reason I'm calling you—so someone knows where I'm going to be. I'll text you a brief report when I get back to the B and B in an hour or so. If you don't get a text in two hours, call the National Guard."

"Great. Not only do I have my own crazy daughters to worry about, but now I've got a crazy editor to worry about too. Honestly, your safety is worth more than this potential book deal. Not much more, mind you, but more, okay? So don't do anything stupid, or allow Devon Deepfreeze—"

"De Vries."

"—*whatever* his name is to even *try* to do anything stupid."

"Don't worry. I know what I'm doing. And I've got a very good feeling we're close to finding that unfindable author."

"Okay. I'm going back to bed now, but I won't really sleep until you text me."

"Will do, I promise," she said and hung up.

She might have known what she was doing, but when she turned all of her attention back to the deserted road she was on, she wasn't completely sure where she was going to be doing it. There were, of course, no streetlights. Nor were there lights at any of the turnoffs or intersections. Worse still, there were no lights from the houses because there were no houses. Occasionally, she would glimpse some distant light coming from something half a mile from the road, but whether it was a house or a barn or a warren of witches with torches in the woods, she couldn't tell. And the further she drove, the more distant and distantly spaced these eerie lights became. Devon had texted her very clear directions, but in the pitch darkness, nothing was clear. He said it would take her ten minutes, so when she'd gone half an hour and still saw nothing of Devon's "pocket of civilization," she was forced to assume that she was, if not completely lost, at least not where she wanted to be. She knew she needed to stop and call Devon to tell him she was running a little late, but stopping on a deserted road in a darkness that seemed darker than black was not something she wanted to do. She drove another five minutes, hoping to come to some road with a sign or a place with a comforting light, but instead, the road she was on narrowed and started to wind into the mountains. And once the road began to rise, there was no shoulder and no place for her to pull over without being in the middle of the road itself. Worse, there was no place to turn around. Up and up she went through an ever thicker and, if she could believe it, darker forest. She knew now that she was very lost as she drove further and further from anything vaguely familiar. When something—a raccoon, a skunk, a bobcat, a mountain lion—ran across the road just in front of her car, she screeched to a stop just in time to prevent whatever it was from becoming another potential roadkill roommate. Keeping her engine running and the car in drive, she quickly called Devon. Before he answered, she took a deep breath and tried to control herself. She didn't want him to hear how frightened this gutsy New Yorker really was at that moment.

"Devon?" she said when he picked up, "Devon, I'm lost."

"Lost? Where are you?"

"Um, well, if I knew, I wouldn't be lost."

"I mean, what street are you on and what do you see?"

"I thought I was on Happy Canyon, but I've been driving for more than thirty minutes and I can't see anything out my window. It's all black, there are no lights or houses or anything, and the road just started to go up into some mountains, and there's no place to turn around, and... and... I'm kinda"—she took another deep breath—"concerned."

"Wow, you sound it. Do you remember anything particular that you passed?"

"About the last thing I remember before everything went completely dark with trees and mountains and a ridiculously dark sky was an arch over a dirt road or driveway with some weird design in the middle of a circle."

"Like a cattle brand?"

"I don't honestly know. I don't think I've ever seen a cattle brand."

"Do you have GPS on your phone?"

"I... I don't know... It's not really necessary in New York."

"Okay, okay. The best thing to do is to go back the way you came and get back to town. You said you've been driving half an hour, so why don't we meet in front of the bookstore in thirty minutes. We can sit in my car or yours, and I'll tell you who I think Loretta is, and where—surprisingly—you'll find her."

"That sounds great, Devon. I just met some cowboy in the Black Barn who says he's Loretta's friend and agent."

"A cowboy?"

"He looked and talked like one—which I guess doesn't mean much, but, well... I'll tell you all about it when I see you. Right now... I'd really like to get out of here. It's... it's kind of creepy. I'll see you in half an hour, if I can find a place where I can turn around."

"I'm sure you'll find some place to turn around before you get to Nevada," he said with a chuckle.

Catherine was not feeling quite so lighthearted and simply said, "I hope so. I'll see you in front of the bookstore."

"Yes. And drive carefully."

"I'll try..."

She eased her car further up the steep and winding road, and, a couple of unpleasant minutes later, she came to a wide curve and decided to turn around right then and there. She wasn't so concerned about hitting or being hit by another car. She hadn't seen one in over twenty minutes. She was worried, however, about not being able to see the edge of the road and, before she could do anything about it, driving right off a cliff. To say she accomplished her move carefully would be an understatement. She inched back and forth twelve times before finally completing her turn. With great relief, she much less cautiously sped back the way she'd come, relieved that soon she'd be back in town.

However, not knowing how she'd gotten to where she was, she was not sure how to get back to where she'd begun. What few roads there were all looked the same and when she finally found one, instead of turning right, she turned left and, once again, drove away from town and toward another mountain road.

For a while, things looked familiar, as if she'd passed that gate, that collection of lights blinking at her from behind trees, and that noisy grating in the road. Now that she was paying more attention, she noticed that pretty much every driveway, if such dirt roads could be called driveways, had some sort of arch from which hung either a name or one of those weird "cattle brands" Devon had referred to. As she glided along roads distantly dotted with these signs of ownership and possession, the thought struck her that, out West, the whole idea of possession was brutally—and beautifully—honest. She came from and lived in a world of complex territorial claims—who owned what, who'd thought of it first, who held the patent or copyright— but the demarcation of ownership was, if it wasn't owned by some ostentatious billionaire who'd put his name all over everything, less clear. Branding, the pressing of hot iron into the flesh of that which you claimed as yours, was what it was all about. And here, there was even a calligraphy of possession—bold, unembarrassed, and clear.

This was, however, about the only thing that was clear to her as the road she was on unexpectedly narrowed and started to rise into the mountains. Catherine slowed down, and as she started to climb through a steeply mounting curve, she realized this wasn't the same road she'd been on before. Same darkness. Same deserted countryside. Same mountains... but somewhere else. She was lost— again. Angrier this time than anything else, she pulled as far to the side as she could and swiped on Devon's number.

"Hello," he said cheerfully. "Are you having a hard time finding a place to park?"

"No. I'm parked, if you can call it that, in the middle of nowhere. Again."

"But... didn't you just come back down the road?"

"Yes. But apparently it wasn't the same road. I'm lost. And I'm about to drive into these ridiculous mountains again."

"Well, wow... I don't know what to say. Here I am, and there you are. I... I'm so sorry I'm not there. Can you tell me where you are, any clear hints, so maybe I could come out?"

"Darkness—everywhere—and mountains. And no, don't try to come out here because I really don't know where 'here' is. I'll turn around and try it again. Eventually, I'll make it back."

"Should I wait?"

"No, no. I've wasted enough of your night."

"Well, so let's meet for coffee tomorrow morning."

"Want to meet at the Saddle Up Café, say, at eight-thirty?"

"How about nine-thirty? You're gonna love what I've figured out."

"I'm sure I will, if I can ever get out of these mountains."

"You will. Just get back into the valley, and you'll eventually get here. Maybe you should text me when you get back, or if you're still lost in an hour?"

"If I'm still lost, I'll text you... and I'll call the police. Otherwise, I'll see you at the Saddle Up in the morning."

"Looking forward to it. I'd really love to come out and find you, but—neither of us knows where you are. I mean, maybe I could drive out and try to find you... I don't know."

"No, no. Don't worry about it. Probably the worst thing that could happen is that I'd hit a skunk in the road and watch it come back to haunt me in my room later tonight."

"It's a good thing smell isn't a part of our bad dreams."

"It won't be a dream if it happens. It's an odd little detail about Violet's place... but I'll tell you about it later."

"Oh... okay. So you get back safe and sound. *À demain*, as they say," and he hung up.

*À demain* indeed, Catherine thought with a resigned chuckle, aware by the luminous clock on the rental car dashboard that it was less than an hour until *demain*, and she was still lost. For a while she simply sat there, and between occasional sighs, she considered how strange the day had been from its Violet beginning to its pitch-black end.

Slowly though, she realized that things weren't quite so pitch black. Despite the seemingly utter darkness surrounding her, she could see the ragged shapes of the mountains she was headed into. Wanting to see them more clearly, she reached for the door handle— but stopped. They were beautiful, yes—but it was dangerous out there. She decided to stay inside the car with the engine running, just in case, though she lowered the window to get a better look. With no moon in the sky, Catherine realized it was the stars and nothing but the stars that gave visible shape to the blue-gray mountains surrounding her. The landscape was serene and silent and like nothing she'd ever experienced before. It was enchanting, and for a few minutes she hardly even breathed, not wanting to disturb the quiet.

No one knew where she was. *She* didn't even know where she was. She was simply where she was and it was beautiful—that is, until something rustled in the brush nearby. She rolled her window back up and, with a shudder and a quick, apprehensive glance in every direction, she turned her car around and started back down the road, not relieved this time, but neither quite so nervously indifferent to the details of place. As she bumped over another one of those strangely placed gratings in the road, she saw lights in a clearing and could just make out a house. It was a large white Victorian farmhouse with two stories and a porch. Someone lived there and was comfortable. It was far too removed from the things she loved for her to really imagine such comfort, but at least they were home, possibly with someone they loved, or at least with a much-loved cat.

On she drove, and half an hour later a promising dome of light appeared in the distance. Eventually, Catherine found herself traveling west on Cota Road and, five minutes later, through the deserted heart of Sisquoc, her temporary home.

She parked her car in front of Violet's B&B and texted Vito. Got completely lost—did not meet the contact. Will tomorrow. Back at B&B. NOW sleep tight. When she got in the door, she got a response from Vito: Thank you. I will. Good luck tomorrow.

She nodded to her phone then texted Devon, Back at Violet's finally. Thanks for your concern. Sleep well, see you tomorrow.

His response, PHEW! I was worried. See you in the sunny part of the morning... sweet dreams, came in after she'd gone to sleep, but she was very happy to discover it when she woke.

# CHAPTER 18

The clock in the stomach of a raccoon read 8:47 when Catherine opened her eyes. That was later than she'd thought she'd be getting up, but it was still early enough for a shower and a quick bite to eat.

After an unimprovably tepid shower, she confronted her face in the mirror. She was not a woman who cared much for makeup. In fact, she believed that no one worth her while would fall for such cheap and easy manipulations, but that conviction did not prevent her from observing a careful, if brief, daily routine—the slight darkening of the eyelashes, the rubbing on of some subtle base, the application of lip gloss—a routine she performed somewhat more carefully on this particular morning. She was aware of whom she was about to see and, even more importantly, who was about to see her.

She made her way down the hallway to the breakfast room and was abruptly stopped by a couple that was spilling out of one of the rooms. They were so passionately entwined in one another's arms that she couldn't get past them. With their limbs groping about in all directions, Catherine felt as if she'd been forced to dance with an epileptic octopus. The couple, both in their late thirties, appeared to be either in the first throes of the affair that would ruin their respective marriages or the first month of their second marriage.

When this coupled obstacle finally laughed and jerked its way out of her path, she walked into the sun-bright breakfast room and saw a most surprising and discomforting sight. Seated at the table wearing perfectly fitting jeans, a ballet-necked hunter-green sweater, and matching stilettos was Sharie Blanchard, her newly discovered counterpart in the business of finding Loretta de Bonnair.

"Ah," exclaimed Violet, as Catherine came into the room, "here's our other New York girl. Catherine," she said to her, then turned with a nod to Sharie, "this is Sharie. But maybe you've already met? You're both in books, both work in New York, and Sharie arrived from New York just ten minutes before you did two nights ago. You probably even passed each other getting here."

"Yes," Catherine replied as pleasantly as she could, "we've met."

"We share a common interest," Sharie said with a big smile and an ambiguous tone.

Violet paused, noted the tone, then turned to Catherine. "I'm surprised to see you up so early, my dear, after you came in so late. I trust you found some local attraction?"

"To be honest, I got lost..." Catherine began, but seeing a satisfied smile broaden on Sharie's face, she went in another direction, "completely lost in the beauty of your California night. I went for a drive up one of your canyons. I had business to do, and then I became enchanted by all of the rugged, quiet space. Very different from New York City." She laid it on a bit thick, but at least the smile on Sharie's face was forced to freeze with the mention of "business."

"Yes," Violet said, warmly, "this is our little piece of paradise, so different from a place like New York. None of the hurly-burly, hustle-bustle. Just good, simple living and good, simple folk, with a beautiful sky overhead."

With wide-eyed and calculated innocence, Sharie added, "And I've noticed it is especially beautiful at sunset when the whole sky turns a wonderful shade of... well, violet."

Turning to the oblique flattery, Violet bowed her head slightly. Then she turned back to Catherine and said, "Have some eggs, dear, while they're still hot. And do try some of that wonderful lavender-flavored butter. It's local, both the butter and the lavender."

"It looks wonderful. Your breakfasts really are as good as you said they'd be," Catherine said while plopping a spoonful of violet eggs on her plate. She did, however, forgo the lavender butter by willfully resisting both scone and toast. "Speaking of these wonderful breakfasts," she continued, taking a seat as far from Sharie as she could, "I think I'd like to be able to have one or two more of your breakfasts. My business in Sisquoc is going to take another day or two, so I'd love to reserve my room, if it's still available."

"If Ezekiel's little monsters don't scare you, then yes. You are very lucky you're not squeamish. There isn't going to be a room available from tonight through the weekend anywhere around here because of the de Bonnair festival."

Sharie stopped spreading lavender butter on her purple scone and looked up. "I thought it was going to be a more general 'fans of romance' convention. But maybe I misunderstood," Sharie quietly concluded, now buttering Violet with attractive humility.

"No, you're right, dear. It is for fans of romance, but, honestly, is there anyone more important in the field right now than Loretta de Bonnair? I don't think so—and neither does anyone else, really. And though I don't think she'll even show up for the award we've decided to give her, we will certainly be talking about her more than anyone else."

"If she's so popular," asked Sharie, still cloaked in a tone of innocence, "why would she not be there? Is she just too frail to travel?"

"Or," Catherine added, "does she not even really live around here—anymore?"

"Oh," Violet said, chortling, "it's nice to see such keen interest in a romance writer by the younger generation, even if it is 'just business.'"

The two editors glanced at each other without expression.

"People say," Violet continued, "that she lives on a ranch not far from town but… I'm not so sure that Loretta de Bonnair isn't living right here in Sisquoc under everyone's nose."

"What's so debonair about Loretta?" asked a very much older man at the breakfast table.

"Loretta DAY Bonnair," Violet articulated with emphasis, "is a local writer who just happens to have written a very successful and beautiful romance novel. Our town is hosting a convention for the fans and aficionados of romance literature, all of whom will undoubtedly be most interested in what Ms. de Bonnair wrote. Her book is the number one bestseller in America right now. You have, perhaps, heard of *Rancho de Amor?*"

He turned to his wife and said, "I don't know—have we heard of it?"

"Yes," his wife replied, "I told you about it last week and said we should buy a copy."

Turning back to Loretta, he asked, "Is it that big pink thing you see in whatever bookstores are left?"

Bristling, Violet replied, "It has a beautiful pink cover; it is ample, both in size and literary delight; and you can find it in pretty much any bookstore that is left, yes."

"Well, your little convention sounds fascinating, but I think we'll push on down the road to check out the newest messy diapers in the family, at least, on the young end of things." The couple had stopped in Sisquoc overnight on their way from Portland to San Diego to see their first great-grandchild.

"Raymond!" his wife hissed sharply. "*Pl-ease!*"

"Sorry. Got carried away. First great-granddaughter. I'm too excited for polite company. Great lavender butter, BTW."

"BTW?" Violet repeated with a cool, inquisitive look.

"By the way."

"Ah," she said, relaxing slightly. "Thank you."

"So you see no chance of Ms. de Bonnair showing up?" Sharie asked, now in a more businesslike tone.

"Unfortunately, dear, I really don't. She writes a good romance, but that woman lives a good mystery."

Again, Catherine and Sharie glanced at one another. This time, there was something akin to sympathy in their eyes, albeit a sympathy wrapped in nettles.

Catherine took a final forkful of eggs, bussed her plate, and, as she started out of the room, glanced back at Violet. "I'd love to talk to you more about the area, but right now, I have to meet someone at the—well, somewhere in town," she said, stumbling away from revealing too much to a very quiet, very attentive Sharie Blanchard. Catherine enjoyed the idea of leaving Sharie to wonder and worry about who she was seeing, where, and why.

# CHAPTER 19

When Catherine walked into the Saddle Up, Devon was seated at a table next to a window bathed in early morning light. His head was down, his glasses on, his hand and mind busy writing something that looked, from a distance, like a poem. Promising, she thought... very promising.

Although she didn't look at him directly while she was ordering her coffee, she was peripherally aware that he'd looked up at least once, seemed to stare in her direction for a moment, then went back to his writing.

"Don't let me interrupt," she said as she slid her cup of coffee onto his table. It was, indeed, a poem he was writing. Sitting down and pulling out her phone, she said, "I'll just catch up with the *Times.*"

"LA, of course..." Devon playfully challenged.

"Sorry... New York. It's a little bigger and will keep me busy while you write."

Whenever she was asked if she had ever wanted to be a writer herself, Catherine would reply with glib finality, "Why would I want to feel like I have homework to do every single moment of the day? It's easier and far more entertaining to read someone else's prose than to struggle to write my own." True as this was for her, she could think of few more enjoyable ways to spend an hour or two than to read while sitting with someone who did write. It was the sort of intimate parallel-play she longed for but had experienced only fleetingly.

"No, no, we have much to discuss," Devon said as he arranged his papers. "I'll finish this later."

"I'm so sorry about last night. I don't know what I did but—"

"Don't worry about it. You're here now—safe and sound. I have to admit, I was a little worried."

"So was I. It's so dark and isolated out there. Are you actually comfortable living so far from other people?"

"I don't, actually. I live in something of a suburban development. My house is about one hundred feet from my neighbors on both sides. They can't hear much when I crank up the Shostakovich on my speakers, but I'm hardly out in the middle of nowhere, which is where it sounds like you ended up last night."

"I certainly wasn't in any pocket of civilization. There was no one and nothing around… well, except for some trees and mountains. Did you grow up around here?"

"Santa Barbara, just over the hill," he said, waving his hand toward the window.

Catherine looked out and asked, "You call those hills?"

"Well, I guess technically they're mountains, but they aren't very big."

"If you say so. So why'd you come over those 'hills'?"

"I love the peace and quiet, I love the bookstore, I love the people I get to meet—present company very much included—and I needed a job, and this is where it was. It's a bit off the beaten path, but we do occasionally get people all the way from New York out here, even if they think that their *Times* is better than our *Times*," he said with a smile.

"The poor fools." She smiled back. "And what do you think of them—the people, not the newspaper, as a rule?"

"As a rule, I avoid all rules, but I can say that those I've met most recently seem to be very bright and *very* alluring. They're even leading me to discover things I didn't know about where I live—and who lives here."

"Like… maybe, Loretta de Bonnair?"

"Like… for example, that very lady."

"So," Catherine said, leaning toward him with excited anticipation, "what did you find?"

"Oh, a few things," he said temptingly.

Catherine's eyes widened, and she said with amused impatience, "Tell me!"

"It might be nothing, but there's someone who comes in the bookstore who has a peculiar interest in romance novels."

"For better or worse," Catherine said, on the brink of disappointment, "a whole lot of people are interested in that stuff."

"Yes, but not only is this particular woman obsessed with the genre and buys every new romance that comes in, she knows more about Ms. de Bonnair than anyone else I've ever met, which *these* days in *this* town is impressive. And then there are these." Devon pulled a folder from under the poem he'd been writing and extracted a small stack of handwritten letters. "These are letters she has written to me, sixteen of them in the last six months, requesting that I order certain titles. Each letter is at least two pages long and goes into elaborate detail about the book she's requesting and why it is, in her opinion, so very important for me to stock it in the bookstore. These are the letters of a writer who knows *way* too much about romance novels. And then there are the similarities between herself and Loretta."

"Really? Oh, this is good, Devon. Very good. Give me a few 'for instances.'"

"I remember one night recently when I was bored out of my mind, she came into the bookstore and I let her rattle on about her favorite writer, Ms. de Bonnair. She told me all sorts of things I don't remember now, but I do very distinctly remember that she told me she's done a careful count of the number of times Loretta uses words to describe colors, and one color stands out above all the others."

"Pink?"

"Close."

Raising an eyebrow, Catherine said, "Violet?"

Devon nodded. "Do you see where I'm going?"

"Do you know where I'm staying?" she asked.

"Yes."

"Wow. This could be it, Devon. Violet certainly loves violet and she is obsessed—almost over-the-top obsessed—with Loretta de Bonnair. It's a perfect cover. And it makes so much sense psychologically. She's a typical writer—self-absorbed, and yet she talks about everything, including herself, with a narrator's distance. She even just said this morning that she thinks Loretta is in disguise and hiding right here in town. Wink, wink!"

"Yep," Devon said with a very satisfied smile.

"I do wonder though why she'd hide this... and not even ask what business I want with Loretta."

"Who knows, maybe she plagiarized the whole thing, or she's playing some game and is waiting for the right moment to dramatically reveal herself and make herself available to more publishers. She's a savvy businesswoman, coy—and smart."

"You're right. This could be good, *very* good, Devon," Catherine said, beaming. Then she paused. "Except that, if it's true, I just left Violet alone with a very determined rival."

"A rival? Since when did you acquire a rival?"

"You know the book business. A lot of publishers would like to sign a contract with Loretta de Bonnair, but there's only one publisher desperate enough and another publisher well connected enough to send someone out here on this wild goose chase. My rival is the connected one. She works for Loretta's current publisher, though even *they*, apparently, don't know where Loretta is. Their rep is out here and also staying at Violet's—where I just left her talking with Violet about Loretta."

"Hmm… Well, if I'm right, that's probably not so good."

"No," Catherine said, getting up quickly, "if you're right, it's not so good. I think I should get back there and head her off at the pass." She put her hands on the table and leaned toward Devon. "I owe you—big time."

"Yes, you do. But you can pay it all back, with interest, if you let me take you out to dinner—tonight, to a good local place."

Hesitantly, Catherine asked, "The Black Barn?"

"That's local, but *not* very good, unless you need to eat half a cow to be happy. There's a place in Tres Robles, La Parodie de la Campagne." His pronunciation was almost perfect, though not quite.

"La Parodie? The parody of the country?" Catherine asked, confused.

"No, the Paradise of the Country."

"Ah, Le Paradis de la Campagne," Catherine replied.

"Yes."

With a good ear and four years of college French, her French was good enough to gently adjust Devon's pronunciation and, in so doing, remove the parody from paradise. "Well then, I'd be delighted to pay off my debt at Le Paradis de la Campagne."

"I'll pick you up at seven o'clock in front of Loretta's… I mean, Violet's. I'll drive because, well…" He didn't finish the thought.

"About all I can say is that I never get lost on the subways. I don't particularly like driving—I'd rather watch the ride than the road."

Then she rubbed her hands together with excitement. "I can't tell you, Devon, how good this would be. The idea that Violet might be the real Loretta de Bonnair! It would definitely simplify things and make that storytelling cowboy nothing more than an irrelevant nuisance."

"Oh. Right. You were going to tell me about your meeting at the Black Barn with Loretta's ranch hand, best friend, book agent. Whatever it was sounded pretty insane."

"It was, but it's not worth talking about now. Anyway, I've gotta run. I can't let that other woman work on the best Loretta we've found so far. We really need this contract. Boy, do we need it." She put her hands on his and gave a quick squeeze. "Thanks again."

Devon, taking hold of her hands, stood up and gently kissed her cheek. "See you tonight," he whispered.

Catherine smiled broadly then almost ran out of the café. All of a sudden, so many things were on the verge of being so very right.

# CHAPTER 20

As Catherine strode back to the B&B, a red convertible pulled up next to her and stopped.

"Did you forget something for your 'business meeting'—or is it already over?" Sharie called out.

"I... I forgot something," Catherine mumbled as she walked past Sharie's car.

"Right," said Sharie mockingly. She waved, gunned her engine, and took off down the street.

With increased concern, Catherine hurried back to Violet's. What if Violet and Sharie had already talked and Violet had accepted Sharie's offer?

But no, there hadn't been enough time for that. And anyway, maybe Violet wasn't Loretta. And yet, given what Devon had just said and what she had inadvertently observed, it seemed possible that Violet could be the hidden author everyone was looking for.

Catherine went straight to the kitchen when she got to Violet's. The colorful proprietress wasn't there, but her husband was humming an unrecognizable tune and noisily washing the breakfast dishes.

"Um... hello?" Catherine said to his back.

He stopped humming, looked up, turned around, and when he saw Catherine, quickly walked over with a wet hand extended. "Hello there."

Catherine looked at the soapy, dripping fingers, and hesitated.

He quickly pulled his hand back and wiped it on his pants while saying, "You're, yes, you're the one I scared the other night with my, well, my new raccoon. I feel terrible, really terrible about that."

"Don't, please. There was no harm done. I went right back to sleep."

"And you don't mind, well, you don't mind rooming with my frightening little friends?" He proffered his somewhat drier hand which Catherine shook gingerly.

"They're not so frightening. You do a nice job."

"Thank you. Poor things, I do try to give them something of a... well, a second life."

"They are very lively, yes," she said, then jumped to the business at hand. "Is Violet around, by any chance?"

"Not right now. Is there... um," he paused with habitual, somewhat awkward, somewhat endearing hesitation, "is there anything I can help you with?"

"Not really." Then she paused and thought better of that response. "Well, actually, maybe you can. I was wondering... does your wife like to write things?"

"Oh, she's writing all, well, a lot of the time. Baking, writing, and reading romances are her, yes, her three favorite things to do. Why? Do you need her to write something?"

"No, though she seems to be so observant, she could write any number of interesting things, I'm sure. Has she ever shown you what she's written?"

"Almost never, no." He shook his head and repeated, "No. She's very secretive about it, and I'm not much of a, well, not an avid reader. She steers clear of my hobby, and I steer clear of hers. It's one of the things that makes us such a happy, yes, such a happy couple."

"Ah... the secret to a successful relationship," she said, both to give a polite response and to articulate what, at that moment, she thought might just be the secret she'd been missing.

"It's no secret, no secret for us. We met and got married when we were young and just got used to, well, used to being used to each other. I like how she likes what she does, and, well, she seems to like that I like what I do, and we both like that we don't have to like the same things if, well... if that makes sense."

"Yes... yes," she said hesitantly, not completely sure she had understood all of what he'd said. She did, however, know what she wanted to know. "So Violet has liked to read and write for a long time?"

"Yes. Reading, writing, both of them. Yes."

"Interesting. And she definitely *seems* to know a lot about one author in particular, Loretta de Bonnair."

"Yes. I think she knows more about Loretta than, well, than Loretta does herself."

"You know, a few people are beginning to think that she might actually *be* Loretta. I'm not one of them, but..." Catherine trailed her baited line.

"What a funny, well, an interesting thought," Ezekiel responded to the lure. "My wife, a famous romance writer? It would certainly make it possible for us to travel, or, well, go more places." He got a distant look in his eyes as if he were imagining the taxidermic possibilities of various distant roads.

Breaking into his silent reverie, Catherine asked, "Yes, it does seem unlikely that she's Loretta herself, but do you think she's at least met her? Has she ever mentioned anything to you that might indicate that she knows Ms. de Bonnair?"

"Mention to me? No... not to me, definitely. You'd really have to ask her about all of that."

"Right," Catherine replied with a polite and pensive expression. "Will she be back soon?"

"I don't think so. All of this convention business has her running around to meetings and... well, and other errands all day. She said she'd be back at about five."

"Ah. Well then, I'll come back around five. Thanks." She was about to leave when she thought of one more question. "Do you happen to know if the other young woman who's staying here—Sharie, I believe, is her name—talked to your wife before she left this morning?"

"I can't, no, I can't really say, but they couldn't have talked for long. Violet was out of here right after breakfast. She was in... well, in a rush."

"Oh." She shrugged. "Oh well. Thanks again. I'll see you later."

It certainly didn't seem likely that Violet had committed her next book to Blushing Dove, or that she had even talked to Blushing Dove's busy representative yet. This was good, thought Catherine as she left the kitchen. But if Violet actually were Loretta, she knew she had to finish reading her book before talking to her. She'd intended to finish it that morning, but in her rush to see Devon she'd forgotten to bring it. She now went back to her room, grabbed *Rancho de Amor*, stuffed it into a bag, and left for the small local library she had seen at the end of Cota Road the day before.

On her way back downtown, she amused herself with the thought that Violet Smith might actually be Loretta de Bonnair.

If she really were, she was, indeed, playing a clever game waiting for the right time to unmask herself. Violet could write about the area as knowledgeably as she could because she lived right in the midst of those who would "string her up" if they knew who she was. But they wouldn't know—not yet, in any event. They were looking for an old rancher in a skirt. Instead, the real Loretta ran a romantic bed and breakfast and, with a typical artistic conceit, hid in the hues of herself. Of course de Bonnair was her favorite writer. What writer doesn't prefer the mirror to the window? But what about that cowboy of hers? With a start, Catherine wondered if she and that cowboy-costumed regular at the Black Barn were actually in cahoots. Was he part of her ruse: a red herring in cowboy boots?

She started to walk faster. She just *had* to stop by the bookstore and tell Devon about it. She rounded the corner onto Cota then slowed down with second thoughts. Their relationship was still too new for this sort of spontaneous exuberance. A text would be enough, she thought, as she pulled out her phone. Violet not home. Hubby confused. Your guess as intriguing as ever, just needs confirmation. Could cowboy last night be part of her game—red herring?

With her message sent, she continued toward the library with her phone in her hand in anticipation of a quick text response. Devon's response was quick, but it was a call, not a text.

"Catherine?"

"Devon, you get my text?"

"Yes, and responding by text would take longer than a quick chat. Plus, I do like hearing your voice."

Catherine couldn't help smiling, then she said, "It's probably foolish, but it does make some sense to add a *Rancho* touch to her game by getting some cowboy type to help pull suspicion away from her. And it certainly explains that weird stuff at the Black Barn last night."

"So what *was* that weird cowboy stuff last night?"

"Well, after walking into the Black Barn and seeing this guy in the middle of some absurd arm-wrestling contest, I go up to the bartender and say I'm looking for Ms. de Bonnair. The bartender, who must also be a part of this little conspiracy"—Catherine mused for a moment, then continued—"he talks to this cowboy who then gets Sharie—that's the woman from Dove—and me to sit with him at some table in the back. He tells us to keep it all hush-hush and says he's Loretta's friend and agent, and we have to talk to him and only him about our offers."

"He's got both of you there—at the same time—at the same table?"

"Yes. He probably thought that it would make us compete more and raise our offers."

"And he'd just been arm wrestling."

"And the night before, I saw him in a barroom fight."

"Seems to be a pattern here."

"Yeah, and it's not a very pretty one. But he sure does pull attention away from everything else."

Devon took a deep breath and then said, "Maybe he's a red herring and is working with Violet, but I've met and talked to Violet many, many times. She's living in a different world, a world of fluffy romance, and I can't really see her getting involved with some combative cowpoke in the Black Barn just to set up a diversion. I mean, what does this crackpot cowboy give her little story that her own husband in a cowboy hat wouldn't give her?"

"I don't know." She paused to consider. "I guess not much. I'm just trying to make sense of that cowboy's story, which really doesn't make much sense."

"Oh, I don't know about that. I think it makes perfect sense in a different sense. He sounds like some juiced-up dude who, when he isn't punching either cows or other cowboys, tries to corral some out-of-town fillies with an impossible, but enticing, story. It's classic. With the help of the bartender, he finds out what the out-of-town women want, tells them he's the only one who can get it for them, and hopes that at least one falls for it long enough for him to get... well, what he wants."

"You seem to know this routine," she teased wryly.

"Only in the abstract, I assure you."

Catherine laughed. "A good response. So it looks like our cowboy probably has nothing to do with any of this."

"Sure looks like it."

Catherine paused, sighed with relief, and said, "Good. I'm telling you, Devon, everything about that man is so... unnerving. Violence and lies, lies and violence."

"Not a good combination."

"No, not a good combination. I was even going to see him at noon—no, one o'clock—today at the Saddle Up so he could give me 'the details,' but I don't have to worry about that anymore. I definitely won't be there to meet him. I'll just go back and have a chat with Violet at five and, until then, concentrate on finishing *Rancho de Amor*."

"You're *actually* reading it?"

"I have to say, and... well, I don't have too far to go," she said, veering away from what she'd intended to admit. She was actually enjoying that big pink book but didn't want Devon to question her taste in literature so early in their relationship. "I guess you haven't read it?"

"I haven't yet had the opportunity. I'll let you tell me all about it."

"With pleasure."

"Tonight," he said with a voice resonant with anticipation.

"Tonight." She smiled to herself, put her phone back in her purse, and started off toward the Sisquoc Library.

When she'd walked past it the day before on her stroll into "de Bonnair country," she thought that it looked like a great place to spend a few undisturbed hours. It was housed in one of the cutest and tiniest buildings she had ever seen. Some fieldworker might have lived in this clapboard box a hundred years ago, but if he'd had more than a small bed and a pot-bellied stove for cooking and heating, he wouldn't have had room for himself.

As she walked up the three steps to the door, she read the hand-painted sign:

SISQUOC PUBLIC LIBRARY, MAINTAINED BY
THE VOLUNTEER LIBRARIANS ASSOCIATION OF
GREATER SISQUOC

She was heartened to know that there were others somewhere close by who liked books as much as she did, though as she walked up to the door, she realized that there weren't quite enough of them to keep that library open for more than a few hours a week.

NOON TO 5 P.M., WEDNESDAY, THURSDAY, AND FRIDAY;
9 A.M. TO 3 P.M., SATURDAY

This meant that she would have to wait an hour to discover its pleasures.

Before leaving, Catherine stood and looked at the colorful collage of posters taped to the glass of the door announcing various local artistic events: Doug Strathmore and his bluegrass band playing at the Howling Owl in Tres Robles on Friday nights for the next month; the Stray Cats Jazz Quintet at Lydia's Inn on Highway 56; Chata Gutierrez singing at Christie's in Buellton this Friday and Saturday; the Valley Vixens performing at the Chumash Casino Resort, indefinitely; local poet Anja Van Houten reading from her new book *Lovers and Liars* at the Stone Hinge Café in Ballard; and the Lompoc Chamber Orchestra giving an all-Vivaldi concert at First Church on the coming Sunday in Buellton. Prominent in the middle of the door was a large purple poster announcing FORC, the Fans of Romance Convention, and listing the events that would take place on Saturday at various sites on the campus of East Valley High School, "Home of the Mighty Cougars." Both surprised and pleased, Catherine reflected that culture seemed to be moving along steadily, if unhurriedly, in this remote part of the world.

# Chapter 21

With an hour free before the library opened, Catherine decided to walk next door and check out the Sisquoc Museum of Folk Art and History. It was open, though it certainly wasn't crowded. The donation box just inside the front door was empty, and no one was in the first room of historical displays. She slipped five dollars through the slot of the clear plastic box, then turned her attention to a display of local rocks. The arrangement was attractive, but the subject was not enthralling, and so she moved on to the next part of the exhibit, which featured the local flora. There were some very pretty flowers, but this display also did not hold her interest for long.

Walking counterclockwise around the room, she left the flora and moved on to the fauna: the raccoons, skunks, bobcats, deer, hawks, mountain lions, etc. arranged in poses much like the poses of the animals who were her current bed and breakfast roommates. She glanced at one of the identification labels; underneath both the common name and the Latin name of the dead beast, the label noted, *Taxidermy by Ezekiel Smith.* Catherine smiled. She'd been in Sisquoc barely two days, and she already knew the local taxidermist. It was oddly comforting.

As she turned to the final wall of displays in the first room, the Chumash and pre-Chumash wall, a man wearing jeans and a well-ironed dress shirt, with short brown-going-gray hair and glasses, walked in from a small adjoining room.

"Ah, a visitor," he exclaimed with delight. "Welcome." It wasn't clear whether he was English and had spent a few accent-softening decades in the States, was American and had spent a few enunciation-enhancing decades in England, or simply wished he'd spent a few decades in England and had adopted an accent that projected his dream persona. Whatever the reason, he spoke with almost infectious clarity. "I am Mr. Landon, the curator. If you have any questions or queries, I'm here to address them."

"That's great since, well, I do have a question, or more like a query. Do you, by any chance, know of Loretta de Bonnair?"

"How could anyone in this town not know of her, by reputation at least?"

"True, but are you one of the privileged few who know her personally?"

He paused to consider the possibilities, then replied, "Perhaps."

"Perhaps? That sounds mysterious."

"Indeed. As Ms. de Bonnair has thoroughly obfuscated her identity, no one can be quite sure who she might be, or whether or not we have already met her."

"Interesting." Catherine then politely asked, "So do you have any suspicions about who she might actually be?"

With a hint of a smile, he replied with laconic precision, "Yes."

There was an awkward pause. The curator seemed reluctant to volunteer his suspicions, perhaps because he was sensitive to Ms. de Bonnair's apparent desire to remain unfound, or perhaps because he enjoyed adding to the aura of secrecy about her very existence. His slight smile was ambiguous, so Catherine pressed on.

"I'm here representing a New York publisher, and I'd like to offer her a very nice book deal, but she'll never get it if I can't find her. And that would be a real shame."

The curator pursed his lips, took a slow breath, then said, "Well... in that case, let me hazard a guess. You might want to talk to Violet Smith. She owns the local bed and breakfast. If she's not Loretta de Bonnair herself, she will undoubtedly know who she is. She's an expert in all things romantic and seems to know more about this mysterious author than anyone else around here. Just a week ago, she persuaded me to put *Rancho de Amor* on display in our little museum. She described it as 'a noteworthy work of a shy—or disguised—local.'"

"So you think Violet might actually be that shy—or disguised—local?"

"Perhaps," said the man with a sly smile.

"You know, you're not the only one who thinks it's possible. The man who works at Shelf-Discovery Bookstore thinks the same thing."

"Hmm," the curator hummed with a wistful look, "Devon. Yes, quite a clever boy." He sighed.

Catherine sensed their possibly overlapping interests in Devon and decided to let the subject drop. "Well, I'll definitely be talking to Violet later today. I'm staying at her B and B."

"And will you be sojourning in Sisquoc very long?"

"As soon as I talk to Ms. de Bonnair, I'm out of here." Realizing that this might sound a little harsh to a man whose job it was to protect and present the wonders of a place she couldn't wait to get out of, she added, "I'm hoping that won't be for a few more days though. I haven't, for example, finished seeing your museum."

"It is... diminutive, but fairly comprehensive. And don't miss the folk art exhibition on the other side of the courtyard. The display of quilts is transporting."

"I'll make it my goal. Thanks for your help."

The curator smiled and bowed slightly. "Good luck on your quest." Then he turned and walked through a small door marked *MUSEUM CURATOR*.

When he had left, Catherine turned her attention to the wall of aboriginal displays: metates, arrowheads, soapstone figurines, abalone jewelry, beautifully decorated baskets, and a dozen photographs of Chumash cave paintings. She was struck by how powerful those paintings seemed to be. With only three colors—black, white, and red—they created a universe of evocative images. Circles within circles, writhing snakes and centipedes, the penetrating eyes of ravens—the recurring images that covered cave walls in the mountains nearby. A shiver ran down Catherine's spine. Unlike in the East, the clear and moving vestiges of a prior civilization were close, very close, in this part of the West. Other people with other ways had lived right here and had left countless hints of the ways they'd lived—and died.

Catherine stared at a particularly provocative photograph of a painted wall with an image of what might have been a Spanish galleon. According to the caption, the conjectured date of the painting coincided with the arrival of the first white men—an event which would have catastrophic consequences for the native culture. Also painted on that wall was the red and frenzied image of a raven with a disturbingly large and probing eye. Catherine looked away. It was a little too unsettling. She quickly looked at another caption as much for distraction as anything else and read that the word Sisquoc meant "stopping or resting place" in the Chumash language. At that particular moment it seemed to be a sadly appropriate term for the Chumash. It also seemed oddly appropriate for her at that moment. Here she was, stopped, and here, briefly, she wondered how close she might have been to some of those art-rich caves last night as she blindly drove into the neighboring mountains.

The next room was cluttered along all four walls with the vestiges of the Spanish, the Mexican, and the Gold Rush periods. In the first display, the one piled with items from the Spanish period, she saw swords belonging to soldiers, muskets belonging to bandits, and a knife said to have been taken from one of the men in the invading party under French Captain Hippolyte de Bocluse, known as "California's only pirate," who had attacked the Orlando Rancho along the coast just west of Santa Barbara. The pirates didn't get any gold, but, according to the brief history of the display written in a careful hand on a series of index cards, one of those pirates stole Señorita Isabella Orlando's heart. Catherine reread the words "stole Señorita Orlando's heart," then blinked as she realized she'd just read this story somewhere else: a pirate steals the heart of the daughter of the domineering Don of a large rancho on the coast of California.

Catherine was dumbstruck; this was the storyline of *Rancho de Amor*. And right next to the pirate knife and its romantic little story hung a wedding dress, the wedding dress Señorita Orlando purportedly wore at her very morganatic marriage to her pirate-lover. Catherine did not know if Isabella Orlando had, in real life, been lucky in her marriage, but looking at the dress, she saw how lucky Señorita Orlando had been to have worn that dress. It was at once striking, shapely, and beautifully refined.

As her eyes moved down a string of black pearls stitched along a jet-black sleeve, she remembered a passage in *Rancho de Amor* that described a very similar dress. It was the dress worn by the fictional Señorita Isabella Guerrero at *her* wedding to the fictional English pirate, John Powell. She pulled her copy of the book out of her purse and quickly flipped through the pages until she found the passage she was looking for. De Bonnair's description fit the dress like that shapely dress must have fit the young bride. And even more intriguing, Catherine saw that the caption echoed the wording used in the book—or was that the other way around? Phrases like "the black Majorcan pearls running down the sleeves" or "worn at the sumptuous nuptials on the coast of Alta California" were, if not identical, almost identical—Loretta using the word "wedding" in the place of "nuptials" and reversing "the coast of Alta California" to read "the Alta California coast." Catherine was almost breathless as it sank in that none of this could be coincidental. Loretta de Bonnair knew this story, knew this dress, knew this library, knew this very spot in this library.

Breaking into a broad grin, she quickly turned and walked back to the door in the first room marked *MUSEUM CURATOR*. She knocked softly but insistently. Seconds later, the dapper man she'd met before came to the door.

He said, looking delighted, "You have another question?"

"Yes, I do. I just noticed something in the second room, the Spanish, Gold Rush room, and... well, can I show you what it is?"

The man nodded, and Catherine led him to the display and handed him her copy of *Rancho de Amor*. "Take a look at the description," she said, pointing to the middle of the page.

The curator leaned down, quickly read the passage, then looked at the dress in the display case.

"Good heavens, that's the dress right here in Loretta's book."

"And look at how that dress is described on the label."

Mr. Landon did as he was bid, looked back at de Bonnair's book, then said with a chuckle, "Well, well, there are a good few similarities there too. What do you make of it?"

"Well, the words aren't always the same, but it sure seems like the people, or *person*, who wrote each of these was looking at this very dress."

"I know who wrote one of them," Mr. Landon volunteered suggestively.

Catherine smiled, raised an eyebrow, and paused.

The curator understood the implication. "No, I only wrote one of them."

Catherine still said nothing but now raised her other eyebrow expectantly.

"It would be wonderful to claim that I am the one and only Loretta de Bonnair, but I am, have always been, and will always only be Brian David Landon."

"You are sure of that?" she asked, only half-playfully.

"For better or worse, yes, I know who I am."

"Well then, Brian, someone else has been here, and I think we both know who that was. Not only are the details of this dress identical to the details of the dress in the book, but the story of the book itself is the story of the woman who wore that dress—the story that's told on index cards in this very display case."

Now it was Mr. Landon's turn to raise an eyebrow and smile.

"So," Catherine continued with a sly, anxious smile, "have you, by chance, seen anyone who might have fit Ms. de Bonnair's description showing a particular interest in that display?"

"We're a small museum, and, I'm embarrassed to say, we are never very busy, but we do get a good few people through here, and many, if not most, would fit a description of Ms. de Bonnair. I can't honestly recall anyone showing uncommon interest in that particular display. It is an object that inspires romantic fantasies in many of our visitors, I suspect."

"It definitely seems to have inspired someone in particular," she said, staring at the most relevant index card. "How long has this display with these cards been here?"

"Four years, at least. It was in my second year here. I'd decided to redo all of the displays and their cards, not that there was anything wrong with the displays *or* the cards before, but I did want to make my mark, literally."

Catherine turned to Mr. Landon and said with a very genuine smile, "Well, it seems as if you have—literally. Someone used your words in the writing of the most successful recent romance in America. Congratulations. I'd suggest that you sue for a cut of the royalties, but apparently the author doesn't even get royalties."

"Oh, that is a shame for both of us."

"Sorry. I do have to thank you, however, personally, for giving me proof that Loretta de Bonnair was here, right here, sometime in the last four years. Now, all I have to do is find out who she is and where she is now."

"I must admit, I think I might have liked being Loretta de Bonnair, though I don't think I'd ever have written a Western romance, and I would never have chosen that silly title, even if I had written it: *Rancho de Amor*," he said with a grimace. "Anyway, good luck with your search. And come get me if you find anything else in here from which Ms. de Bonnair may have derived any significant inspiration. It certainly supports my hope that this little museum is, from time to time, genuinely useful." The curator gave a slight bow, then walked back toward his office.

Catherine remained rooted in front of the dress for a while, thinking about how Loretta de Bonnair, whoever she was, had been there. If Violet Smith were Loretta de Bonnair, she most surely would have been in the museum numerous times, and not just to make sure her finished book was on display. But even if Loretta were someone else, whoever she was had to have stood here—right here! It was unsettling, perplexing, and exciting all at once. Catherine glanced down at the tiled floor where she was standing and where Ms. de Bonnair once stood. She then looked back up to the gorgeous dress that both she and Loretta clearly admired. She realized that she might never find the real Loretta de Bonnair—if she were dead, if she'd moved away, if she lived up where no one could find her—but still, she was at least sure that she had found where the real Loretta de Bonnair had once been.

Energized by this thought, Catherine carefully scanned the rest of the Spanish-era display looking for any other details that might suggest Ms. de Bonnair's prior presence. As far as she could tell, however, there were none. And quickly enough, the Spanish items gave way to a display of Mexican-era objects, followed by Gold Rush objects, and finally the preserved objects and images of early farming and ranching in the Santa Ynez Valley, all periods ever more distant from the historical period of de Bonnair's novel.

The only thing that caught her eye in these later displays was a collection of black-and-white photographs of cowboys doing their dusty cowboy thing, circa 1930—images of brandings, ropings, castrations, calvings, and cuttings. It all looked exciting, dirty, and dangerous.

The last room was devoted to Sisquoc in the recent past, up to the present moment. Crowded in the display cases were the pictures and objects of the new "important" people in the area. Michael Jackson was, of course, prominent, although even he was upstaged by Ronald Reagan, who, in a series of carefully staged photographs, posed as the quintessential American cowboy, tall and proud in his saddle. Catherine couldn't help noting the striking difference between these posed pictures of the former president as a cowboy and the unposed photos she'd just seen of unknown men who were actually doing the work of the cowboy. Despite her stated distaste for the swaggering, dirty, and violent cowboy, she much preferred looking at a cowboy in action than one cleaned up and posed on a motionless horse.

The final display in this room was dedicated to the most recent celebrities. And sure enough, there was that big pink book behind glass. It was accompanied by the terse caption, *Rancho de Amor is the bestselling romance novel by local author Loretta de Bonnair.* Catherine wondered if Loretta had been in to check the display of this little piece of herself or whether she was long gone, one way or another.

The last display case in the museum celebrated another wildly popular, land-grabbing prima donna: *Vitis vinifera*, the grape. According to the captions, grapes had been grown in the Santa Ynez Valley for over a century, but it was only in the last thirty years or so that the wines produced locally had become world famous. There was even a reference to a couple of successful movies about the local grape and what it could do in a glass. As Catherine walked out of the room and started across the courtyard toward the part of the museum dedicated to folk art, she reflected with some amusement that, at least in this part of the West, the corkscrew was replacing the cowboy.

Catherine had never been a fan of folk art exhibitions. With so much bad art pretending to be good art, she didn't like to waste time on art that didn't even *pretend* to be good. She walked quickly past lifeless drawings of cows, horses, and cowboys; static still lifes; bombastic seascapes; melodramatic sunsets; and endless photos of trees and awkwardly posed nudes. She was about to walk out the door at the far end of the exhibition when she saw a room with the sign *QUILTS* over the door. She stopped and remembered that she'd told the curator that she would give this display a look. Glancing at her watch, she saw that she still had five minutes to kill before the library would open. This was as good a way to kill five minutes as any, though she had her doubts about this little exhibit being "transporting," as Mr. Landon had suggested it would be. Catherine walked in hurriedly to give the room a perfunctory once-over. Seventeen minutes later, however, she was still there looking at displays and carefully reading captions.

Particularly poignant was the display of two tiny quilts with patterns typical of the era. The woman who had made these quilts had finished them just before crossing the Sierras. They were for the twins to whom she'd given birth while crossing Nebraska in 1851. Caught in an early snow while coming down the west side of the mountains, both of her children survived the bitter cold thanks, in part, to those quilts. Three weeks later, however, the boy, wrapped in a little Bear Claw quilt, had suddenly died one night just before the family arrived in the Valley. The girl survived into adulthood and passed her Road to California quilt and her brother's never-to-be-used-again quilt to her daughter. The daughter, in turn, passed both quilts to her own daughter who, ten years ago, had given them to the museum. The Road to California was tattered, stained, and frayed. It had obviously been used for many years. The Bear Claw was still in pristine condition.

Catherine backed away from these tiny quilts and their stories and stood for a while in the middle of the room. The colors, the craft, the practical importance, the clever thrift—the whole exhibit was, as the curator had said it would be, "transporting." Out of almost nothing, the woman who had stitched these quilts had brought together form and function in beautifully useful ways—delight and necessity made from scratch with scraps. Catherine had seen beautiful quilts back East, but these, though perhaps not the most beautiful she'd ever seen, were the work of a woman facing huge and daily challenges while moving West, and yet she had made something of beauty out of the next to nothing she'd had. It was inspiring, almost heroic.

Catherine walked out of the room, recrossed the courtyard, and went back to the museum entrance. She reached into her purse, pulled out a twenty-dollar bill, and slipped it quietly into the donation box. If to be moved is to be transported, Catherine had just gone places she had never imagined she'd go.

# Chapter 22

After grabbing a sandwich and a Diet Coke from the gas station convenience store, Catherine quickly walked to the library. A tiny bell tinkled on the door as she entered. A small, frail woman looked up from her desk and peered around her computer. Her eyes were bright and large in a slender face made all the slenderer by the unforgiving bun imprisoning her tightly curled hair. "Welcome to the Sisquoc Library."

"Thank you," Catherine replied. Glancing around at the cramped, though carefully arranged, bookshelves, she said, "What a cute place. I'm so glad you're here."

"We are so glad we're here for you," replied the librarian in a kind voice wobbling with age. "Can I help you find anything?"

"No, thanks, I'm just going to sit here and read, if you don't mind."

"Not at all. We'd be delighted. I know we're here because of the books, but sometimes I think the greatest service we provide is the peace and quiet that people can use any way they like. When you think of it," she said, thinking of it, "it's the cheapest thing we do, and probably the most valuable."

"You're absolutely right." Catherine smiled broadly at this superannuated sage and volunteer for the cause of peace and quiet. She then walked over to the one reading table in the library, put her book down, and was about to sit when she turned back to the librarian. She scrutinized her as discreetly as she could, then said, "You know, there is, actually, something I'm looking for—the author of *Rancho de Amor*. No one seems to know who she is or where she can be found." Faithful to the notion that Loretta de Bonnair was very likely Violet, she nonetheless thought it wise to eliminate any other possible candidates and here was one—a witty woman who was the right age in the right town and with an obvious love of books. It was certainly an intriguing combination, and if she weren't Loretta herself, she might very well know who she was.

"You didn't, maybe, write *Rancho de Amor* yourself, did you?" Catherine asked with an inflection of hope.

"No," she chuckled, "but I did read on the dust jacket that a young, rich Spanish woman falls in love with a poor Englishman, which causes big problems for her family..." She paused, then added humorously, "That and the fact that the young man is a pirate. Being of mixed race and in a mixed marriage myself, I certainly could have written about a few of their challenges."

"You could definitely write more knowledgeably about them than most people."

"Yes, though I do seriously wonder if it's only the people who have lived certain experiences who can and should write about them. As far as we know, Shakespeare was a man, and yet his Juliet is a much deeper, more interesting, and more believable character than that pretty flirt, Romeo—in my humble opinion."

"Yes, yes, I agree," Catherine replied brightly. "We know he's cute, we know he's a good talker, but he doesn't have a lot of... what... complexity and depth."

"Not a lot, you're right. Writers who only write about what they see in the mirror don't have a lot of characters to play with."

Catherine smiled and nodded, then brought the conversation back to her purpose. "You clearly know a lot about writing... Are you sure you're not Loretta de Bonnair?"

"I hate to disappoint you, dear, but no, I'm not. I was born Laura Lee Johnson, and after I married Alex Gonzales, the principal of the Santa Maria Middle School where I was the very young school librarian, I became Laura Lee Gonzales, which is who I'll be for as long as I'll be—even though my Alex died three years ago." She took a short, deep breath, briefly looked down and off to the side, then quickly returned her amused attention to Catherine and the subject at hand. "Unfortunately, although I know what Ms. de Bonnair has done, I don't have a clue about who she is."

"You're in good company around here. No one seems to know who she is, and it would really be unfortunate for *her* if I can't find her."

"Not if she likes her privacy."

"True enough," Catherine conceded, "but the poor woman was taken advantage of by her publisher. She made essentially no money at all from her book. The publisher seems to have gotten it all."

"That is certainly a shame."

"Yes, and I hope to correct that. I am an editor with a different publishing company, and if I could find her, I'd make her an offer I don't think she'd refuse. She must have written another book or two, and we would like to buy at least one of them for a good price."

"Yes, I imagine she does have other books. Possibly drawers full of them. It's sad to think of all those drawers out there full of fine manuscripts that will never be published and never even be read..."

"And we wouldn't like that to happen with any of Ms. de Bonnair's books. So, you don't happen to have a good guess about who she might be?"

"I'm sorry, dear, but I haven't the faintest idea who she might be. And to be perfectly honest, I haven't read a word of her book, just the dust jacket. I don't really like modern romance novels. In fact, I don't much like novels, period, unless they're very depressing. The happier the life, the more important it is to read unhappy books. Except for the problems I've had with people who didn't like the color of my skin, I've had a mostly happy life, so I balance it out with a dose of Morrison, Dostoyevsky, and Kundera from time to time. As for finding Ms. de Bonnair," she said, then pursed her lips in reflection, "I'll bet it isn't who most people think it is."

"Why?"

"Well, let's think about it," she said, sounding very much like the librarian she was. "She might like her privacy, but she did send her book to a publisher. It's not as if it's a book of private revelations. It's entertainment and probably not much more. That kind of person doesn't hide her identity unless she's got something to hide. And if she's clever, and most writers are at least that, she's got a clever disguise. Does that make sense?"

"Yes, unfortunately it does. But she also could just be playing a coy game with false modesty. Kind of like pretending you're dead so that you can attend your own funeral and see how people react."

"True, except that she's already got many, many responses and would get even more if she'd come out of hiding. No, I think there's a twist here, dear, and I hope you can figure it out."

"Yeah. So do I. And I guess I should settle down and finally finish reading it."

"You haven't read it either?"

"I hadn't, until I was given this assignment. I also don't like modern romances, though I have to admit, this one's pretty good, so far. She writes with an intelligent, energetic style."

"Well, if her book goes bad on you, let me know, and I'll help you find something else. We don't have much, but the books we do have tend to be pretty good, and we have one of the best collections of Westerns in the area—though I haven't read many of them either. They're not depressing enough."

Catherine laughed then said, "Thanks, but I think *Rancho de Amor* is about as close as I'm likely to get to a Western. I'm not a particular fan of cowboy hats, boots, guns, and swagger. And if I can't get through the sentimental end of this"—Catherine held up her copy of the pink book—"I'll let you guide me somewhere else."

So saying, she sat down and dove into the last ten chapters of de Bonnair's book.

An hour later and with six chapters to go, Catherine started to climb to the climax of the novel. Isabella had just slapped the sneering face of a general who believed he could buy her affections with some of his vast wealth, and she was now headed to the jail where her true love, the former pirate John Powell, was imprisoned and gravely ill. Her intention? To break him out of jail and hide him in a cabin in the mountains above Santa Barbara.

At this dramatic moment in the book, someone else walked into the library. Catherine was too engrossed in her book to care—until she heard his voice. Her breathing tightened and almost stopped as she paused to listen.

"Howdy, Laura Lee. How you doin'?"

"Very well, very well."

"Good." He looked around, saw someone seated at the table, and continued in a loud whisper, "Did you get those persimmons I left on the doorstep yesterday morning? Right off the tree next to the house."

"Yes, I did. I took them home and made persimmon pudding. You come in here this Saturday, I'll have some for you."

"That's an awful tempting offer, but I think I'll have to forgo the persimmon pudding this time. I wouldn't be caught dead anywhere near town this Saturday, not with all that 'fans of romance' thing happening and everybody making a fuss about that de Bonnair gal."

"It is an awful lot of hullabaloo for someone who's a romance writer, I have to agree."

"Yeah"—he chuckled tightly—"imagine that, someone who wrote something called *Rancho de Amor* getting all that attention."

"I don't personally have much interest in that sort of book, though I just heard a good recommendation for it, and it might not hurt you to read it, single as you still are."

"Only thing that's gonna change that is finding the right woman, and until then, I'm not gonna waste my time reading somebody else's fantasy. *Rancho de Amor?* No, no, definitely not for me. You know my taste in books—catchy metaphors, mysteries, murders, or anything Melville. I leave the 'amor' stuff for others to enjoy."

Catherine looked up and stared at the wall of books in front of her. She didn't dare turn around to see if this man was who she thought it was. It couldn't be. It was impossible. And yet...

"Sam Wilson, I do believe you are actually afraid of love. I may share some of your taste in books, but not to mix a good dose of 'amor' in there from time to time seems to me to be more than just a question of taste."

Sam paused, then said in a surprisingly serious tone, "No... no... I'm not afraid of it. I'm just afraid of never finding it the way I want it, and so I ignore the disappointments and have as much fun as a loner like me can."

"Ignore it? Really now, Sam," Laura Lee said, "I think it's time you got off your high horse and started looking around with your feet on the ground. I'm sure there are a few women around here who'd be good enough for your elevated taste."

"'Good enough' isn't good enough for me, but I'm still lookin'. In fact, the only reason I'm in town is because I was supposed to meet a couple of fillies at the Saddle Up."

"A couple? Wouldn't one be enough?"

"In the end, only one of them showed up, and unfortunately she wasn't the one that..."

Catherine blinked and stifled a gasp.

Sam sighed, then changed direction. "Well, it doesn't matter.

The one who did show up was plenty cute and did make me a nice offer."

"They make you offers these days?!" Laura Lee asked, half-horrified. "I do not understand modern romance."

"I mean, she just seemed to have a lot to offer..." Sam paused and tried to find the right words to get out of the embarrassing and not just slightly suspicious impression he'd talked his way into. He didn't think Laura Lee would guess that he was Loretta de Bonnair, but suspicion is contagious, and he didn't want to inspire someone as smart as Laura Lee to start wondering what he was up to with these two "fillies."

Before he could come up with the right words to get her thinking in the wrong direction, however, he heard something fall on the floor behind him. He turned and saw a pen rolling away from the library patron seated at the table. Whoever it was glanced down, started to reach back for it, then quickly turned away and went back to her book. Sam walked over, picked up the pen, and extended it to the woman at the table. She didn't turn, but, seeing the pen out of the corner of her eye, reached out, took it, and said quietly, "Thank you."

Sam squinted, craned his head around, then, after breaking into a tight smile, said, "Well, well, if it ain't the gal who didn't show up. I guess you got lost in a book."

"Yes," she said, turning and confronting him face to face, then averting her gaze from those unsettling blue eyes. "I'm sorry I didn't show up. If I'd had your phone number, I would have called, but what I've discovered since last night made our meeting unnecessary for both of us."

"What you've discovered..." Sam repeated slowly. He was at a loss for words. He couldn't talk about what she'd discovered, even though it was undoubtedly false, because he'd then have to talk about his connection to Loretta as her agent and friend, and this right in front of the town librarian who'd just heard that he'd never even read her book. That subject was clearly off limits. And he couldn't try to convince Catherine that he really wanted to talk to her, and for reasons other than a potential book deal; it would sound contrived and would force him to admit that he was more interested in this alluringly restrained New Yorker than he wanted to admit even to himself. The best he could do was to back out of the situation altogether, which he did, awkwardly.

"Ya know, it's kinda, well, unfortunate that you don't really know me, but if you did—"

"Fortunately," she said, sure the man was relentlessly pestering her for a date, "I don't really have to. I'm here to find Loretta de Bonnair and only Loretta de Bonnair, and I have a decent chance to do that at five this afternoon."

"Really... at five this afternoon? Well, I wish you much luck with that. If you ever find her, I imagine the two of you'll have a lot in common."

"I certainly hope that's true. Even you and I have at least one thing in common. I'm not a real fan of romance in fiction, but this book is an exception. It could use a bit of editing, but really, it isn't bad at all. Maybe you should actually *read* it someday," she said, clearly reminding him of his comment the night before when he'd said he'd not only read this book but was almost finished reading her second book!

Sam did his best to avoid that problem and pursued another topic near and dear to any author. "But if you're not a fan of romance, why do you like this one?"

"It's spunky, smart, observant, and it's even got an occasional 'catchy metaphor.'"

"Occasional metaphor or occasionally catchy?"

"Both—in the right places at the right times."

Sam suppressed a smile while saying, "Ya know, I think I gave you the wrong impression last night."

"No, I think I got the right one. Look, don't take it personally, but I'm just out here on business, and," she paused, momentarily distracted by the look in his eyes, then she forged ahead with her purpose, "and that's all I want to do." She turned back to her book.

Sam nodded, and in a resigned, though serious tone, said, "Well, I really hope you find that author. I know you don't believe it, but someday I may even be able to help your efforts, so until then"—he bowed slightly and lightly tipped his hat—"have a good day."

As he walked to the door, he called back to the librarian, who was still pretending to be busy at something on her desk. "Gotta go, Laura Lee. I've been here a lot longer than I shoulda been. We're calving, which is not a good time for me to be takin' long lunches in town. I'll see you in a week or two and bring you some walnuts. They're starting to drop, and the ones I've tasted so far are good and sweet."

"Just don't get into one of those solitary moods of yours and stay away from town for too long. I start to miss you if I don't see you regularly."

"If for no other reason, I'll come in special to see you. So long." And with that, he stepped out the door and closed it, quietly, behind him.

Catherine went back to her book and tried to read.

Laura Lee went back to her computer and tried to work.

Neither one was very successful. After a minute or two, Laura Lee broke the unproductive silence and said, "So, you've met Sam."

"Yes," Catherine replied, "and I wish I hadn't. He..." She paused, and turned to the librarian, intending to tell her all the unbelievable things he'd told her the night before. She wanted to get some sort of public support for her somewhat impolite and increasingly shaky resolve to ignore Cowboy Sam. And yet, when she looked at Laura Lee, she was calmly smiling. There was nothing about that smile that suggested she felt any of Catherine's concerns. She was a friend of Sam, and she was entitled to believe what she wanted to about the man. Why trouble the lady with a conflicting opinion about someone she liked, someone who brought her fresh persimmons and walnuts?

Catherine shifted gears. "Well, he seems very complex."

"Yes. He's a complex man who unfortunately thinks he can be satisfied living what appears to be a simple life."

"Yes. Well, that is too bad," Catherine said, hoping that this would end the discussion on a note of bland, noncommittal agreement.

It didn't.

"I've got to say though, I'd certainly rather spend my time with a complex man who tries to live simply than with a simple man who makes things complex."

"If those were my only choices, yes, I'd have to agree."

But, as she turned back to her book, she felt with a surge of conviction that she wouldn't have to settle for just one of those two choices. At least she didn't *intend* to have to settle for either. Someone like Devon didn't present such a narrow choice. Life was complex, and people needed to be complex enough to deal with it. Pretending to be simple was simply silly—and a lie. Which was the problem with Sam. Lies, nothing but lies—and for no good reason. Devon, on the other hand, didn't lie, and, without having to tell crazy stories, he had recognized the complexity of finding Loretta and had probably figured out who she was. After being riled up by Sam, it was calming to think that she would likely meet Loretta at 5 p.m., and then have dinner with the interesting young man who'd cleverly divined who that Loretta had to be.

# Chapter 23

True to his word, Devon picked up Catherine at Violet's at seven o'clock sharp. The town to which Devon took her for dinner was no larger than Sisquoc, but it was a good deal fancier. Whereas Sisquoc was true to its farming and cattle ranching past and present, Tres Robles was faithful to, or at least eagerly flirtatious with, its probable future. More than half of the ranches in the Upper Valley had been sold in the last fifty years to people who either wanted to turn them into white-fenced, high-end horse farms or stonewalled, high-end vineyards. Tres Robles had remodeled itself to be of service to these changes and the new sort of clientele that came with them. Instead of the Saddle Up for a Cup Café, there was a large Starbucks, and that was the least upscale of the three cafés in town. Instead of boasting of the largest feed store in the area, Tres Robles boasted of the largest number of boutique wine stores in the area. And instead of the Black Barn, there was Le Paradis de la Campagne.

The owners of this nominal slice of heaven didn't live in Tres Robles. The wealthy French-descended husband and his wife lived somewhere in Silicon Valley. Absent as they were from the daily grime of restaurant work, they nonetheless controlled the hiring and firing of the staff. When they were lucky—and not too meddlesome— they got and were able to keep a good chef. When they weren't so lucky, or spoiled the broth with too much advice, things were not so good. The restaurant was in one of those confused periods: three weeks prior and in the middle of dinner, their former chef had bellowed as he stormed out the front door, "I won't be told how to make a proper bordelaise by two idiots from Northern California!" and the new chef, though talented, was too young and inexperienced to stand up to the befuddling culinary advice of the distant, well-read, but not terribly experienced owners. As a result, the meals were hit or miss. Luckily though, most of the patrons were so sauced on expensive wine by the time the food came that few noticed and even fewer cared to point out any problems. This was the only place to find "haute cuisine" in the neighborhood, and so, if the neighborhood wanted haute at all, it needed to be more supportive than critical. This suited pretty much everyone, except for the occasional visitor from out of town who, for whatever reason, might have been a bit less forgiving.

Catherine, though very much a visitor, was not in a particularly critical mood when she walked into Le Paradis with Devon. She felt that warm anticipation of genuine possibilities with her handsome and helpful date. He was so many things she wanted in a man. He loved books and he spoke beautifully well, particularly in comparison to the "howdy" crowd with whom she was becoming all too familiar. He also seemed kind and considerate, and though he may have had his ulterior motives for wanting to help her, those motives weren't baffling; he wanted to go out with her and see how far things could go. Typical and innocent enough—as long as he didn't try to push things further than she wanted them to go.

They sat by a window, though because it was dark outside and almost as dark inside, they could only really see each other by the flickering candlelight on the table. As soon as they were seated, a waiter ghosted out of the shadows and presented menus and an embossed, leather-bound tome listing the available beverages, mostly wine, mostly from California. Devon chose a bottle of local pinot noir—good, but on the inexpensive end of things. When the waiter left, Devon asked Catherine if she would have preferred a different wine, or none at all. She smiled and eased his brief concern by telling him that she loved pinot noir, which, in as much as she could tell the difference between pinot noir and any other red wine, was true.

After taking a sip of his water, Devon changed topic, apologetically. "I got sidetracked on the way here talking about the differences between Sisquoc and Tres Robles, and I didn't ask you what happened when you went back to Violet's." Devon lowered his head slightly for emphasis. "So, am I right—Violet *is* Loretta de Bonnair?"

"Well," Catherine began, trying to find the right tone, "I am absolutely sure you're right about who she'd like to be, but... I'm not so sure she is that person."

"Oh?" Devon asked, gently disbelieving.

"I mean, I've read most of her book, Loretta's book, and so I asked Violet about some details, things she'd know if she'd researched or written it herself. The problem was..." Catherine paused and made a goofy face.

"She didn't know anything about them," Devon completed the thought flatly.

"Well, we start talking and I ask her if she's interested in the local history since it's kind of a *big* part of the book, and she says yes and tries to impress me with a couple of details like when the Spanish first came to California—she says 1750—and where they first landed, which she says was San Francisco. The problem was, what she said was a 225-year and a 250-mile mistake. I was just in your local museum this morning. The Spanish first came to California in the early 1500s, and the place was around Santa Barbara, right on the other side of those 'hills,' in fact. I checked the book and Loretta got it right, but Violet didn't."

"Could she have been distracted at that moment and just tossed out any date and any place?"

"Sure. Maybe. But I've only been here two days, and I already knew that."

"A temporary memory lapse... or you're a better historian than either Violet or her pseudonym," Devon smiled as the waiter popped out of the surrounding darkness with a bottle of wine. As he was opening and pouring it, Devon rhapsodized knowledgeably about the local conditions that made this and other regional wines so good and different, say, from all those Northern California wines. Catherine didn't understand a thing he was saying, but she was impressed with his knowledge—although to her untrained palate, the wine they were drinking tasted just a little sour.

After they'd both taken a few sips, Devon offered up a toast.

"To a new and exciting friendship," he said.

"And maybe even," added Catherine, raising her glass to Devon's, "to finding the real Loretta de Bonnair."

"Yes," said Devon, slightly deflated. "So you think Violet is not Loretta because she missed a couple of questions about some details in her book, huh?"

"There is that, but the thing that gets me is the fact that when I told Violet how I wanted to see Loretta and offer her an impressive advance on her next book, Violet didn't drop the disguise and ask how impressive that advance might be and when she could get it. I'm essentially offering this woman a contract that could eventually be worth more than a million dollars, and she's not the least bit interested. If Violet were Loretta, she would have betrayed at least some interest in that little detail. It was a good guess, Devon. Even the curator at the museum said he thought Violet was Loretta, but this seems to be a dead end. Maybe you've got another suspect or two in mind?" she asked hopefully.

Devon smiled and shook his head. "No. No idea. But I promise, first thing tomorrow morning, I'm going to take another look at those lists I made and see if I can't conjure up any other likely suspects for you, and I'll try to give them a history test before you meet them."

"I ran into an interesting suspect myself earlier. I was in the library reading and I have to admit that the older, wise, and witty woman working there did seem—possible."

"Laura Lee Gonzales?"

"She's old enough and she knows books, although she said she hates romances and hasn't even read *Rancho*, which could, of course, be a cover-up."

"And did you tell her you were an editor come to offer a big, fat advance?"

"Yes, and unfortunately she didn't bite the bait either. She's a happy reader, not writer."

"Sometimes you can be both. I love to read, but I love to write too."

"You're not Loretta by any chance, are you?" Catherine asked playfully.

"Sorry, romance novels are not my style. I'm a poet. In fact, I've just finished a new book of poems. Do you read poetry?"

"Some, yes, and what I like I really like."

"Well, it just so happens I've got a copy here, if you'd like to see it."

"Absolutely."

"I really believe there is no better way to know who someone is than to read their writing. And... since we're getting to know each other..."

Catherine smiled broadly and nodded encouragingly.

He reached into his satchel and pulled out a copy of his book. It seemed to be the only thing in his bag.

Taking it and holding it against her chest with both hands as if it were a precious gift, Catherine said, "Thank you. I look forward to meeting more of you as I read it."

"I call it *Variations of (Form and) Passion.* They're very modern or, as I like to say, poetry that's beyond the zeitgeist."

"I'm not an expert in modern poetry, but I'm intrigued to read poetry that's, as you say, beyond the zeitgeist."

Devon, now more excited, frothed with clever insight. "People who chase the zeitgeist arrive late to the future, if you see what I mean."

Unfortunately, Catherine didn't, though at that impassioned moment in Devon's discourse, she was loath to admit it. "Kind of, yeah," she said, nodding slowly. She took a large swig of wine and looked away, quickly hoping to be struck by what all of that had meant.

Instead of seeing that, she saw something far more difficult to ponder. Out of the dark and past her table walked Sam Wilson and Sharie Blanchard following the hostess to a table. Catherine and Sam looked at each other, were about to say something, but, thinking better of it, both turned away, Sam to look toward his table, Catherine to look out the dark window. In its reflection, she could see Sharie smiling as she followed Sam and the hostess out of view.

Devon saw this strange reaction and couldn't help asking, "Do you know them?"

Catherine turned back to Devon and asked in a whisper, "Where are they sitting?"

"Three, four tables away. Why?"

Catherine let out a relieved sigh and then said in a nearly normal voice, "That's him—the cowboy I told you about, the one I saw in the Black Barn last night who said he was Loretta's good friend. And that woman he's with works for Loretta's present publisher, Blushing Dove."

"Wow. Looks like she fell for his line, all right. I actually saw her this afternoon when I got off work. She was walking out of the Western-wear shop on Cota with a couple of bags." Then Devon glanced over at Sam and said, "And I've met him before. He comes into the bookstore every once in a while, though I don't remember what he's bought, if he's bought anything. So what did this ranch hand tell you, exactly?"

"That he was 'Loretta's friend and business agent' and that any offers we—that is to say, my Blushing Dove rival and I—might want to make would have to go through him, Loretta being *far* too frail to see us personally."

"He's got quite an active imagination—and he's using it to try to get one of you two book editors into bed. What a scam."

"He even came up to me in the library this afternoon and tried to keep the story going. I mean, there's something about him that's—"

"Kind of creepy?"

"Not exactly creepy, no. I mean, he seemed nice to the librarian. They talked about books and persimmons."

"Books? What did he say about them?"

"He said he liked Melville, but he also said he liked books with mystery and murder in them."

"Ah-ha. I'll bet he did."

"But he really does seem genuinely clever, and—"

"He was in a barroom brawl two nights ago, and last night he was wrestling or something in a restaurant. He sounds genuinely charming."

"He is, which is one of the problems."

"Yeah, when he's lying. The guy's a violent liar. I mean, his lies aren't violent, but—"

"He tells lies and he's a violent man, which means he's, well..."

"Dangerous." Devon leaned toward her and almost whispered, "What if, for example, he really *did* know Loretta and really did know that she wanted a new deal with a publisher, and he 'convinced' her to make him the executor of her estate so that he could not only negotiate the deal but also keep the money if she weren't around anymore."

"So not just the executor, but the beneficiary as well."

"Yeah, whatever it would take."

"Well, I suppose it is possible, though with lawyers and contracts and whatnot, it'd be a little hard to pull off. And I'm pretty sure he's not *that* violent."

"Except that no one's seen or heard from Ms. de Bonnair since she became famous, have they? She's supposed to live 'out there' somewhere," Devon said, waving his hand vaguely toward the surrounding country. "And maybe she did at one fine time, until a guy who knows this country really well helped her to have an accident in the back country. She 'falls off a horse,' say, and no one has found the body—yet. There's 'mystery and murder,' but that doesn't keep the checks from coming in for poor, dead Loretta de Bonnair."

"Except that there's only been one check, as far as I know, which, by the way, has never been cashed, and he just doesn't seem like someone who'd kill a person, well, just for money."

"A guy like that? I can imagine he'd do it just for the fun of it."

"And he brings persimmons to the librarian—"

"Potentially poisoned, if need be."

"And, well, I just don't know."

"You seem to be looking for excuses for the guy."

"No, no, not at all. I know he's telling a story—"

"Lying."

"Okay, lying, but I don't know why."

"Because he's either killed Loretta or he wants to make love to you—or both. This guy's story is no more nuanced than that."

"I don't know, Devon. I'm beginning to wonder if it isn't a lot more nuanced, or at least complicated, but I don't really want to talk about him and the whole de Bonnair business anymore. They've become nothing but an upsetting and endless mess. I'd much prefer to talk about you, your poetry, what you read, where you've been, where you want to go," she said, believing her own pivoting enthusiasm.

And so did Devon, who immediately satisfied her desire by telling her all about himself. As they ate their faux-haute entrées, he told her about his plans to move to Paris and why Paris is still so important for poets; about how he grew up in Orange County, California; and about how he was the class outcast in high school, having preferred late Beethoven quartets to surfing. He had just begun to tell her that he was reading almost nothing other than modern Japanese writers, his current favorite being Murakami, when their waiter suddenly appeared at their table to bus their dishes and ask if they wanted any dessert or an after-dinner drink. They decided to share a crème brûlée and Devon ordered himself an Armagnac.

"The hors d'age, please," he specified.

After ordering dessert, Devon dropped his discussion of other writers and turned his and Catherine's attention back to his own poetry, a topic that eventually led him to ask, "Banter House has been known, occasionally, to publish something a little more literary than Western romances written by Loretta de Bonnair, hasn't it?"

Catherine laughed then said, "This whole *Rancho de Amor* thing is so embarrassing for us. My boss, Vito, he's not the most imaginative guy in the world; it was his grandfather who started the company in the 1940s and who set the tone for its priorities, but I've gotta say, he does try hard to remain faithful to old granddad's vision. So, yes, if we can survive long enough to publish more of it, we would love to see more poetry, if, of course, it's good poetry."

There was a pause—during which she realized that her last "if" might have seemed directed at him. Quickly she added, "Which I'm sure yours is."

"I suspect you'll like the whole gestalt of it," Devon replied as he lifted the brandy snifter to his nose. "I sometimes think I should call these poems 'zippers' because I put two different, semantically coherent poems side by side and slip them together line after line like a zipper. It's formal, yes, but there's passion there. Lots of passion." He took a satisfied sniff, sipped some Armagnac, looked at her probingly over the top edge of his glass, and asked, "So whose poetry do you really like? Thomas, Hejinian, Plath, Ferlinghetti, or maybe some rap artists...?"

As she was about to answer, Sharie quickly walked past, presumably on her way to the restroom. She smiled at Devon as she passed. He smiled back.

"It looks like she'll be keeping that killer cowboy busy and out of your hair."

Catherine slowly nodded.

A moment later, however, that killer cowboy walked up to the table.

"Pardon the interruption, once again," he said with a deep voice that had lost almost all of its Western flair. "I was going to leave this note for you at Violet's tonight, but here you are, so"—he looked toward where Sharie had just disappeared as if concerned she, or someone else, might witness this transaction—"may I deliver it now?"

"A letter—for me? From you?"

"Yes," he said, handing it to her. She took it, gingerly, then quickly stuffed it out of sight into her purse.

Beginning to puff himself up into relevance, Devon asked, "And why would you be writing a letter to her?"

"I'm not absolutely sure that concerns you, but Catherine may wish to share that with you once she's read it. Or maybe not."

"More improbable mysteries about Loretta?" Devon asked facetiously. "Catherine has just been telling me about some of those stories she's recently heard."

"Then I may be interrupting at a critical moment and should let her continue to relate all that she knows."

Just then, Sharie walked back into the light and said, "Sorry. I forgot something in my purse under the table. You haven't told them any secrets while I was gone, have you?" she asked as she gave a sly grin and turned to face Sam.

"And has he been telling you secrets too?" Devon said to Sharie, laughing. "I hope, for your sake, you haven't fallen for any of them." Devon was on an after-dinner drink roll, and he was rolling right into Sam. "Isn't it funny how much he seems to know about Loretta, but Loretta hasn't been seen in months?"

"Have you *ever* seen her?" Sam asked coldly.

"No. Which proves my point. Well, actually, it doesn't, but the point is, Loretta is missing, and I'd be a little concerned about where she really is, if I were you."

"What, exactly, are you implying?" asked Sam.

"All I'm saying, my friend, is if you're so close to this woman, a woman these two women need to see, I'd habeas corpus—that is to say, 'produce the body.'"

"Well, you know the Latin, but you don't know the law. No one is being held in prison and needs a writ of habeus corpus."

"Whatever." Devon shrugged off this meaningless detail. "Someone is clearly missing, and that person needs to be produced, otherwise—"

"Otherwise what?" Sam replied with rising anger.

"Don't get upset. We are not in the Black Barn here," Devon said with a hint of concern.

"Unfortunately," Sam grumbled, then continued more clearly, "I'd mind my own business if I were you. People who..."—he took a deep breath, relaxed his face, and went in a different, calmer direction—"people should just do that. My apologies to both of you for the interruption. Good evening." Sam turned on his heel and began to walk away.

To his back, Devon bravely clarified, "All I'm saying is that I think you might introduce these women to Loretta de Bonnair. They came all the way out here to see her."

Sam paused, turned around, and said slowly, carefully, and forcefully, "Loretta de Bonnair is frail, tired, and close to death, and I won't let her be bothered, no matter what these women have to offer."

"Well," Devon suggested with a softer, more constrained voice, "they should at least—maybe—be able to see her."

Sam turned to Catherine and said, almost painfully, "Do you believe *anything* I've told you?"

"No," Catherine replied with more conviction than she felt, "but I might start to if I could at least *see* Loretta. I mean, I don't want to bother her, really I don't. But just to see that she exists would be good."

Sam blinked a few times then turned to Sharie. "You too?"

"I'm having a wonderful evening and I don't want to ruin it with business, but... I would definitely feel better making my offers directly to her."

Sam bit his lip then, with an audible heave of breath, said, "Fine. I'll talk with her and see what she's willing—and able—to do. Maybe a phone call?"

"We really can't see her at all?" Sharie asked coyly.

"Maybe... maybe. Let me see what I can do. I've got your phone number," he said to Sharie, then he turned to Catherine and asked, "but, how should I, well, how should I get in touch with you? I could call Violet's, or...?"

Catherine opened her mouth, not sure whether to give this confusing man her phone number or not, but before she'd decided, Devon quickly jumped in.

"Call the bookstore by 3 p.m. tomorrow. That's when I get off."

"I gotta go through *you* to get in touch with her?" Sam asked.

Catherine lowered her eyes and said, softly, as she reached into her purse, "Well, if you really are going to get us in touch with the real Loretta de Bonnair, here"—she handed her business card to him—"you can call me directly, but by three would be best."

"Fine. I'll get in touch with both of you sometime tomorrow during the day."

"By 3 p.m.—please," Devon quietly reminded a visibly angry Sam.

Smoldering, Sam took another deep breath, then exhaled. "By 3 p.m. Yeah." Then he gave Catherine a crooked smile. "Again, pardon for the... for the intrusion. I don't mean to be a bother, but I don't seem to be able to avoid it while trying to help." As if defeated, he shrugged, shook his head slightly, then, with Sharie, walked back to their table.

Devon watched as Sam took his seat, but Sharie bent down, quickly retrieved her purse, and started back toward the restroom. She didn't smile at Devon this time around. In fact, she didn't even look at either him or Catherine as she briskly walked past their table.

When she'd passed, Devon leaned toward Catherine and said with a crooked smile, "Makes you wonder what she forgot as she prepares to leave with handsome Sam."

Catherine, wondering far too many things at once, had no suggestion.

# CHAPTER 24

Catherine's mood had deepened and darkened as the evening progressed. If both Violet and Laura Lee were now unlikely candidates, she was no closer to finding Loretta than she'd been when she arrived two days ago. And Sharie Blanchard was following a very different lead. It was dangerous and undoubtedly on the wrong track, but at least she was going somewhere, which was better than where Catherine was now going.

Then there was Sam's letter. They'd seen each other five times, and every new meeting was more unnerving than the last. If he'd actually tried to upset her more, he couldn't have done much better than he'd already done without trying. But it wasn't just what he did or who he was that bothered her. It was her own responses—sharp, confused, and increasingly contradictory. At most, he should have been an occasional, almost laughable annoyance, as if he were a cowboy-costumed actor who'd burst onto the wrong sound stage with guns ablazing during the filming of, say, *Sleepless in Seattle*. Instead, he was becoming an insistent distraction even when he wasn't around. And now, she had a letter from him. What in the world could he have to say to her in a letter anyway?

By the time she got into Devon's car, her feelings had descended into confused concern about pretty much everything. And this feeling was not lightened when Devon clicked his seatbelt, turned to her, and said with jaunty practicality, "Your place or mine?"

"Oh, mine, if you don't mind."

"Not at all. I love Violet's novel and violet bed and breakfast. It's a little over the top, but it works. And I'm still not sure she's not the one and only Loretta de Bonnair. Maybe we can find a clue or two around the house." Clearly, he wasn't ready to admit defeat.

As they started to drive back to Sisquoc, Devon launched into a clever, if slightly presumptuous, attack on Sam, "that storytelling ranch hand." To Devon, Sam's occasional visits to the bookstore and library were nothing more than a part of his show. Devon reasoned that if Sam were such a good friend of an author, he would have to pretend to actually like books. "But did he mention anything about any books just now? No!" And then there was Cowboy Sam's angry, almost violent outburst. "Clearly," Devon said with disgust, "that lying, conniving cowboy had essentially exhausted any civilized way to discuss anything and just wanted to take me to the Black Barn and fight." Devon turned toward Catherine and continued to look at her while saying, "He's a barbarian. Hopefully he will not call tomorrow, and you won't ever have to see him again." He glanced back to the road and quickly adjusted his course before hitting a parked car, then he looked back at Catherine and said, "Instead, you can see me."

Catherine barely heard a word of all this. She was, instead, nervously aware of Devon's almost exclusive attention to her, accompanied with grand gestures and many excessively long glances her way, and that all of this might, at any moment, drive them abruptly into an oncoming car or an immovable tree.

"Mm," she murmured as politely as she could, while keeping her eyes glued to the dark and potentially deadly road ahead.

When Devon finally turned his attention back to driving, she relaxed enough to say, "I'm a little concerned for that Blushing Dove rep though."

"I wouldn't be," Devon said, once again turning to Catherine. "She definitely looks like she can take care of herself."

Inadvertently, she eased her foot onto an imaginary brake pedal. If he didn't see the stop sign looming up out of the night, at least she did.

Eventually, he, too, saw the sign and came to a fast and jerky stop. Luckily, it was the last stop they'd have to make before rolling into Sisquoc.

Catherine had already decided that the night was over by the time they drove up to Violet's. She was sure it wasn't anything Devon had or hadn't done. He was fine—just maybe not quite as interesting as she might have hoped he'd be, so far. Nor was he quite as funny as she'd hoped. And he did seem a bit more taken with himself than she felt completely comfortable with. And that awkward kind of "macho thing" he'd done with Sam in the restaurant had been—

well, awkward. Still, he did seem right in so many ways, and this had just been their first real date. As everyone knew, first dates were always tricky. Things would undoubtedly be better the next time.

Devon, however, didn't seem to sense any of this. Instead, he slid out of his seat, walked around the car, opened her door, and offered her a warm hand. "I've only been in a couple of Violet's 'romance-themed' rooms and never in the back room you say you're in. I'd love to see what she's done with it. Georgette Heyer or Danielle Steel?"

"Neither. This one has a little more of Ezekiel's touch, which..." She paused, looking for the right way to describe it.

Devon rushed to finish her thought with a thought of his own as he opened Violet's lace-curtained front door. "I'm sure we'll make out just fine no matter what it looks like."

Catherine decided not to say anything more about it. She figured her room would do the talking for her, saving them that awkward conversation by which desires and expectations would need to be abruptly adjusted. A stuffed skunk would give them both excuses by which those adjustments could discreetly be made.

And indeed, the menagerie of stuffed roadkill did surprise Devon. Unfortunately, it did not put him off his purpose. In fact, it seemed to have the opposite effect. Instead of distracting and thereby postponing his ardor, the wild and aggressive aspects of many of Ezekiel's critters seemed to strengthen it.

Eventually, Catherine had to take both of his busy hands, put them together, give them and his lips a quick kiss, and conclude this deft parry of a young man's seemingly imperturbable passion with the earnest appeal, "Will you be able to join me for Loretta's 'coming out' tomorrow if that slick cowboy actually gets it together? I'll go alone if I have to, but I've got to tell you, after what you've suggested about him, I'd feel a little safer—and a lot happier—if you'd come along."

His one goal halted, Devon paused, regrouped, and said with almost equal conviction, "I would love to see what all of this is about. I get off work at three tomorrow, so as long as it's after then, I'll be able to."

"That's great. Really, Devon. So, until tomorrow..."

"Yes. It was an interesting evening, though I can't wait to get beyond Sam and Loretta and just concentrate on us."

"Me too." She gave Devon another quick peck on the lips while gently but firmly holding his hands and ever so gently pushing them and the rest of him to the door.

As Devon started out the door, Catherine said, softly, "I'm looking forward to quietly reading your poetry. Good poetry needs to be settled into, and this is a perfect night for that, thank you."

"No, no, thank you. Enjoy where it takes you." He gave her a nod and said, "I'll see you tomorrow," then smiled—and left.

She shut the door, leaned back against it, and stood there for a moment, aware and surprised that she had just heaved a sigh of relief. She then pulled her phone from her purse and punched in Vito's number.

"Catherine?"

"Hi, Vito. Sorry it's still late, but it's at least not as late as last night. If you want, I can hang up and text you."

"Don't be silly. Being awakened at twelve-fifteen is *so* much better than being awakened at twelve-thirty," he said facetiously. "At least you're going in the right direction."

"Sorry. I should've called at six, nine your time, but I was peppering a possible Loretta with questions and then I, well, I had a date with that bookstore guy I told you about who's helping me."

"Is he really helping you"—Vito yawned loudly—"or is he just helping himself to you?"

"Don't go there, Vito. So far, he's just a friend. It might get more serious, but up to now, he's really just given me some advice... and a manuscript of his poems."

"Ah-ha. A reason for his kind advice. He's a poet—you're an editor. And he thinks he's found his way to fame and fortune."

"He couldn't just be interested in me, could he?" she said playfully.

"Oh, well, I *suppose* he could," he teased, "but the important question is, has he helped you find our famous recluse?"

"Not so far. There were two promising paths, but they've ended up nowhere. Have you read or heard anything new about Loretta de Bonnair, her whereabouts, her new novels, her real name, the date of her funeral?"

"Bubkes. And other than publishing new and astounding sales figures, the trades aren't saying anything more about her. I guess there's nothing more to say. Do you have any other leads?"

"It's insane, but that cowboy from last night who says he's Loretta's friend, he says he *may* let us meet her tomorrow."

"Us?"

"That rep from Blushing Dove Press I told you about last night."

"At twelve-thirty in the morning, I'm not sure what I hear, and that's something I'm still having a hard time hearing. Her own publisher doesn't know who or where de Bonnair is? Is she dead, in prison, or a murderer on the run?"

"Any one of those ideas is as likely as anything I've heard out here. All I know is that the cowboy who says he's Loretta's friend and business agent and might get us a meeting with Loretta tomorrow had a date with the Blushing Dove rep tonight. She's a complete flirt and he's—he's incomprehensible."

"Is there any chance he could be the 'genu-wine article,' you know, a real cowboy who really does know the real Loretta de Bonnair?"

"I doubt it. On the other hand, right now, there's not much else to go on. If he calls tomorrow and says he will actually produce Loretta, I'll go, and Devon said he'll come with me, just in case."

"So this cowboy fellow, he took out the other editor?"

"I think it was more like she took him out, but yeah, he went out with her."

"And he actually said he was going to get both of you an audience with de Bonnair?"

"He said he'd try, that's all he really said, except to tell us how frail she was. He made it sound like she's at death's door."

"So maybe he really is doing de Bonnair a final favor?"

"Well, maybe..."

"And if that's the case, the way to her heart and mind would be through him?"

"If you believe this crooked scenario."

"Have we got any other scenario to believe?"

"Only dead ends."

There was a pause, then Vito said, "Did he, you know, that cowboy guy, look happy with his date?"

"Given how aggressively she seemed to be courting him, I imagine he was very happy with his prospects."

There was another pause, which Catherine broke with inquisitive concern. "You're not thinking I should go out with that guy?"

"Absolutely not! I forbid it."

"Good. That saves you from a lawsuit and me from murdering the man."

"Short of that, however, you have my blessings to do whatever it takes—rent an ambulance and a doctor for the ailing author, lock her in, and drive her back here. I need to convince Ms. de Bonnair of all the things Banter can do for her and her long-lived reputation. *Then* she can die if she wants *after* signing with us."

Catherine sighed. "I'll do the best I can, with or without an ambulance."

"Still, Catherine, keep that bookstore guy with you if you have to deal with that cagey cowboy. He's playing at something, and it could be dangerous."

"Understood."

Both tired and disheartened by the stubborn realities of the situation, they had nothing more to say beyond their goodbyes, good nights, and sleep tights, after which they hung up.

Catherine got into bed with every intention to put the day and all of its challenges behind her with Devon's poetry. There was, of course, that letter, but she wanted to ignore it and everything it was about for as long as possible. She didn't want—and didn't even know how—to deal with her increasingly confused responses to Sam, and so she'd do the next best thing: she would put it out of her mind for as long as she could. She wanted to settle all of her thoughts and feelings somewhere else. Unfortunately, Devon's poetry didn't give her many places to settle. It was full of sophisticated language and literary devices (he seemed particularly fond of oxymorons), but there was something "jumpy" about it all. Instead of inspiring much thought or feeling, his poems had her almost perspiring with the effort of figuring out what all of his aggressive juxtapositions meant. After working through five poems, she was nervous and exhausted. This was not how she wanted to escape the present.

She put Devon's *Variations* on her nightstand and returned to what she knew would provide nothing but an escape from her complicated present—*Rancho de Amor*. Soon she lost herself reading the last two action-packed chapters and their compelling improbabilities.

At 12:37, she finished the book. The very end was satisfying. She wondered, however, as an editor and potential publisher, should she be at all concerned by the end being simply "satisfying" as opposed to "stunning"? The book did end as she'd been sure it would, with an "unavoidably happy ending." But she had to admit that, at least as a reader, she was happy with how happily it had all come together. And the journey... well, the journey had been so much more enjoyable than she'd thought it would be. Overwritten at times, yes, but nothing a good editor couldn't fix. *Rancho de Amor*, despite its predictable resolution, was a genuinely good read. It was well crafted and often quite meaningful, two important aspects that to her made it truly a work of literature, with or without capital letters.

Yes, if she could find this mysterious writer, she would be happy to sign her as an author for Banter House Books. She heaved a sigh of relief and put the book down on the nightstand.

She paused, uncomfortably, remembering that she'd have to confront Sam's letter before she could completely let the day go. Reluctantly, she reached over to her purse and took the letter out. She lay back and considered; everything about this man was like a maelstrom, an inward, downward spiral toward him and an impenetrable, troubling obscurity. Who was this guy, why was he bothering her, and why was she so bothered by him?

The envelope was a plain business envelope on which he had printed her first name. Nothing more. She tore the envelope open and saw that the letter was at least relatively short.

She propped her head on her pillow and read.

Dear Catherine,
Though seeming to be little more than a barroom-
brawling, filly-chasing fella in a cowboy hat and boots who
lives somewhere near that frontier outpost to which you
have been sent on business, I am sufficiently perceptive
to sense the disdain of others and even understand its
largely legitimate origins. Three of the four times we have
seen one another, I have either knocked you onto a pile of
fertilizer or been unappealingly embroiled in a barroom
conflict or a noisy barroom competition. On the one other
occasion of our meeting, you overheard me refer to you

and your flirtatious rival as "fillies," a term that, to some (in this case, completely unintended) degree, implies the depersonalization of women. And on all occasions, I have worn the hat, boots, and other sartorial flourishes of those who either genuinely are, or would genuinely like to appear to be, the cow-punching opposite of a well-dressed man about town. None of this I can deny.

Furthermore, claiming to be the friend and business agent of the one person you have been sent to meet out here has forced you either to believe the unbelievable or to reject any possibility that this could be true. And why, indeed, should you believe me? If I am Loretta de Bonnair's friend and agent, I must know where she is. And if I know where she is, then why, if I am anxious to help both you and her, don't I take you to her or at least tell you how she can be reached? Yes, something appears not quite right about all of this. You say you don't believe me and don't want to know a thing more about me. Although your suspicions are justified by the appearance of things, not to entertain the possibility of another interpretation would be unfortunate for all concerned. There are legitimate and compelling reasons why Ms. de Bonnair is unable to meet with you directly. And although there may be other ways to reach her, there is truly no more direct route than through my awkward intercession. I am, indeed, a "local" who claims to have more information than I should believably be able to have, and yet, however incredible this claim may seem, it is true. Fiction has to be believable, but truth is held to a lower standard. It just has to be true. Unbelievable as it may appear, it is true that Loretta de Bonnair and I are very close to one another, and that I do, and must continue to, take care of her interests as best I can.

You have judged me with your well-educated mind and your sophisticated expectations. Clearly, I do not appear to be someone you could either like or trust. But is the mind truly the best judge of character? Please entertain the possibility that your best business and personal interests might better be served by believing me. I have shared with

Loretta the fact that two women have flown out here to meet her and deliver offers of further publication. As I described both of you to her, she expressed a particular interest in hearing from you. I, myself, may be wrong and may have incorrectly inferred from insufficient details, but I told her you seemed to be more curious, independent, intelligent, genuine, and kind than Ms. Blanchard. All I ask of you is to suspend your disbelief for a day or two and trust me with your confidence, either to be your spokesman or to be your postman in further communication with Ms. de Bonnair.

Loretta has, for some time now, wished to reveal herself as someone somewhat different from the image her current publisher has presented to the world. I suspect you could offer a more profound change to her image than she has thought possible. Doubt me, dislike me, dismiss me completely from your thoughts if you must, but please do not dismiss the possibility of reaching Loretta de Bonnair through my privileged contact with her. Loretta's well-being depends, in no small way, upon your response.

Yours very seriously,
Sam Wilson

Catherine finished the letter open-mouthed and completely befuddled. She looked at the signature again. Sam Wilson. Sam Wilson wrote this letter to her.

But what did it *mean*?

What, for example, was the earnest appeal to dismiss him completely but not to dismiss Loretta's well-being? Would a man such as Sam care about any of this if he weren't somehow attached to this author? To go to these lengths on behalf of Loretta de Bonnair suggested that, despite appearances, this brawling, baffling man was what he said he was. Maybe the ranch where Sam lived bordered the ranch where Loretta lived, and they'd developed an almost tribal rural bond. Or maybe she really was so old and infirm that she needed him to be something of a neighboring caregiver? Whatever the reasons, this letter suggested in the clearest terms that Sam not only knew Loretta but was truly committed to serving her needs in this business.

Catherine put the letter down, turned her light out, and relaxed into bed. She felt briefly relieved. It seemed that she'd actually and unwittingly stumbled upon Loretta de Bonnair and was likely going to see her in not too many hours. It was too bad she'd have to share the stage with Sharie, her chameleon-like counterpart—a woman who would dress and say and probably do anything to get what she wanted. Catherine snorted in self-righteous reproach. She, Catherine, could never—and would never—change her colors like that. She'd do her honest best to present her company's honorable interests, but she certainly wouldn't stoop so low as to flirt with the go-between and then date that man with the clear intention of sleeping with him. It was disgusting. Surely, she thought, Sam would see through it. Well, maybe he would, and maybe he wouldn't. He had, after all, described Sharie as "plenty cute"—and she had certainly put all that cuteness on display earlier that evening.

But if Sam really believed that, why had he written this letter to her *after* their awful, awkward conversation in the library? It didn't make any sense if he really believed Sharie had, as he'd said, "a lot to offer." Whatever it was though, Sharie seemed to believe his stories and had apparently already made some offer. But maybe Sharie's offer wasn't very good—which was why Sam was still interested in courting her interest. Yes, that was probably all it was, Catherine nodded to herself, but as she lay there temporarily satisfied with her analysis, another thought needled into consciousness. Was Sharie *really* "plenty cute"? Catherine twitched angrily in bed. Sharie Blanchard was all makeup, a big smile, and a tight dress—nothing more. Well... and that hair. That damned hair. And... she *was* thinner...

She paused and let her feelings subside a bit. Why, she wondered, why did she care about any of this anyway? If Sam was so easily attracted by Sharie's sort of tricks, that was his problem, not hers. He'd essentially promised to get her offer to de Bonnair, and she was possibly going to see de Bonnair herself tomorrow. She didn't need Sam's good opinion of her—didn't need it at all. Let that tart take him to heaven and back for the rest of eternity, she thought. It wouldn't change anything. Yes, Sam was meaningless, she sighed. She fluffed her pillow up, winked at the anxious little field mouse at the foot of her bed, and settled on her side.

But she wasn't settled for long. Could she really say—and did she really believe—that Sam was meaningless? If nothing else, he was still the go-between and—she quickly shifted sides to get comfortable—and maybe there *was* something else. Why had he written those things about her in the letter? She reached out, grabbed his letter from her nightstand, turned on her light, and read—*you seemed to be more curious, independent, intelligent, genuine, and kind.* She put the letter back down on her nightstand slowly. Why did he bother to include any of that? And that line about the mind not being the best judge of character. He seemed to be asking her to search her feelings—about *him.* Why? Was this just a misleading exaggeration that came from an overblown writing style, or was there more? Did he want her to search her feelings about him because, well, because maybe he had feelings for her? She sat up suddenly and replied loudly to her own question, "No!"

She took a few quick breaths then, more quietly, thought of the things that would justify her sudden declaration. There was no reason for him to feel anything for her, and so, no way that he could feel anything for her, except—except in the library, he had started to say that only one of the two reps showed up and "unfortunately she wasn't the one that—" Not the one that *what?* Showed up? And why "unfortunately"? Did she have something the other "filly" didn't have? Certainly it wasn't the support of a publisher with lots of money, certainly it wasn't a perfect wardrobe and a perfectly slender figure, certainly it wasn't her willingness to do anything to get and keep this cowboy's interest. No, it made no sense, no sense at all, she thought as she shrugged her shoulders, turned off her light, and relaxed back onto the bed with that conclusion, for the moment.

But, she considered from a slightly different angle, even if he *did* have some very confused and confusing feelings for her—which seemed pretty unlikely—that would really be too bad for him, because it *definitely* wasn't reciprocal. True, Sam Wilson in the library was a little different from Sam Wilson in the Black Barn. Well, more than a little different with those persimmons and walnuts and metaphors and Melville. Yes, more than a little different. Then she remembered him saying, "Unfortunately, you don't really know me, but if you did..." and, now blushing in the dark, she remembered her snarky response, "Fortunately, I don't really have to..." which, she was beginning to feel, hadn't been completely true even then. Every time she'd looked at the man, something had moved in her—off rhythm, out of place, unwanted—but there, definitely there. She sighed and whispered, "Did I have to be so cuttingly clever? 'Fortunately, I don't have to'? *'Fortunately'?!*" Catherine sat there and let her feelings jostle for attention. And the one that kept popping to the top was the one she was least ready to acknowledge, but there it was—silly, unjustifiable, alone: the feeling that there *was* something attractive about this man.

"And I insulted him at dinner—in front of everyone," she confided to her stuffed, sympathetic field mouse. "What should I do?"

There was no response.

She fell back onto her pillow and stared at the ceiling. Could he, would he, after all she'd said not only at the library and the feed store but at dinner, prevent her from meeting de Bonnair? Of course he could—and he probably would—particularly after a lovely date with Sharie. The very thought of that entanglement made her flinch. Still, he did say he wanted what was best for "Loretta," and having two completely different offers from two completely different publishers would definitely be best for Loretta. But that would be that. It would be business and nothing more. Almost certainly, he would have no interest in speaking to her again. He'd even said as much at the restaurant, so she'd probably never find out why he seemed so contradictory, so complex, and why he'd said he liked "anything by Melville." She'd also never find out for sure if he actually had or hadn't read de Bonnair's book... at which thought, Catherine rose on her elbows, stared at her frozen mouse, and said out loud, "But what does *that* matter? What I know for sure is that, one way or the other, he's lied!" Catherine groaned, "Lied."

She eased back onto her pillow and now both sighed and groaned. Devon was right. This guy was playing a clever and possibly dangerous game. He was undoubtedly the one who'd tried to get de Bonnair's mail at the post office. And now, after he'd gotten his aging "friend" and neighbor to change her will and name him as the sole beneficiary, he'd caused a fatal accident which had yet to be discovered. Catherine could see it now, the broken body of poor Loretta de Bonnair mangled on the side of some steep slope up in those dark and frightening mountains. Now Sam was trying to get some contract for a book she'd written before she was killed and for which he'd get the money if she or Sharie were stupid enough to fall for it. "Which," she said to her motionless mouse, "we seem to be. I get a pretty-sounding letter, and I'm ready to believe anything except... except that..."

She sank back onto the bed and concluded in a whisper, "That doesn't make sense either." She thought about how he'd been *way* too open about *way* too much of this with *way* too many people. Even more confoundingly, why had he said they might actually be able to meet Ms. de Bonnair the next day if he'd killed her? She bit her upper lip. What to think, what to feel? Back and forth and back again, she thought she should go to the police, she thought she shouldn't worry, she thought she was on the brink of success, she thought she was going insane. She felt afraid, felt hopeful, felt embarrassed, and felt more, much more, for someone she didn't want to feel for—but did.

# CHAPTER 25

When Catherine finally pulled herself out of bed from a few hours of short, disconnected nightmares, she felt physically exhausted, mentally confused, and more than slightly excited. Although she was supposed to care more about her meeting with Loretta, try as she might, she thought far more about her meeting with Sam. And though she'd been sure she'd feel excited about seeing Devon later in the day, as the day progressed, it was the prospect of seeing Sam that excited her more. As Catherine didn't believe in divine intervention, the inexplicable pull of the stars, or the inscrutable demands of fate, her best explanation was that because she was tired (she never slept well in strange places), nervous about not yet having done what she'd been sent out to do, and thoroughly disconnected from her normal and comforting routines, she was temporarily vulnerable to emotional intrusions. Whether or not it was wise to let such intrusions have their sway, she knew that there was a reason for these intrusions beyond reason.

Making it all the more confusing was the fact that Catherine never fell for the proverbial "dangerous guy." She liked courage as much as anyone, and certainly didn't mind complex, even troubled, depth. But someone who liked danger for the sake of danger? She didn't understand why certain people liked, or liked lovers who liked, death-defying acts. The "into thin air" crowd wasn't her crowd. She was glad someone was into it and even more glad that someone was writing about it, but she took her doses of excessive daring in a warm room and a comfy chair. Even if all those things that a cowboy had to do to be a cowboy were, if not noble, at least admirably necessary things to do, the dangerous, brutal nature of it all held no romantic attraction for her.

So what could it possibly be about this man that "moved" her in such an increasingly insistent way? While standing in the shower, she tried various words in combination and alone, and finally landed on a word of effectively vague clarity: élan, a word that suggested his physical, mental, even emotional vitality but which, as well, implied a certain cocky style and, in his case, unexpected sophistication.

She shut off the water and repeated the word out loud—"élan." Yes, that was the perfect word. There was comfort in finding a word with which she could define, describe, and even conjure the man she now welcomed into her thoughts. But the more she thought of him, the more she thought of the painful reasons they might never get to know one another. The first and most superficially painful was his relationship with Sharie. Just how interested was he in her, and how far had they let this interest go? What she was feeling was jealousy, pure and simple, though she knew that she had no right to indulge that irrational passion yet. Without a relationship to protect, jealousy was, at best, a presumptive fantasy. More profoundly disturbing was her recollection of the various walls she'd built and maintained between Sam and herself right from the start. If the best defense is to be truly offensive, she knew that her very public scorn of him had more than admirably defended her from any tender feelings he might have felt for her now. She had given him more than enough reason to take his élan and go elsewhere—if he hadn't already.

All of this made dressing particularly challenging that morning. Having already worn her one other cotton dress the previous day, there was only one left, a black dress with a V-neck, three-quarter sleeves, and a formfitting waist. This was her "power dress," almost all business except for a fairly tight waistband and the slight décolleté cut. Modeling it in the narrow mirror set between a raccoon and a bobcat, she frowned. It was a very pretty dress with a sort of understated elegance. Not exactly Audrey Hepburn at an executive board meeting, but trending in that direction. Was this, however, the best dress in which to drive out to a cattle ranch and meet the cowboy go-between and the rancher/writer of a Western romance novel? Probably not, but she had no functional alternative. And so, with a dissatisfied smirk, Catherine turned from her reflection and asked her stiff little field mouse, "It's not *that* bad, is it?" Though he remained discreetly silent, she was sure he shared her concern.

Sharie was already at the buffet table and dressed in a more regionally appropriate costume, a rhinestone-studded jean skirt and a very décolleté blouse with a large frilled collar. It read "Western"; it read "romantic"; it read "ready"—none of which Catherine now felt. In fact, about the only thing she felt at that moment was a gut-tightening curiosity. Clearly, Sam hadn't killed her the night before, but had that attractive Blushing Dove editor metaphorically killed him? She glanced at Sharie's bare arms. Had they pulled Sam down to her last night? Catherine closed her eyes and shook herself out of the thought. It was just too disturbing.

Sharie was smiling, but it was a tight, purposeful smile. There was no hint of any soft, reverberant joy. It was business. But that's all her relationship with Sam would have been to her anyway, Catherine reflected. Business. She felt momentarily sorry for Sam, but this feeling quickly shifted into a sharp-edged combination of anger and jealousy, a feeling which, when Violet hailed her from across the room, Catherine instantly pressed into a dark, though not very distant, corner of her thoughts.

"Good morning, my dear. I trust you slept well?"

"Yes, yes, I did, thanks," Catherine lied.

"Aren't you looking very serious this morning. You're not going to a funeral, are you?"

Catherine heard a small chuckle from Sharie, who was serving herself a plate of violet-colored waffles.

"No. A couple of business meetings."

"I imagine those can sometimes be deadly too, no?"

Catherine smiled tightly and nodded.

Prior to reading Sam's letter, Catherine had intended to query Violet one more time to see if maybe, just maybe, she might not be the real Loretta. She hadn't held out much hope for it after her conversation with Violet the previous afternoon, but Devon had thought it was still possible, and while Catherine was thinking that Devon was still "possible," she entertained the idea. Now that Devon's star was fading, she didn't feel any need to confirm what was already clear in her mind. Whoever Loretta was, she was not Violet Smith.

"Surely you have time for some boysenberry waffles."

"Unfortunately, I don't. I really do have some business to take care of."

And indeed, she did have business to attend to that morning.

Catherine was determined to reread parts of *Rancho de Amor* and organize her notes so that she could knowledgeably and competitively comment on the book when she met its author. She decided to go to the Starbucks in Tres Robles, a place presumably far enough away from any chance encounters with the increasing number of people in Sisquoc with whom she was developing increasingly complicated relations. She grabbed a purple scone, thanked Violet, ignored Sharie, and left.

Unlike the nerve-wracking drive from Tres Robles the night before with Devon, this morning's drive was both calming and refreshing. Although she disliked the idea in the abstract, in reality the warm, dry wind blowing out of the northeast on a late November day felt wonderful. The air was so clear and the sun was so bright, everything looked as if it had been fashioned in glass. At the same time, nothing looked the least bit fragile. Everything seemed to stand out, substantial and distinct: the dark green oaks against the gold-colored grass, the black Angus bulls against their white corral fences, the tree-lined, sandstone-knuckled mountains against a light blue sky. Even the smell was distinct—a rich mixture of the sweet and sour smell of hay, oak, and horse manure. She was reluctant to turn off the highway and drive into town. Cute as it was, she knew that Tres Robles wouldn't be able to compete with the sensory excitement she was experiencing in the open country.

Still, she knew that a good Venti Frappuccino would jolt her into the business at hand, and this was precisely what she ordered from the awkward, though earnest, eighteen-year-old barista.

When she sat down to continue her notes on Loretta's book, her concentration was quickly distracted by a nagging concern: was she really dressed for *success* or, as Violet had suggested, a funeral?

Catherine got up and went to the restroom for a look. She was not happy with what she saw. She was trying to do her best, but under the circumstances, was this really the best she could do? In New York City, such a look would have suggested an almost seductive sobriety, a seriousness of purpose, and a quiet but clear appreciation of timeless style. But was it a style anyone would appreciate out here in cattle country? What would Loretta think about it? And what would Sam think? She knew she couldn't do the frilly thing or the tight and tiny thing. Maybe, though, she could keep the dress and do something else to change her image, something like change her hair. She'd wanted to have it trimmed for over a month anyway, and here was a practical excuse to get it done. She left the critical mirror and went straight to the counter where the awkward eighteen-year-old with red hair and pimples stood ready to serve, although he wasn't quite ready for the question he got.

"This is an odd one, but do you know of a good hairdresser in the area?"

The young fellow went slightly pink and stumbled toward an answer. "I, well, I've never been there, but right across the street there's a girl, well, woman, really, Pennie, that's her name, she's real nice and does a lot of hair."

Playing with the poor boy, Catherine said, "But you've never had your hair done there?"

"Ah, no," he replied, turning a slightly deeper pink. "My dad, well, he cuts my hair."

"Too bad he doesn't have a shop. He does a nice job."

The kid didn't know how to respond to this, so just went a bit pinker and smiled tightly.

"Well, since I imagine your dad's already busy today, I'll try Pennie's upon your recommendation. She does do a good job as far as you know?" Catherine asked, more than half-serious now. Letting someone cut your hair, even if just for a minor trim, required a leap of faith that Catherine was never comfortable making.

"Well," said the eighteen-year-old with the conviction of someone who had unconditional admiration for the person he was describing, "everybody who comes out with a haircut from Pennie looks real good."

"That's good enough for me. Thanks." Catherine slipped a dollar into the tip jar. Then she went back to her table, gathered her things, and, as she walked out, saw the *PENNIE'S FROM HEAVEN HAIR SALON* sign right across the street. She took a deep breath, walked quickly across the quiet street, but slowed to a stop just outside the door. What did she really want this hairdresser to do? In the last ten of her twenty-eight years, her hairstyle had changed exactly two times: once to try a more layered and slightly tinted look, the second time to go back to what she'd worn before—shoulder-blade length, untinted, and of uniform length, all to be worn back with either a hair clip, barrette, or in a ponytail. She now stood, hesitant at the door of change, and looked around for help, or at least some timely inspiration. As if on cue, inspiration stepped out of a Range Rover across the street. It was in the form of a tall and tan blond with lots and lots of bouncy waves. Waves seemed to be a Western thing, a local "look" that suggested wealth, sensuality, and independence.

She shrugged, turned, and no sooner had she walked through the door than she was greeted by three different people in quick succession.

"Good morning, miss," said a forty-five-year-old brunette in spandex pants and a leopard-print top, busy adding blue to the white hair of a woman who appeared to be sleeping in the first chair of the salon.

A slender, unnaturally blond young man of about thirty in tight orange jeans smiled at Catherine over the head of a young woman whose hair he was wetting from a spray bottle and said, "Welcome to Pennie's."

"And how can we change your life?" asked an energetic young woman in her mid-twenties seated at a small desk at the back of the salon. Her hair was short and black. She had a discreet lip ring near the left corner of her mouth, three small diamond studs on the right side of her nose, and a tattoo of two roses growing up from the top of her blouse, one flower rising up the right side of her neck and the other rising up the left. "I'm Pennie," she said with a warm, crooked smile.

"You're the owner," Catherine said, somewhat surprised.

"I've got my name on the window, but we're all kind of owners. The one in the flaming orange pants is Randy, and the one in the leopard is Ronnie. I just hope you're not here to make an appointment for any time soon. This 'fans of romance' thing has everybody within a thousand miles getting primped and permed."

"No. It's kind of now or never. I was at Starbucks, and a young man with very red hair said you did a good job. How could I not take his recommendation?"

"Yeah, that would be Alan. Not that he's wrong, but I could be giving everybody buzz cuts and he'd still say I was doing a good job. He's eighteen, and there aren't too many women with tattoos to look at and wonder about around here, if you know what I mean."

Catherine smiled. "Yes. A boy's gotta dream."

"Yep," said Pennie, getting up and looking at Catherine's hair. "I just got a cancellation, so if you've got half an hour and don't want anything complicated, I could probably sneak it in right now."

"Right now is definitely better than never," Catherine said, surrendering to Pennie's confident charm.

"Perfect. Have a seat"—Pennie indicated the only empty chair left—"and tell me what you want."

"I want..." Catherine started, haltingly. "I want to change my look... a little. I'd like to look a bit more country-western, if there is such a look."

"It's mostly waves out here right now."

"That would be fine, I think. Nothing radical. Just something with a little local flair."

"You found something with a little local flair?" Ronnie interjected, having heard the last six words. "Oh, honey, tell me where it is."

"It's standin' right next to you, girlfriend," Randy teased.

Ronnie laughed.

And Pennie asked, "Where are you from?"

"Wait, wait... let me try to guess," Randy interjected while quickly finishing a curl. Then he turned to look at the object of inquiry.

Amused, Catherine turned to meet his gaze. "Okay, and I'll double my tip and give you half if you guess it within one hundred miles."

"One hundred miles? Ha! If I don't get within ten miles, I'll pay your tip myself."

Catherine laughed. "Deal."

Randy turned to face her squarely, crossed his arms, pursed his lips, and inspected her from hair to heels. He wasn't the only one playing the game, however. The two other hairdressers and the two women being coifed, including the one who had formerly been dozing, turned to work on their own silent guesses.

"East Coast," Randy said in a perfunctory tone.

"Good start," Catherine replied, "but the East Coast is even longer than the West Coast."

"If you don't include Alaska," he tossed out correctively. "I'd say, New York."

"Ah, yeah. That's narrowing it down a bit, but—"

"City."

"Yes. And, well, you've won. New York and all of its boroughs aren't thirty miles wide."

"But I said within ten miles," he replied, raising his head and jutting out his chin in the pose of a man undaunted by the challenge.

"Go for it. But this isn't going to be so easy."

Randy shrugged and chuckled. "We'll see." He gave her another careful look, then said, "Shoes—Marc Jacobs, but not paid for at full price. Likely a consignment store in which such lucky finds are not common, but to the watchful and habitual eye, not uncommon. Which means this particular establishment is either close to work or close to home—or both. The dress—Max Mara. Full price. A rare extravagance and, as such, bought at Bloomingdales. Not a place often entered but often passed on the way to, again, either work or home—or both. The scarf—now that's an interesting one. Hmm..." Randy considered for a moment and then said, "A knockoff Hermès. The gift from a former boyfriend who picked it up somewhere on the Champs-Élysées. He wouldn't have ventured far from the river of typical tourists. He pretended to be more adventurous than he actually was, which means you are, if I may be so bold, better off without him."

"Mostly right with the clothing, and absolutely right with the boyfriend." Catherine was thoroughly enjoying the show.

"The tights—a local drugstore. Convenience over—not style, convenience can be perfectly stylish, and I mean that, but over pretense. Discipline like yours is a quality of those with genuine style." He paused. "Now, we put it all together, and... well, it could have been the Upper East Side on a budget, but those funky little Marc Jacobs kitten heels say Greenwich Village to me."

Catherine laughed and coughed at the same time. When she recovered, she said, "You're on a roll. I've got a rent-controlled studio right in the noisy middle of things. But can you get the street address?"

Randy broke into a huge but tight smile and started to do a little dance behind his wide-eyed customer. He ended his dance with a perfectly executed pirouette, then said, "Oh, what the heck. Broadway and Bleecker."

Catherine threw her hands up and shook her head in mock disappointment. "Wrong, wrong, wrong. Sixth Avenue and Bleecker."

Randy laughed.

"Wow," Catherine exclaimed. "Not ten miles. Ten… ten blocks. Very impressive."

Everyone including Catherine gave Randy a round of applause, to which he bowed briefly.

"Even if I end up with a crew cut, you're going to get half of a good tip."

"Please," said Randy, with mock severity, "I can't accept it. The pleasure of being right is twice the pleasure of being paid. Pennie's From Heaven welcomes you to Podunk." He bowed, more deeply this time.

"What are you doing way out here?" Pennie asked.

"I'll guess that one," said the woman being coifed by Randy. "Loretta de Bonnair."

Reluctant to admit it, Catherine paused, then quietly said, "Yes."

"So does that mean I get some of that tip too?" the woman asked playfully.

"Serena, that one's *way* too easy to guess this week." Pennie then turned to Catherine, handed her a smock, and said, "Here, change into this, I'll shampoo you, and we'll get down to business."

When Catherine returned, smocked and shampooed, she settled into her chair and glanced at herself in the mirror. She raised a wary eyebrow, aware that she was looking at a look that was going to change, and she wasn't so sure she was happy about it. She might even have jumped up and fled had she not noticed a photograph taped to the border of the mirror. Too shocked to be subtle, she asked, "Is that your boyfriend?"

The image was of Pennie, a big smile on her face, her arm around the waist and her head resting on the shoulder of the man Catherine knew as Sam Wilson.

Pennie laughed. "Nope. That's my bro."

"Your brother?" Catherine asked, a worried expression slowly fading into genuine curiosity.

Pennie noted this change in her expression and replied, "Yep, my brother. You know him?"

"Ah, yeah," Catherine said, hoping she hadn't revealed too much of her interest with her interest. "He's going to introduce me to Loretta de Bonnair this afternoon."

"No..." Pennie said with broad disbelief. "My brother knows Loretta de Bonnair?"

"That's what he told me. He said he was going to try to set up some meeting. He said he was her friend and business agent."

"Wow. I love him to death, and he can be a pretty private guy, plays his cards close to his chest, but this... I got a feeling there's a misunderstanding."

"Well, he only said he'd *try* to set up a meeting with her. Said he'd call me by three this afternoon if it were happening. Maybe it won't happen, but I should be, you know, prepared."

"I promise, you'll be looking good no matter *what* happens."

"I've gotta say, your brother is one of the more mysterious men I've ever met. Are you close?"

Pennie chuckled then said, "You could say that. After our parents died, he basically became like a parent to me. It was a little weird, but it worked."

Ronnie chimed in, "He led her out of *temptation*."

"Amen," Randy sang.

Catherine gave her a very confused look in the mirror.

"Sam was away in college when our parents died, but he came back here to take care of his wild younger sister"—Pennie gave a quick curtsy—"me. Got a job on a ranch 'cause it was work he'd liked doing summers in high school and because he thought it would be better for me to be living up on a ranch and not so close to some of the things I was getting into in town."

"Sam Wilson, the cowboy, the guy who hangs out at the Black Barn, raised you after your parents died?"

"Yes, he did," Pennie said with a snap of her scissors. "Took care of me from the time I was fifteen, and in a lot of ways, he did it better than my parents."

Ronnie didn't look up from her work but said, "Tell her what he did when you got your first tattoo."

"Yeah, well, that was interesting. At first, he freaked out. I got it for my 'sweet' sixteen, and I didn't start with a tiny little something on my ankle. I started with this one." She gestured to the two roses twisting up from her chest.

"And what you don't see is even better," Randy added.

"What did he say?" Catherine asked.

"Sam's got a little bit of a temper, and he got a little mad." With a vision of Sam flying backward out a set of saloon doors, getting up, and heading back in to continue a fight, all she said was, "Hmm."

"But I'm at least as stubborn as he is, and he was smart enough to realize it, so he stops being mad and instead gets himself a tattoo."

"Really? What's it of?" Catherine asked.

"Wouldn't we all like to know?" Ronnie said.

Catherine glanced at the picture of brother and sister and silently agreed.

Pennie quickly ran her fingers through Catherine's hair to check the evenness of her cut, then asked, "So my brother really said he knows Loretta de Bonnair?"

"That's what he says. She's supposed to live on a ranch somewhere around here. Maybe she's a neighbor of his?"

"I haven't lived up there in more'n five years, so maybe. I didn't really know the neighbors when I was up there. It's kinda isolated."

"I love it," said Ronnie wistfully. "Hunk is a friend of a romance writer."

"Hunk?" Catherine asked.

"It's what we call her brother," Randy replied.

"They both have a little thing for Sam," Pennie acknowledged.

"Little?!" Ronnie blurted out. "I've been trying for years to catch more'n his eye. He's always nice, flirts a little, but I can't get him to pick the good, low-hanging fruit. He's too darn picky, and I can't figure out what he's trying to pick."

"And I," Randy added, "I keep hoping he'll pick from the other side of the tree, but this isn't *Brokeback Mountain*, so I move on, I move on, I move on." With a resigned shrug, he went back to cutting hair.

Serena, the young woman Randy was working on, sat up in her chair and confessed proudly, "I had a thing for him in high school. Me and him even went out a couple of times, but even though he was good at sports and all, he mostly wanted to talk about the books he was reading. I couldn't keep up with all the stuff he was talking about, so that was the end of that. He still looks as good as he ever did—better, even. I kinda wonder if I shouldn't read a few books and give him a call."

She got a chuckle from everyone, except Catherine, who was busy adding these new details to her picture of the man in her mind. No one said anything for a few moments, then, after a couple of snips, Pennie said, "Well, if you actually do meet Loretta, she's gonna like your new cut."

"So will Hunk," Randy added, turning to face Catherine, curious to see how she would react.

Both he and Pennie saw Catherine quickly glance down, briefly bite her lip, then look back up—insistently recomposed. No one said anything for a moment.

To fill what could have become an awkward pause, Catherine said brightly, "I definitely look forward to meeting Ms. de Bonnair."

She punctuated this remark with a nod which didn't please Pennie, who was trying to cut the hair on that nodding head. "No, no, don't move. You don't want me to chop off a couple of these beautiful waves, do you?"

Catherine sat perfectly still and didn't say anything else for a while. For one, she wanted to concentrate on what was happening to her hair, which, for better or worse, was now beyond the point of no return. And as the waves took ever more distinct shape in her hair, the emotional waves in Catherine's mind grew steeper and thicker. She had to meet and win over Loretta—thus besting her flashier and undoubtedly more financially able competition. It was do or die that very afternoon, and the weight of her company's survival was on her shoulders alone. And then there was Sam, the man in the photograph on the mirror right in front of her that she couldn't stop glancing at. Her interest in him was not yet beyond the point of no return, although the things she'd just heard about him had increased her speed down that emotional runway, particularly hearing that he'd given up his private dreams to raise a sister without complaint, and had done it well...

Catherine was definitely running out of runway.

# CHAPTER 26

When her "do" was done, Catherine went to the changing room and stared at herself in the mirror. It was both an intriguing and disturbing experience. Had she not recognized herself under her new hair, she would have thought the woman in the mirror quite attractive. But seeing herself surrounded by an ocean of waves made her feel as if she were drowning in unfamiliar waters, unable to catch her breath as the person she'd always been.

But it was too late for regrets. She would have to make the best of her new image. Unfortunately, she could see that her new hairstyle didn't really work with the dress she was wearing. She looked like a study in ill-advised contrasts.

As she was paying Pennie, she asked if there were any nice dress shops in town.

"Nice might be pushing it, but there are a couple of shops down the street."

"Good enough, I hope," Catherine said, then she turned to give Randy half of the ample tip she'd promised him. As he politely put his hand up to refuse it, she said, "I insist. You earned this—and my eternal respect—for your brilliant fashion profiling. Since you now know where I live, when you come to New York, please look me up." She took a card out of her purse and handed it to him.

"Be careful what you offer. I *love* New York and I might just pop in. I'm gonna want you to show me all the places you like to shop. You've got a good eye."

"I'd like that," she said, then turned to Ronnie and Pennie. "Thanks, you all, or should I say y'all?"

As she started out the door, Pennie yelled after her, "Say hello to my bro when you see him. If he doesn't treat you good, you come back and tell me. I'll straighten him out."

"Will do," Catherine said with a nod, then she left in search

162

of the two dress shops that would hopefully have what she'd need to complete her image adjustment. She walked down the street and found not only the two dress shops but a large thrift store. The fashions displayed in the windows were not the styles Catherine usually wore. Pant suits, frills, and mauve were the common themes. Still, she didn't have the luxury to expect the familiar. Taste being in the eye of the beholder, she knew it wasn't her eye that needed to behold her, it was the combined eye of a female rancher of a certain age who'd written a romance novel and a twenty-something cowboy. That being the case, there was a slightly over-the-top dress that, were she to buy the pink cashmere sweater she'd seen in the thrift store, would make an acceptably fetching adjustment.

She went back to the dress shop where she'd seen the dress and stared at it in the window for a while. It was cut a little lower and a little tighter than she liked, and there was a bit of frill at the collar, sleeves, and hem, but it was relatively subdued while still being perky. Thus far, Sam had seen her cynical and dismissive side. It was time to try perky.

She went in and tried it on. When she stepped out of the dressing room to observe it in one of the larger mirrors, a shop woman with long red, white, and blue nails exclaimed loudly, "Oh, yeah, that dress is *you*." Looking in the mirror, however, Catherine had to glance up at her face to make sure it was really she who was wearing "that dress." It was she all right, in a very contour-complimenting creation. It also fit with her new hair and her sense of what both Loretta and Sam would like to see, an ensemble that suggested exuberant and open-minded youth. She paid for it, had the cashier cut off the tags, and walked out wearing it, her black dress in a bag.

She then went to the secondhand store and bought the pink cashmere sweater. Both for warmth—it was November after all, even if the temperature was a desert-dry seventy-four degrees—and to tone down some of the flash.

The only real problem was that, perky as the clothes and hair might actually have made her look, Catherine didn't *feel* perky. She realized that she didn't know how to wear her new look. Walking down this sunny street on a warm November day in Tres Robles, California, she felt as if she were shrinking into the flower she was wearing. And the more she retreated from her appearance, the more aware she became that that was exactly what she was doing.

When she got to her car, she turned on her radio, hoping to be blasted out of her mood. She had to turn the dial past a number of soul-soothing Christian stations before she found something appropriately energetic. She didn't listen to much rock, particularly not much hard rock, so she didn't know what song she was listening to, but it was loud, boisterous, pounding, and exactly what she needed. By the time she reached Cota Road in Sisquoc, she was feeling, if not truly perky, at least perked up and ready to be what she could be in her new look.

Not wanting to go back to the B&B and risk hearing Violet's observations about her radical costume change, she decided to grab a bite to eat at the convenience store and slip into the library where she could finish her notes and, unseen by anyone but a librarian, wait to see if Sam would actually call.

As she walked out of the convenience store with a tuna sandwich and a Diet Coke, a red-faced middle-aged man walking past stopped and exclaimed, "Well, howdy! Aren't you a sight for sore eyes?" He gave her an encouraging wink.

"I beg your pardon?" she asked, suspecting, but not quite sure, that she should be annoyed.

"You're lookin' real good," he said broadly.

"My apologies. I certainly didn't intend to disturb you."

"No, you don't disturb me one little bit. You make me glad I'm alive."

"Well, hold on to that thought for as long as you can. I've got to run." Which, at least metaphorically, she did—straight to the library.

As Catherine pushed through the door, Laura Lee looked around from her screen and said, "You're back—did you leave something, or are you just anxious to get back to that romance novel?"

"No—well, kind of. I wanted to come to the most comfortable place in town where I could read, discreetly eat a little lunch, and pretend to relax before my meeting with Loretta de Bonnair later this afternoon. I'm supposed to be getting a phone call confirming all of this in a little while, if you don't mind."

"A phone call? Not at all; it'd liven up the place. So you think you've found her. Bravo!"

"Sam did, actually. He says he's her business agent, and he set up this meeting with her."

"Our Sam? The Sam who was in here yesterday and with whom you had a"—she paused to find the right words—"an interesting conversation?"

"Yes, that Sam."

Laura Lee nodded slowly. "I knew he had broad interests, but to be the business agent for a romance writer he said he hasn't even read? That is a surprise. I see you decided to dress up for the occasion, whatever it'll be."

"I don't really know what Loretta expects, but I thought a little Western flair couldn't hurt."

"No, it couldn't hurt. Will Sam be there too?"

"I hope so. I mean, he should be."

Laura Lee smiled, then her face scrunched up as an odd thought crossed her mind. "You don't suppose he's married to her, do you? She could be shy and retiring, one of those writers who's smart and stubbornly antisocial, particularly when confronted with fame, and Sam, gentleman that he is, covers for her to the point of even pretending not to be married..."

"Wow, Sam involved with an older woman. Now that's a thought."

"An older woman? Ms. de Bonnair isn't a young, first-time author?" Laura Lee asked, confused.

"Apparently not. In fact, it seems she's a *good* deal older than Sam."

"Really?" Laura Lee straightened up and gave a slight smile. "Sam is an open-minded fellow, but—no, I just don't see it. He flirts with everybody, even me, but I imagine he'd have to marry someone who could keep up with him, not just intellectually, but physically and emotionally."

She glanced at Catherine.

Catherine didn't see this. She was looking down and asked pensively, "Can Sam be trusted? He says he's setting up this meeting, but..."

"He's got *some* good reason for saying what he's said, I'd bet my life on it, though at eighty-seven, that's a pretty cheap bet." She laughed at her own morbid humor.

"Well," Catherine said, picking up her book and settling back in her chair, "I guess I'll find out soon enough."

"Yes, I guess you will," Laura Lee said with a hint of concern and hope in her voice.

Less than an hour later, Catherine's phone rang. It was Sam.

"Hello, Catherine Doyle?"

"Yes," she replied hesitantly. It sounded like Sam, but his voice was scrubbed of any hint of a country accent and any warmth.

"This is Sam Wilson. I've set up a meeting with Ms. de Bonnair at the ranch where I work, the Circle D Ranch, 2253 Tomol Road. You, or that fellow you were with, indicated that you wanted the meeting to be after three o'clock, so can you make it at three-fifteen?"

"Yes, yes, thank you. I..." Catherine paused. She wanted to say something else, anything else, just to continue talking, but she could think of nothing more to say except, "I appreciate what you're doing."

Sam, also confused about what *he* should or shouldn't say, simply said, "Good. Then we'll see you soon," and hung up.

Catherine sat there, stunned into motionless agitation. She'd heard exactly what she needed to hear: she would meet Loretta de Bonnair to discuss the possibility of signing a book contract with her. She did not, however, hear what she *wanted* to hear. Gone was the slightest hint that Sam was still interested in her for anything but business. She looked up and saw Laura Lee busy at her computer. Hopefully, she hadn't heard anything, or if she had, she hadn't paid it any mind.

Too buffeted by contradictory feelings to sit quietly in a library, and aware that she had to meet Devon before going off to some isolated cattle ranch for a meeting shrouded in mystery, Catherine began to gather up her things. As she did, Laura Lee asked quietly while looking at her computer screen, "Sam?"

"Yes. I'm supposed to be meeting Loretta out at his ranch at three-fifteen."

"You must be happy," she said, now looking at Catherine.

"I guess. Well, yes." She stood up. "This is what I wanted. I'm just nervous about how this will work out."

"One way or the other—it will," Laura Lee said, offering an irrefutable, if banal truth. As Catherine approached the door, she added, "If you wouldn't mind though, I'd love it if you'd stop by tomorrow and let me know how it's all going with Loretta and... and everything else."

166

Catherine blushed slightly and could only manage to say, "Yes... yes, I'll come by and let you know how things are going."

Catherine felt at least as awkward as the situation had become. There she was in an odd costume that made her feel out of place in her own skin. Then there was the fact that she was headed toward a young man she had shown some interest in not twenty-four hours before, whom she now hoped would accompany her to meet a man she was suddenly much more interested in. And that new interest was, itself, a source of confused discomfort.

The day before, she'd convinced herself that this man was a swaggering, superficial, sometimes violent, usually deceitful flirt with whom she wanted nothing to do. Now, having read a letter he'd written to her and reconsidered certain details of their brief, charged interactions, she was increasingly intrigued by him. And yet, no sooner had she begun to change her mind about him than he seemed to have changed his mind about her—and not in a positive direction. His tone during the phone call they'd just had convinced her of that. Worse still, this man apparently was the one person in the world who could put her in contact with the author she'd been sent out to meet and woo. Pretty much every aspect of the situation made her nervous, anxious, almost queasy. What would she think about Loretta de Bonnair when she met her, and what would Ms. de Bonnair think of her and her offers? And what would she think about Sam Wilson this time around—and what, more critically, would he think of her?

It was almost a relief, then, that Devon was undisguised in his reaction to Catherine when she walked into the bookstore.

"Is that you in there, Catherine? It looks like you've just walked out of an episode of *Westworld*."

Resigned to the irreversible extent of her new look, she admitted, "I thought I should change things for Loretta, but this change is a bit more than I thought it would be."

"It is different, yes. I hope she likes it."

"Is it too much?"

"Depends on Loretta, if she's there, and maybe Sam?" The rise of his voice at the end of the sentence made it a last-second question.

Catherine sidestepped the question, though not all of its implications, with a concern for the practical. "I'm not sure you really need to drive me out to this bizarre meeting. In the daylight, I ought to be able to find it on my own."

"Would you prefer that I *not* come?"

"No, no. I'd definitely prefer it if you would come. I don't know my way around here very well, I don't know about this Sam character, and... you are clever and perceptive company."

"Well, in that case, I guess I'll grab my pistol and join you."

"A pistol? You've got one, really?"

"No. But if I did..."

"I've got to admit, I am out of my element here," she said with exasperation. "All I'm trying to do is find an older woman who wrote a romance novel and talk to her about the prospects for her next book, but instead, I could be in the middle of some shoot-out on my way to meet her. How does anything ever get done out here in the West?"

Devon just smiled.

Less than a minute later, Devon's blond, dreadlocked replacement, Amy, showed up twelve minutes early. Amy not only loved books and appreciated her job, but also thought she loved the tall, young man she was replacing, who'd slept with her twice and who she hoped would make it a habit. He had yet to tell her, however, that that was unlikely.

Liberated from work early, Devon sped off with Catherine at 2:50 p.m. toward the Circle D. As they squealed around curves and ignored stop signs on the thankfully sunny and deserted roads, Catherine felt that she had perhaps been too quick to judge him. Here he was driving her into the middle of nowhere, ready and willing to protect her from some strange and possibly violent man, and all she could think about was that other man. How silly. How unfair. How wrong. Whether or not anything would ever grow between them beyond what was already there, Catherine felt a genuine, if temporary, surge of warmth and gratitude. Devon deserved better than she was giving him.

And so, as they sped along a stretch of blessedly straight road, she said, "I really do appreciate all you're doing, and have done for me—your research about who Ms. de Bonnair might be, dinner last night, and now driving out to God knows where for God knows what. You're a good man, Devon."

"My pleasure," he said and gave a deferential nod. "By the way," he continued, "did you get a chance to read my book?"

"You know," Catherine stalled, "I've been so concerned with all of this de Bonnair craziness, I honestly haven't had the chance to give it the time it deserves."

"But you did, at least, *start* to read it?"

"Yes."

"And?"

"And it's interesting, really. You've got some very perceptive insights, and the form, as you say, really is beyond the zeitgeist."

Devon was, indeed, a perceptive fellow. Wisely, he decided not to press for more details.

# CHAPTER 27

The house in which Sam lived had been built in 1887 by a farmer who'd bought the property a decade earlier. The farmer had struggled for the first few years when he'd brought Midwestern farming notions to a Western location, but he eventually learned the error of his ways. He gave up on the wheat and the corn and started running cattle. It took a bit of time to get it producing properly, but soon enough he had a working ranch, so he found himself a local bride, had a family, and, after outgrowing two smaller houses, eventually built the large, white, two-story Victorian Sam Wilson now lived in, the front porch of which Sam Wilson now hurried across to meet his unexpectedly early guests. His face was tight with concern. The success of the arranged meeting with the famed and frail Loretta de Bonnair required that everything and everybody be right where they needed to be at the right time—but they weren't. Catherine was arriving seventeen minutes early.

Sam Wilson hadn't expected he'd ever have the chance to get more from pretending to be Loretta de Bonnair than a finished novel, but those expectations had changed completely. The fanfare he could do without, but when two editors from two different New York publishers flew out to talk to Loretta and make offers for her next books, his imagination took flight. He was writing two other books that he eventually hoped to sell under his own name. But Sam Wilson was a nobody, and he knew it would not be an easy sell. Ah, but if Loretta just happened to have a couple of books in the works— well, she'd be able to get the serious attention of publishers with no trouble at all. He knew, of course, that he'd have to come clean before signing any new contract, which would ultimately be a very good thing. This time, he would pocket the money himself instead of letting the publisher run away with it all. But he, in consultation with his friend and confidant Walt Bruegger, had decided that it would be best to get a firm commitment from a publisher—with numbers, hopefully big numbers, attached—before finally showing *his* cards.

But there was now another complicating dimension to his plans, and she had just arrived. The tight, nervous expression he'd displayed when she first drove up relaxed into a smile when he saw Catherine's smooth and unstockinged legs flutter and extend out of Devon's low-slung car. Not wanting to be seen staring, Sam started to turn away, but stopped when he glimpsed the rest of her body unfold from the small car.

Catherine looked up and saw Sam looking at her. She quickly glanced down and reflexively pulled her sweater more tightly around herself.

When she looked back up, Sam looked embarrassed. He cleared his throat and said, "It's good to see you, Catherine, but, um"—he paused as his worried expression began to reassert itself—"you're a little early, and Loretta, she's still getting herself ready. Why don't you and your... boyfriend come inside for a bit?"

"Oh, he's not my..." Catherine began quickly, though Sam had already turned and was striding to the front door, a fact which saved her from having to explain more than she wanted to at that particular moment. Instead, she followed Sam up the stairs and into the house, where she apologized for arriving so early. "I didn't want to be late, but I didn't realize how quickly we'd get here."

"That's fine, just fine. I'll just go and tell Loretta what's happening and make sure she's comfortable." So saying, Sam briskly walked from the living room, through an open door to the left, down a hallway, and into an adjoining room. He shut the door behind him with a resolute snap. With Sam gone, Catherine looked around the large room she'd just entered. The walls were covered in a textured, burgundy wallpaper against which hung various original paintings— bright Western landscapes and dark, somber portraits, presumably of departed ancestors. All of the trim, the picture rails and window and door frames, was of dark wood. The floor, or what could be seen of it around the borders of a large Oriental rug, was also dark wood. Overhead, an enormous crystal chandelier hung from a twelve-foot ceiling. The room seemed to have been untouched for decades, except that every horizontal surface was covered with books—from both libraries and bookstores.

After walking in, Devon went up to a console covered with six piles of books while Catherine went to inspect the books stacked on an antique sideboard. They were both bent over in the act of perusing these hard- and softbound treasures when Sam walked back into the room. He looked much calmer than when they'd first arrived. The reason was simple. "Loretta feels, well... she feels about as ready as she can be," he announced, "so we'll just wait a bit for the other editor to show up, then get down to business."

In the middle of what Sam was saying, Devon glanced at his vibrating phone, noted a message, then looked over at Sam and asked a question that was needling him. "Is this *your* house?"

"No. The owners, or most of them, live in SoCal. They come up a couple weekends a year, put on cowboy hats, and ride horses. I'm the caretaker of their house—and their cattle."

"It looks like some of them must like to read a lot when they're up here. This is quite a collection of books."

"I gotta thank your bookstore for a lot of this mess. The library's responsible for the rest of it. I got a small room upstairs, so this is where I keep my overflow."

"These are your books?" Devon asked incredulously, then felt his phone vibrate again and discreetly glanced at the screen.

"Hard to believe, *ain't* it?" Sam said. Catherine had the feeling he was waiting for her to say something, but she had no idea what to say or do. She heard a horse whinny outside and the click of Devon's fingers busy on the phone to which he'd returned his attention.

After another beat of unbroken and unspoken tension, Sam quietly said, "Why don't we go out on the porch and wait? It's a little windy, but the view's nice." He turned and started out to the porch. Catherine hesitated, looked back at Devon, who was still engrossed in some online exchange, then followed Sam. He was standing at the railing when she came out. Catherine noticed, as she had in the Black Barn, how broad his shoulders were and now noticed how his upper arms filled the space of his sleeves. She felt a sudden desire to put her hand on his back, but quickly suppressed the urge, surprised and almost angry at feeling such an inappropriate thing. She walked up next to him and looked out across rolling pastures that, less than a mile away, tilted up and blended into the foothills and mountains she'd fearfully explored two nights before.

The crystalline morning had progressed into an even more crystalline afternoon, buffed and buffeted by one of those strong off-shore winds that swept toward the sea every few weeks in the fall. The contrast between the dry, beige grasses and the dark green islands of oaks seemed almost too striking to be natural, more like a stylized painting than a bit of rural reality. What she saw, however, mirrored what she was feeling; everything was slightly exaggerated and she, in the midst of it, was slightly off balance. Somewhere very nearby was Loretta de Bonnair, the woman she had been sent out to meet and woo, but that all-important task was oddly not so all-important as she stood on a porch with a handsome, well-read cowboy who was himself maddeningly hard to read. Taking advantage of Devon's temporary absence, Catherine decided to correct a potentially critical misunderstanding. "Devon's not my boyfriend, by the way. I didn't know how to get here, and he said he'd help."

All she got was a slow nod from Sam and what she thought, from the side, might be a smile. So she ventured a little deeper into things both professional and personal. "After dinner with Devon, I went back to my hotel—well, my B and B—and read your letter."

"Really?" he said, not sure he should believe her. "I got the impression in the restaurant that you'd had more'n enough of my words for one night."

"I thought I had too, but I read it anyway and... it was well written."

He chuckled, "Let's just say Loretta's inspired me."

"It was very compelling—though I have to admit, I'm not sure what it all means."

"Well," Sam replied with a note of pained resignation, "I suspect that letter doesn't mean much anymore. Here you are about to talk to Ms. de Bonnair. Seems you're finally getting what you came out here for. As you said, business—and nothing more."

And for a moment, Catherine didn't say anything more. Maybe it was—and should remain—just business. Maybe she'd read more into that letter and more into those brief, awkward conversations they'd had than was actually there. What if he was just a disappointed flirt, or, even worse, so particular in his romantic taste that, as she remembered him saying in the library, "good enough" (if she was even that) "wasn't good enough." They really were so inescapably different from one another. *Incompatible*, she reflected, was probably a better term. She didn't even know how to ride a horse and had absolutely no interest in learning. It was silly to think she could be happy with him—or he with her. That seemed clear enough. She'd just opened a door for him with mention of his letter, and, very clearly, he wasn't walking through it, so she simply replied wanly, "Yes, that's what I came out here for."

He didn't respond. She didn't add anything. Instead, she quietly focused on the tree-green ridge sharply outlined against a hard, blue sky. Eventually, she moved her focus down to his work-worn hand holding the rail and impulsively declared, "I met your sister in her shop this morning."

Sam turned his head toward her, now with more than a hint of a smile. It was enough encouragement for her to continue.

"There I was looking at myself in the mirror when I saw that you were looking back from a photo she'd taped to the frame."

"Yeah, well, we get along real good, and we're kinda the only family we've got left these days."

For the first time since they'd walked out to the porch, Sam turned his whole body toward her and looked at Catherine full in the face. "So Pennie's the one who did your hair, huh?"

She made a funny face and gave a shrug.

"She did a nice job. Real nice. It's kind of a big change though..."

"I hadn't thought I'd do anything with it until I realized I'd actually be meeting the famous Western romance writer Loretta de Bonnair. I figured it would be better for all sorts of reasons to adjust my East Coast look. When I walked in, one of your sister's coworkers took one look at me and placed me ten blocks from where I live in Manhattan. It was a little scary."

"It suits you, I gotta say. Loretta, though, isn't so particular about those kinds of things. For her, it's kinda how... how open-minded you are."

"I try to be, and I like it in others, so at least we share that," Catherine said, missing the deeper query in his comment. "It's funny, but your sister didn't believe you knew Loretta."

"For better—or worse—I'm not in the habit of sharing everything with everybody, even with my wonderful sister. And Loretta's even more private than I am these days."

"How is she, really? You say that she's sick, or, well, you said she wasn't sick, then you said she was, so..."

"Sick, yes, in a sense, sick and very weak right now. You should consider yourself very lucky to be able to talk to her at all."

"I really do appreciate what you're doing, not just for me, but for her."

"Yeah, she is my biggest concern right now," he said earnestly. Then, less earnestly than probingly, he continued, "and she's yours too, I guess."

"Yes," she said, turning back to the painting-like view from Sam's porch. "Yes... mostly..." she whispered, unwilling to utter any more clearly the thoughts that were becoming ever more clear. She wanted to go back to every moment they'd connected and review them in a new light. She wanted to ask him a thousand questions. She wanted him to ask her a thousand questions, but neither of them said a word...

...until Sam broke the silence with an unexpected comment. "One of these days, maybe I can tell you more about Loretta."

"Yes, yes, I'd like to know more about her, not just what she's written but why, and how she got started."

Sam laughed. "Yeah, it's an interesting story. Might even tell you about how we first came together. That's kind of a funny one," he said with a nervous chuckle as he heard a car rapidly and loudly rattle over the cattle guard at the entrance to the ranch. "Well, we can worry about that later, maybe. It does sound like the Blushing Dove gal is making her usual quiet entrance."

Catherine started to smile at his comment but quickly suppressed it. The moment of truth, at least for the de Bonnair business, had finally come, and Sam and his reflection were temporarily irrelevant.

# CHAPTER 28

Having heard the same noise that Sam and Catherine heard, Devon pocketed his phone and walked out to the porch in time to see Sharie's car slide to a dust-swirling stop in front of the porch.

"Welcome to the Circle D," Sam said with a folksy accent as Sharie popped out of her car looking angry and frustrated.

As soon as she saw Sam looking at her, however, she quickly relaxed her expression. "Sorry. I got a little lost looking for this impressive place." As she said this, she arranged the frills of her low-cut collar then pinched the fabric at her hips and pulled her skirt down, a movement that focused attention on just how short that skirt really was. Although she didn't have as much to show as Catherine, she wasn't shy about showing what she had.

Sam gave a silent chuckle and said, "Well now, here we all are, so let's get started. I'll run in and make sure Loretta's ready."

As Sam walked back in the house to check on Ms. de Bonnair, Sharie noticed Devon smiling at her and said to Catherine while walking up the stairs, "I see you've got an escort." Looking her up and down, she added, "And a new look. Clearly, this is *serious* business."

"It is for both of us, I suspect."

"Yes, though thank heavens Blushing Dove isn't in serious business trouble. I wonder what you really have to offer these days."

Devon stepped forward and offered his skeptical wisdom. "I wonder about this whole thing. Personally, I don't trust that cowboy."

"I'm not sure I do either"—Sharie winked—"but I'm going to get as much out of him as I can."

As she said this, there was a sound in the room at the end of the porch. All three of them turned to see the curtains draw back and Sam walk from the window to a very large chair. They watched as Sam leaned down and appeared to talk to someone in that chair. Unfortunately, the back of the chair was to the window and all they could see of the person was long, gray hair done up in a tight French knot. This had to be Loretta de Bonnair. As they stood there staring at the scene, Sam looked up, smiled, and, with a wave of his hand, a wink, and a nod, indicated that this was, indeed, the real Loretta de Bonnair. Devon raised an eyebrow, not thoroughly convinced. Sharie straightened up and squared her shoulders. Catherine took a deep breath and simply smiled. She might not get a book contract with this woman, but at least she'd get to meet her, which was well beyond her recent expectations.

Sam said a few more words to Loretta, then his face took on a very serious expression as he nodded to something she was obviously telling him. Then he shook his head once, said something to the woman, gently patted the top of her head, and disappeared. Moments later, Sam came back out to the porch.

With a grave look, he said, "Loretta... well, Loretta is feeling very weak right now, what with the, well, the medications and whatnot, but... she would like to hear what you have to say. She wanted me to tell you both how honored she is that you've come all this way just to see her."

"Sam," Sharie said, dripping with conviction, "I would be so honored and happy to meet her and shake her hand. She is *such* an *amazing* writer."

"Sharie," Sam replied, "she would love to have you both come in and chat, but she is feeling so weak right now, and she is such a lady, if she don't look right, she'd rather not be looked at—and that surgery—well, we both think it best that y'all come to the door and talk to her that way. She's just horrified that you two beautiful young women would have to see her in her present condition. Her nose, well, it's just not what it used to be."

"That's fine," Catherine said quickly. "Whatever she wants is fine with me."

"Oh, yes," Sharie echoed, "absolutely fine. Whatever she wants. But Sam, is this where she lives—with you on the Circle D?"

"Well now, no, Sharie, it isn't. As I had to take her to the doctor early this morning—it was, you see, an appointment we knew about last night—and because she lives further up in the mountains on a spread that's kinda hard to find, we agreed that it'd be best just to stop here and have y'all come out to my place instead of driving all

177

over kingdom come and forcing her to worry about getting her place cleaned up for guests. It was just overall more practical to have you meet her here. I'm sure you understand."

"Perfectly," said Sharie with a tone of excessive credulity. "It is an honor to meet her anytime, anywhere."

"You can tell her that yourself in just a second."

So saying, Sam ushered all three down the narrow hallway to the room Catherine had seen him enter before.

As he opened the door, a cat rushed in from out of nowhere and jumped onto the lap of what appeared to be Loretta de Bonnair engulfed in a huge upholstered chair. How it happened Catherine didn't have time to think about, but, somehow, the chair Ms. de Bonnair was sitting in had been rotated ninety degrees so that the back was now turned to face the door. Once again, all anyone could see of her was the well-coifed top of her gray hair.

Devon whispered to Catherine, "Unless she's sitting on ten cushions, little Loretta is six feet four."

Catherine frowned, annoyed by the impolite and unnecessary disruption, though aware that there definitely was something to Devon's observation.

Sam quickly walked over to the chair and lifted the cat from Loretta's lap. As he gently tossed the very large, clearly spoiled, and obviously annoyed cat back out the door, he said, "You can't be a part of this, Herman. When we're all done, you can come back and make yourself comfortable with Loretta. Until then, skedaddle."

As Catherine watched the cat slowly lumber off, she asked, "Herman, as in Melville?"

"Yep." Sam gave a quick smile, slipped back into the room, and moved the door to a semi-closed position. He then stood, visible to those at the door, halfway between them and Loretta, and said as a preface to the proceedings, "Loretta is feeble of body but definitely not feeble of mind. She's already heard what you offered yesterday, Sharie, and she thought it was a real fine start from the publisher that launched her but hasn't paid her very much. So she came up with this efficient way to improve her chances—one meeting, short and to the point, with the two of you showing your cards and adjusting your offers, if need be. Kinda like a game of Texas Hold'em. A little cutthroat, but it is a great way to increase the pot. And, well..." Sam trailed off, as if slightly embarrassed by his financial focus.

His friend Walt, at the moment pretending to be Loretta, wasn't the least bit embarrassed by the appearance of "Loretta's" business interests. He was supposed to play one part and one part only: an aging author hidden from view in a huge, well-placed chair, who, politely, though clearly, was interested in getting the best contract "she" could get. To this end, "she" added to Sam's remark a remark of her own in a breathy, wavering falsetto that sounded, if not convincingly female, at least convincingly close to death, "At my age"—she paused to catch her breath—"I'm just in it for the money."

This was the strangest contract negotiation Catherine had ever heard of, and it was getting stranger by the moment. Not only was she in a very uncomfortable bidding war being hosted by an author who was veritably auctioning off the first right of refusal and the subsequent advance for her next book to the highest bidder, but that author was apparently too sick and too vain to be seen, which obliged the competing editors to shout their bids to the back of her head. Again, the thought crossed her mind that Devon might be right and this tall lady with the wavering voice hidden in the chair before them wasn't actually Loretta but some imposter. And yet, this made no sense. Including Devon, there were three witnesses to this odd event. It may not have seemed real, but it was too weird not to be, which meant, as well, that Sam had apparently told her the truth. He did know Loretta de Bonnair.

A pang of regret shot through her as Sam, with a voice like a stockyard auctioneer, began, "Yesterday, we heard an offer from Blushing Dove Press for an advance of one hundred thousand dollars. Now, just so I understand, that's an advance on the next book, not something to kinda balance out what wasn't paid for the first book that's done a little better than anyone expected, right?"

"Actually, Sam, I talked with our editor-in-chief last night, and we would now like to add one hundred thousand to yesterday's offer as an acknowledgment of how pleased we are with *Rancho de Amor*'s success. Ms. de Bonnair deserves to see our appreciation."

"Two hundred thousand dollars is now the opening bid, two hundred thousand. Do I hear a higher bid?"

Catherine blinked, suddenly more than a little worried. She knew that Vito didn't have the resources to outbid Blushing Dove Press, and

Blushing Dove's opening bid was already close to a reasonable limit for Banter. She knew she'd have to keep any additional increments small and try to sweeten the pot with all the things Banter House could offer that Blushing Dove couldn't and somehow—*somehow*—do what she'd been sent out there to do: find Ms. de Bonnair and get her to sign with Banter. She took a quick breath and said, "Two hundred and *ten* thousand dollars and the excellent literary reputation Banter, alone, can offer."

"Two hundred and *ten* thousand dollars. Nice... nice," Sam said with a smile.

Ms. de Bonnair's response, however, was not quite as encouraging. In a voice that seemed to have gained a bit of strength, she said, "But that's only ten thousand dollars more than the other."

"That's true, Loretta, but it is more, so you just sit back, *quietly*, and let's see what happens."

"Yes, Sam, it's just so"—she coughed discreetly—"exciting," her weak and wavering falsetto restored. Then she coughed again, weakly. Clearly, she was not well.

"Two hundred and ten thousand dollars is the last bid," Sam, the auctioneer, resumed. "Do I hear another bid?"

"Three hundred thousand with a publisher who is far more appreciative of romance *and* its writers." Sharie cocked her head, smiled, and winked at Sam.

Sam gave no apparent response to Sharie but continued with his patter, "Three hundred thousand, three hundred thousand dollars is the bid. Do I hear higher?"

Catherine bit her lip and ventured, "Three hundred and *ten* thousand, and the best editorial staff in the business."

"Three hundred and ten thousand dollars is the bid. Going once, going twice..."

"Three hundred and twenty thousand from Blushing Dove, a business that isn't going out of business." Sharie turned and smiled at Catherine.

"Three hundred twenty is the bid. Three hundred and twenty thousand dollars. Do I hear another bid?" Sam glanced at Catherine.

"Three hundred and thirty," she said quickly, with more defiance than confidence.

"Three hundred and forty."

"Three hundred and fifty."

"Four hundred!" Sharie said and smiled broadly to no one in particular. She was sure she'd win this useless competition sooner or later, and she now wanted that to be sooner.

"That sounds good, doesn't it, Sam?" Loretta said, sounding a little too good herself.

"Yes, it does, but you're getting excited again and that's not good for you. And maybe we're not done yet. Four hundred thousand dollars is the bid," he repeated slowly and flatly, giving Catherine an encouraging glance. "Do I hear anything else?"

"Ms. de Bonnair," Catherine asserted around Sharie's shoulder, "you *really* ought to consider the kind of care, concern, and reputation you will be getting when you choose a publisher—"

"You certainly can afford to talk," Sharie sneered, "but can you afford anything else?"

"Four hundred and *one* thousand dollars."

"Very good, very good," Sam said, almost relieved. "Four hundred and one thousand dollars going once, going twice, going—"

"Four hundred and fifty," Sharie said coolly, giving a little laugh.

There was a pause. Loretta cleared her throat.

"Four hundred fifty and... and *two* thousand," Catherine said, sounding increasingly desperate.

Sam began the auction count again, seemingly anxious to end the bidding, but Sharie jumped in confidently. "Five hundred thousand dollars."

Trying to control a rising sense of panic, Catherine advised, "You really have to consider who you'd like to be with in the long run. I mean..."

Sharie turned to watch Catherine writhe. Sam looked at Catherine with a resigned, almost pitying expression.

Catherine took a deep breath. She couldn't lose this contract. Vito's words—"do whatever it takes"—echoed in her mind. And to lose to Sharie Blanchard right there in front of the new and much-improved Sam Wilson? She took another deep breath and aggressively declared, "Banter House Books offers you *one million dollars.*" Then she turned to Sharie and whispered in her ear, "Perhaps Blushing Dove would like to beat that."

"One million dollars?!" Sharie almost spat. "That's absurd."

"It may be absurd, but I'll take it, if I don't hear a better offer. Do I?" asked Loretta energetically. The offer seemed to have had restorative qualities. The frailty for which Loretta was currently known seemed a thing of the past.

Sharie turned around and glared at Catherine. "No, Blushing Dove won't try to top that offer. We're not that stupid. There hasn't been a million-dollar advance for this sort of book in years. That's almost as high as our net profit on *Rancho.*"

"Well, I sure don't find anything wrong with a million dollars," Loretta announced with an increasingly husky Western accent.

Sharie gave the chair in which Loretta was seated a scrutinizing look, then said, "I think we should all—and most especially you, Ms. de Bonnair—like to know how Banter plans to pay this amount since—"

A phone in the room started to ring. Sharie paused to see if Sam would answer it.

He didn't, though he paused indecisively for three rings, then said, "Let's, ah, not worry about too much right now. I think we should just leave things as they are." He quickly leaned over, looked at Loretta, then insisted, "Loretta is looking very tired and shouldn't be talking anymore at all, really."

"Fine," Sharie snapped, "but as Ms. de Bonnair's business agent, you should be concerned with how Banter—"

She was interrupted now by a different ringtone of a cow mooing in one of Sam's pockets.

"Well, someone's got an issue," Sam said apologetically. "Could be trouble with some calving. Let me just grab this." Sam took his phone out and answered, "This is Sam…" As he listened, he went pale and his jaw dropped.

# Chapter 29

What!?" Sam asked, shocked. "Where? Well, damn, I... I'll be right there, yes, with the truck.... You bet!"

Sam quickly clicked his phone off and said, "There's a fire started over on the Sedgwick place. Brushfire—headed toward their corrals, their barns, their house. Y'all just—you just run along back to town now, and we'll get back to you tonight. And please, let's not disturb Loretta any longer. No matter what she says, she's not up for this without me." He looked back to Loretta sternly, then walked out the door, herding his guests further into the hallway. Closing the door resolutely, he said, "Loretta looks very strained right now. I may even need to take her to the doctor when I get back."

As he started toward the front door, Catherine reacted before she knew what she was doing, "Wait!"

Sam turned and stopped as she almost bumped into him.

"I should come with you."

"What?" Sam asked, thoroughly confused.

"I once helped a neighbor put out a fire in her kitchen."

"This is a little different."

"It's a fire, and I'm sure you could use another body or two out there," she said as she looked at Devon and Sharie.

With a quick, condescending smile, Sam said, "Yeah, but it's dirty, dangerous, and not a place for a, well..."

"A woman?"

Sam didn't know what to say, so he said nothing.

"There are horses and houses and maybe even people in danger, right?"

"Yes."

"So let's go." Then she turned back to Sharie and asked, "You coming?"

"Are you kidding? I don't know the first thing about any of this."

"Devon?" Catherine asked, turning her head to him.

"I really don't think I could be useful. In fact—"

"Well," Sam interrupted with a confused glance to Catherine, "whoever's coming, let's go."

He rushed out the front door. Catherine followed as quickly as she could, but she wasn't going anywhere fast in her heels. "Sam," she yelled, "are there any other shoes I could wear?"

He turned back to her just before he entered the tractor barn. "In the tack room," he said, pointing to a small shed, "there are some extra boots. Maybe something'll fit."

Something did, if an extra inch of room in the toe was considered a fit. In these oversized boots, Catherine ran from the tack room with all of the grace of an ice skater rushing across a thick rug. But the boots were better than the heels. She might not be able to outrun the fire, but she could, at least, place her feet firmly in the face of doom.

As she approached the large barn into which Sam had disappeared, he noisily reappeared driving an ancient water truck. This was an essential piece of equipment on a backcountry ranch in California. On the wealthiest ranches, these water trucks tended to be recently decommissioned fire rigs. On most of the rest of the ranches, the water truck was an old, noisy, uncomfortable thing that had usually served a road-building crew over half a century before. The truck on the Circle D was one of the oldest, noisiest, and most uncomfortable, but it also boasted one of the largest water tanks. Sam and his truck came to a dusty, water-sloshing stop, after which Catherine climbed in. "Those boots fit?" he asked, smiling and glancing down at her feet.

"Not really, but they'll work for now."

Sam revved the engine, but before easing out the clutch, he looked at Catherine and almost pleaded, "Seriously, I don't think you should do this."

"Would it help, even a little?"

"Well, yeah, maybe, but..." Sam took a deep breath and exhaled, slowly, both flustered and impressed. Then he quickly released the clutch and said, "Hold on!"

The truck rattled over the cattle guard at the front gate, then swung with a frightening tilt onto the paved road.

When the truck stopped rocking back and forth, Sam remarked, "The Sedgwicks are good ranchers, been owner-operators for generations and are the last like that around here. They take good care of their cattle and their land. It's a real shame they're getting hit with this. And if we can't stop it, the Circle D's next. We're right next door."

Catherine looked out the side window and saw a dark plume of smoke rising three to four miles in front and to the right. "That's it, right?" Catherine pointed, yelling over the roar of the engine.

"Yep. That's it all right," Sam yelled back.

"You call that 'right next door'?"

"We got big backyards between our doors."

Catherine stared at the smoke for a while. It was thick and dark and being blown almost horizontally across the countryside.

"Is the fire department going to be there?" she yelled over the motor, trying not to sound concerned.

"More like the CDF guys with the state, but yeah, eventually."

"Eventually" was not what Catherine wanted to hear. Although she could feel it, she wouldn't succumb to the fear rising in her mind. The fire needed to be put out, they needed help, and there she was, willing to do what she could to help. Still, she had to ask, "Have you done this before?"

"Brushfire? Yeah, unfortunately. Kinda got to when you live out here. What I don't know is what you're doing here with me. For your own good, I really should drop you off on the road. There are going to be fire trucks and police here soon enough. And maybe Derek, or whatever his name is—you know, the guy you came with—could come get you."

"I'm not going to stand on some road and watch a house and horses and whatever burn up. I know how to hold a hose."

Sam pushed the clutch in and, as the engine quieted down, he said with a wry smile, "I'm sure you do, but I don't want to risk losing... well, I don't want *Loretta* to lose her editor before she's signed a contract." He released the clutch, and instantly the engine roared back into noisy action.

"She's got another editor who can't wait to take my place."

"Yeah, but you're..." He glanced at her quickly, stopped himself, held his breath a moment, exhaled, and concluded quietly, "I'm just concerned about your safety."

Catherine, however, voiced some concerns of her own, though

they were a bit more abstract. "Why did you tell Laura Lee in the library that you didn't like romances and wouldn't read *Rancho de Amor*?"

"Well, it's complicated. When you're a cowboy, you got a certain reputation to uphold around town. I know it's kinda silly, like I'm not tough enough to let people know I read romance novels, but, well, a few people know. People I like, people like... you."

"And Miss Blushing Dove."

"For her, it was for business, Loretta's business. For you... yeah, it was also for business, but it's also personal, definitely personal."

She turned, looked at him, and said, "Thank you," then, as she slowly turned away, she repeated, more to herself than for him, "thank you." As the words left her lips, something seemed to turn upside down inside of her. She felt powerful and dizzy all at once and hoped he'd tell her more, much more, about his friend Loretta, about himself, about anything and everything.

But he didn't.

He couldn't, really—even though he wanted to. He knew he was attracted to her, but as long as she didn't seem to care about him, he was sad, but safe. Things seemed to be shifting, however. Her questions, her answers, the way she looked at him, the way she moved—yes, things were finally shifting. He knew he would have to come clean soon, very soon, but it was still too soon—or at least still too hard.

When he didn't say anything else, Catherine turned back to the fire. It looked much larger now—because they were getting closer, because it was growing, because it was frightening, and because she was beginning to feel something bigger, or at least more overwhelming, than even fear. It wasn't daring, but something similar—a sort of careless willingness to be a part of whatever was going to happen. It had something to do with the immediate need to put out a fire, but it had more to do with what she was feeling for the man next to her. Of course he'd been upsetting her right from the start. On the surface, he wasn't at all what she wanted, but the things he talked about, the things he cared about, how he looked at her, how he moved, well... she wasn't sure, not sure at all, not sure about anything, but she was more willing than she'd ever been to see just how far this thing she was feeling *could* go. She sat back and suddenly felt as if she had just fallen off the moon and was drifting through space, lost, weightless—and surprisingly content.

"What we're gonna do," Sam said over the roar of the engine, "is try to save any structures that are in the way by getting them and everything around them good and wet. The problem is that we'll be in the path of the fire, and so you gotta stay with me, real close, and when I say we move, we move. At any moment, we may need to get back in the truck and hightail it outa there, got it? Brushfires move fast, which is both a good and a bad thing."

Catherine gave a decisive nod.

"Or we might need to help put out spot fires if they've got a blade out there cutting a break. We won't know till we're there."

"I'll do whatever you say," she yelled back.

"Yeah," Sam said with a nervous half smile, "I just hope I say the right thing!"

BACK AT THE RANCH, Sharie, too, was hoping she'd say the right thing. She seemed to have lost the bidding war, but the unexpected absence of both her winning rival and the unnecessary go-between allowed her an opportunity to speak directly to Loretta de Bonnair. She turned to Devon and asked, "Do you think it would kill her if I just poked my head back in and talked to her a little more?"

"Well, she may be frail, but she certainly seemed to gain strength, at least in her voice, as the offers got higher and higher. I think she'd have strength enough to talk a little more."

"Yes, and it would be doing her a favor. Blushing Dove won't go as high as Banter. One million dollars? That's ridiculous! But some of the other things we can offer make us the better choice. We're a romance publisher, and Banter definitely isn't. Wouldn't you want to know about that if you were an author?"

"Yes, I would, because I *am* an author."

"Oh, really? What kinds of things do you write?"

"Poetry, mostly."

"Oh, I love poetry. I've been thinking Blushing Dove should expand into that market. It's about time for some good romantic poetry to sweep the nation, don't you think?"

"I do. America is ready for a new poetic awakening and... I'm sure I could do romantic poetry as well as anyone. I'm also quite good at writing more challenging forms of poetry. I like to think of my work as beyond the zeitgeist."

Sharie didn't know what all of that meant, but she purposefully let the subject die. She didn't want to have to deal with the inflated egos and expectations of two authors in the same afternoon. "So do you mind poking your head in with me to have a little chat with Ms. de Bonnair?"

"I don't mind at all," said Devon, brightening from the mood he'd been in since the hasty end of his date the night before. "I'd love to help you get her to understand the choice that would truly be in her best interest."

So saying, Devon manfully took control of the doorknob that Sharie seemed reluctant to touch, and gave it a decisive turn to the right. With a gentle push, the door opened and Devon stood back to let Sharie enter the room first. As they walked in, however, they saw a surprising sight: the bottom two-thirds of a man on its way out the window. Neither Sharie nor Devon could see who it was, but he had a beefy paunch and was wearing jeans and two very large cowboy boots. Whoever it was didn't seem to know that anyone had come into the room as he was in the process of leaving it. And even if he was aware of this, he didn't turn around to chat. Sharie and Devon heard the heavy and hurried footsteps of the mystery man cross the porch, go down the stairs, and scrunch across the dirt in front of the house. As they approached the window, they saw him jump into the oldest and muddiest pickup truck in the yard, start it with a roar, and, spinning dirt up from behind his tires, speed off down the lane that left the ranch.

"Who was *that*?" Devon asked, genuinely confused.

"Definitely not Loretta," Sharie said, whispering excitedly. "It looked, though I couldn't tell for sure, like that guy who pulls beer at the Black Barn."

"Walt," Devon whispered loudly with a slightly amused expression.

Both then turned and slowly walked around to the front of Loretta's chair. A wig, a robe, and a pair of oversized slippers were the only things left of her.

A smirking Sharie turned to a smiling Devon and said, "Someone's been playing a little game."

"Yes," Devon said, "and if we have anything to do with it, that game is about to end."

# Chapter 30

After noisily downshifting and driving over the hill at the entrance of the Sedgwick Ranch, Sam coasted down into the shallow valley and toward the heart of the property. It was filled with smoke, behind which a long, thin ribbon of fire was advancing quickly across the short, dry grass to the south. Because the fire had jumped the dirt road Sam was on, they would have to drive through the blinding smoke and burning western flank of the fire to get to the central complex of the ranch where the house and barns were.

"Quick, roll up your window!" he told Catherine. "And if you're religious, start praying."

So saying, Sam revved his engine, downshifted again, and roared into the blinding smoke. All that he could see were flames, which allowed him to see where the road had to be, that narrow place in the dark where he couldn't see any fire. With the slightest mistake, they'd end up off the road and in the fire, and if he couldn't get out of it almost immediately, they'd burn to death.

Catherine had never been so frightened in her life. She had thought they were going to fight a fire, not drive straight into it. As they drove into the thick fist of eye- and lung-burning smoke, she clasped her hand over her mouth and nose. She would endure her fate silently, hope that the man who shared that fate knew what he was doing, and hope that whatever he'd do, he'd do it quickly.

Eight interminable seconds later, they drove out of the fire and into the large dirt lot around which the central ranch complex had been built. The fire line had just passed, and with its passing it lit the hay barn on fire, ignited one corner of the cow barn, would have burned the horse barn and tack room had one of the Sedgwick ranch hands not hosed enough water on both to keep them safe, and burned around and past the metal tractor barn. The fire had very nearly engulfed the main house; two ranch hands and one of the

189

owners were still spraying as much water as they could suck from the one water truck and a garden hose onto the swirl of embers that threatened to ignite any unattended part of the structure.

Almost immediately after driving through the fire line and the thickest of the smoke, Sam had to slam on his brakes to avoid hitting the eighty-five-year-old ranch owner, John Sedgwick. Addled by Alzheimer's, all the poor man could do while standing in the middle of the swirling smoke, confused and frightened, was to repeat the plaintive question, "Where's my dog? Where's my dog?"

"Rex is fine, John. Don't worry. He'll be just fine," Sam said, trying to soothe the poor man's panic with a show of confidence he didn't actually feel.

"Do you have my dog?" the man yelled, thoroughly lost in his narrow concern.

"He's in the house, John. He's just in the house and he's okay," Sam lied. He had no idea where the dog was, but a lie might at least reduce the man's anguish for a while. Sam smiled, yelled a final reassurance, "Rex is fine, you'll see," then he gunned his engine, jostled around the poor man, then roared up to where John's wife, Megan Janeway, and two of the four Sedgwick ranch hands were still working to save the house.

"Back your truck up here, Sam," Megan yelled over the commotion. "We could use your water. And then go see what you can do for the heifers in the cow barn."

Sam looked over at Catherine and asked, more afraid of the answer than the situation, "Are you really up for this?"

"I'm not here to watch. I want to do something—anything."

Sam gave a nod. "Well then, let's go." After backing it into position, he jumped out of the truck.

Catherine clambered down from her seat, tore off her unnecessary sweater and tossed it back in the truck, and ran with Sam toward the cow barn, now close to half-engulfed in flames.

When they got to the barn, Sam stopped to explain quickly. "All the ranches out here are calving right now, and this barn's where the first-year cows are put if they're having problems. I don't know how many we can save, but if we gotta choose, we'll take the cow and leave the calf."

"Okay," Catherine said, not sure she understood all of what he'd said but sure they didn't have time to stop and discuss it.

When they ran inside, they saw two cows lying on their sides tethered to posts in two of the four stalls. Each cow had a weak calf at her side. The third stall had a swollen heifer that had not yet given birth to the calf bulging in her belly. Pulling chains hung ready from the partition wall. Some ranch hand had been about to pull the calf from the cow's womb but abandoned the task when the fire broke out. Now, one whole wall and much of the roof of the barn were on fire. Flames were beginning to drip onto the hay, which quickly burst into flame. With no time to lose, Sam rushed into one stall, untethered the cow, yanked her to her feet, and sent her out the door of the burning barn. Catherine did the same thing, although Sam, on his return, helped her yank the unwilling cow to her feet. Then they both went back in to pull the inert calves to safety. Sam lifted his and carried it out, but sixty pounds of moist, frightened, and bony weight was not easy for Catherine to lift. Still, she had just found a way to pull the poor calf out by grabbing the bony legs a few inches above the fetlocks when Sam grabbed her around her waist and yanked her backward. He pulled so forcefully that she had to release the calf's front legs.

"No!" she yelled, struggling. "I have to—"

But before she could finish, part of the roof collapsed into the barn right where she'd been.

Sam spun her around quickly, grabbed her arm, and yelled, "Run!" They dashed out of the barn. Once safely outside, they turned around and watched the rest of the roof cave in.

There was nothing more they could do.

For a few long moments, they stood and watched, Catherine horrified, Sam resigned, as the barn and everything in it exploded into flame then collapsed into a pile of burning rubble.

Eventually, Catherine turned around and saw the house still standing and the smoke from the advancing fire thinning out. The state fire crews and a bulldozer from the ranch had apparently cut a containment break that was choking the fire out.

Just then, one of the CDF trucks, no longer needed in the field, roared up to where Catherine and Sam were standing. It was there to douse what was left of the burning barn. Clearly, there was nothing more she and Sam could do, and at that moment, they were more in the way than anything else. Sam gently took her arm and walked her out to the charred field behind the unburned tractor barn. Still charged with adrenaline, fear, and a frustrated desire to do something more, they stood in the barn's shadow and stared, unfocused and softly panting, at the mountains beyond, orange in the late afternoon sun.

Eventually, Sam mumbled, "I'm sorry." It was all he could say.

Catherine didn't respond. She was afraid to say anything, sure that to utter a sound would open the floodgates of profound distress; the sight of the calf she had to leave behind kept flashing in her mind. She simply blinked and stared at the slowly darkening landscape to the east. After a minute, she sighed loudly, paused, then whispered, "We did the best we could, didn't we?"

"Yes, we did. We saved two cows and a calf... and there wasn't anything else we coulda done."

"I hope that's true," Catherine said without emotion. "Thanks for letting me at least try. And"—she looked down at the ground— "thanks for yanking me out of there."

Sam turned and stared at her. She was so different from the woman he thought he would love, and yet here, in an unexpected package, were the qualities he most admired: brains, independence, courage, and beauty. He stood there trying to crowd his mind with every detail he could see—her dirt- and charcoal-streaked face, the sweeping curves of her body, her dark, disheveled, hay-streaked hair. He felt as if he'd been punched, softly, deep in the gut.

Without needing to see a thing, Catherine sensed what Sam was feeling, sensed why he wasn't talking, sensed why he was staring at her. She raised her eyes slowly, turned her head, and looked into those frighteningly beautiful eyes. Then she looked down at his chest. The snaps of his shirt had been ripped open. It was a wide, strong chest, and on the left side near his heart, Catherine saw part of a tattoo. With one finger, she gently moved his shirt aside and saw a date, April 27, written in a florid script. She looked up with an inquiringly raised eyebrow.

"The day my parents died. My sister and I commemorate it every year by having a picnic at one of our parents' favorite places in the hills."

"So that's the tattoo Pennie was talking about," Catherine mused.

"My sister told you about my tattoo?"

"Yeah. She said you raised her real well after your parents died, even got a tattoo of your own after she got hers. She thought you were really cool for doing that—and wise."

"I don't know how wise it was. Taking care of Pennie, I just did the best I could and hoped it would work out, and I got lucky." He shrugged then said, "It's funny, thinking about my sister doing your hair. It really does look good."

"Better than before?" she asked, playfully fishing.

"I like *you* better'n before, though to be honest, you had me at that first 'no, thank you.' Seeing you right now, seeing what you just did out here, seeing all the things you know and can do, I swear, Pennie coulda given you a lopsided mullet and it wouldn't make a bit of difference." He leaned back slightly to get a more complete look at her and said, "You are a very, very attractive woman"—he leaned toward her, gently lifted her face to his, and almost hummed—"in so many ways."

Catherine closed her eyes and let his lips slowly meet hers. Again—and more intensely now—she felt the falling part of falling in love—and loved it.

When, slowly, they pulled apart, Sam cleared his throat and started to speak. He couldn't avoid telling her the truth any longer. "Later" was now. He, too, was falling in love, and this time, he wanted to do it the right way and as close to the start as he could.

"Catherine, we don't really know each other, and, well, I have to tell you—"

Catherine raised her hand and gently put her fingers to his lips. "You don't have to say anything. I'm the one who has to say something. I was wrong. You are definitely *not* the man I thought you were when I first saw you flying backward out of the Black Barn and I said that first, apparently irresistible, 'no, thank you.' You are strong enough not just to be strong, but to honestly be who you are."

"Well, but ya see, that's the thing—" He stopped abruptly when he saw someone he hadn't expected to see walking up.

After stripping off his wig, robe, and slippers and dashing out a window, Walt had jumped in his truck and rushed off to help fight the Sedgwick fire. He arrived only a couple of minutes after Sam, but he had joined the state fire crew out in the field. He hadn't seen Sam until he walked behind the tractor barn looking for hot spots that might potentially flare up.

He found one, and it flared up right in his face.

"Walt?" Sam choked.

"Sam?" Walt exclaimed, almost equally surprised.

"What the heck are you doing here?"

"In case ya hadn't noticed, there was a fire."

"Yeah, but, ah... what about, you know, back at... the ranch?"

"Everything's fine. Just"—Walt darted a glance at Catherine—"it's just as it should be."

"Everyone, or everything—"

"Yes."

"Were you there too?" Catherine asked, far too lost in the moment to be anything but slightly confused. "I didn't see you."

"Oh, well," Walt started unsurely. "Sam can tell you better'n me."

"Yeah, well, ya see," Sam began, stalling until he could find a credible way back to the make-believe, "Walt was, as sometimes he does, working..." Sam trailed off, not yet sure of the details of this part of his lie.

"At the Circle D?"

"Yeah, well, you see, Sam and I do some work together sometimes on the ranch," Walt said vaguely, but with conviction.

Sam took the narrative baton and continued, "It's ranch stuff out, well, way out in the fields, and Walt was working and then had to leave when he saw the fire, right?" Sam turned to his friend with the hope that he would play along properly.

He did, almost.

"Right. I saw that fire, jumped in my truck, and headed right here, and before that, I was culling some cattle."

Sam gave him a surprised look. Walt knew his beers but not his beef. In late November, the Circle D was not culling much of anything. Instead, they were calving, but at least Walt had said what he'd said with convincing brio.

"Culling," however, was not what Catherine heard. "You were *calling* some cattle?" she asked, somewhat confused. She had a vision of Walt standing in a very Swiss-looking pasture, singing out names like Daisy and Elsie. It was a strange image.

"No, you know, culling," he said, pausing in the hope that Sam would come to the rescue. Walt's knowledge of the activity was dangerously limited.

"It's, ah," Sam jumped in awkwardly, "separating out the unproductive cattle from the herds. Gotta do it every once in a while and, ah, we are doing it a little early this season and, so... Walt was helping."

"Oh," she said, believing every word he said. She turned to Walt and asked, "So do you have to do roping and bucking and all that business too?"

"Well, I'm not a professional like Sam here, but yes, I do it— sometimes."

Sam was wilting, though he did manage to corroborate with a quiet "Yeah, sometimes." Then he looked at Catherine with pain and disappointment. He had been on the brink of confessing how he'd lied and why he'd lied, which, once confessed, would allow him to clear an unencumbered path to Catherine's heart, but now he had to sink back into his increasingly troublesome, if not completely ruinous, deception. He just couldn't say what he had to say to Catherine with Walt standing there trying to tell a completely different story. He would have to wait to tell her who he was and what he really felt—and in waiting, he worried, would the moment be lost... forever?

Making matters worse, he was now aware that Sharie and Devon might have discovered that Loretta was not really Loretta. And if they'd uncovered that little fact and somehow got word to Catherine about this lie, things would get *very* complicated. This unexpected turn of events was a hot spot that could burn rapidly across Sam's delicate field of dreams.

He didn't have much time to wonder and worry about any of it, however, as Megan Janeway ran up to him with new urgency. "Sam, oh Sam, the horses, they're all loose and running around scared to death. And we've only got one corral that we can put them in. Can you stay and help us get 'em under control? You're so good with horses."

"Sure," he said quickly. Megan gave him a quick wave of thanks before hurrying back to the house.

Sam turned to Walt and asked, "Could you maybe take Catherine back to town? She's gonna want to shower and"—he turned to her— "and, well..." He turned back to Walt and asked, "Can she and I just talk for a second, you know—alone?"

"Oh, yeah. Sure." Walt walked away from the barn to stand out of sight and out of earshot.

When he'd gone, Sam moved close to Catherine. "I... I meant everything I said with that kiss, Catherine," he declared softly. "I want to know you, everything about you, and really try to see if we can—like each other, or, hell, I..." He looked away, then quickly looked back and admitted with a steady, unwavering voice, "I feel something I haven't felt in a long time, and I've never, ever felt like this. You challenge me, intrigue me, and increasingly delight me in so many ways. But our lives and experiences are so different. I'd like to make a go of getting to know you and... and having you know me, the *real* me. So let's talk tonight... about ourselves. Eight o'clock at the Black Barn, unless you'd feel better going somewhere else?"

"No, no, the Black Barn is my second favorite place to eat in Sisquoc."

"What's the first?"

"The gas station."

"Ah, yes. A fine selection of goods, but the seating's a little limited. You mind going to the second-best place tonight?"

"It might become my sentimental first choice soon."

"Well then, I'll meet you there. Eight o'clock."

"Good." Catherine nodded. "And Sam, be careful, please. I won't be here to help you," she said, both teasing and pleading at the same time.

"Don't you worry, Catherine," he said as he kissed her forehead. "I'll be there in one piece and maybe even cleaned up."

As they walked out from behind the barn, Sam said, "Why don't you go to his truck? It's that dirty red one over by the house. I just need to talk to Walt a sec." So saying, he angled over to his friend and stopped. Catherine continued walking toward that dirty red truck and heard Sam and Walt, talking quietly, though urgently, about ranch business, she was sure.

The ride back to town began pleasantly enough. Catherine would have preferred riding back with Sam, but Walt was polite company. He mostly asked about where she lived and what she did and how she liked California so far. He also answered a few questions Catherine asked, first about Loretta—was she all right now at Sam's ranch, how would she get home, and where was her ranch?—and then about

196

Sam. Had she been in a suspicious frame of mind, she might have thought Walt was being evasively brief and imprecise in his answers, but after her recent and moving experiences with two very different kinds of fire, she chose to see it as the typical awkward brevity of a man who was forced to sit next to a woman he'd just caught kissing his best friend. Whatever the reason, she enjoyed the first few long silences between them in which she could quietly indulge her warm musings and admire the countryside that surrounded the ranch where Sam worked. This was the perfect, almost ennobling, setting for Sam Wilson, the man whom she had stubbornly misunderstood until reality had shown, or let her finally see, who he really was.

The fourth time she and Walt fell silent after a brief burst of conversation, however, Catherine's recollections slipped past the numbingly wonderful thoughts of Sam and stumbled on some of the details of her meeting with Loretta de Bonnair. And all of a sudden, she broke into a sweat of panic. Yes, it was good to have finally met, or at least talked to, her. Yes, it was great to have won the bidding war and presumably gotten Ms. de Bonnair to join Banter House. But at what price? A million dollars?! She bit her tongue at the thought. How could she have gone so high? Sharie was right, it was absurd. Yes, she'd had to win, but this was surely going to be a Pyrrhic victory. What would she tell Vito? What would he tell her? And what would she have to tell Loretta? Her present success with Ms. de Bonnair was built on a lie, a lie she would soon have to face and deal with. And what would Sam think about her? She'd made a mistake in the heat of the moment, bowed to pressure and her own desire, but the mistake might cost her pretty much everything.

While she was thinking all of this, Walt asked, "Are you all right?"

"Yes. Why?"

" 'Cause it sounded like you were groaning in pain just now."

"Me? Oh, no. I'm just fine. Just... fine. Maybe a little tired and, you know, watching that barn collapse on those cows..."

"Yeah, that musta been tough."

Catherine sighed. "Yes. It's been a very strange afternoon."

# CHAPTER 31

In the past, she certainly hadn't been a prude, but Catherine had always been prudent. Her prudence had protected her from feeling too much too fast. It had protected her from making unwise choices. It had protected her from being vulnerable to feelings and sensations that she couldn't control. In other words, it had protected her from passion. She hadn't really tried to avoid it; it had seemed, instead, to have avoided her. No one had been clever enough, persistent enough, and convincing enough to move her past her well-established standards and expectations. And probably no one would have had someone not ridden in from left field to subvert both expectation and standard.

Right from the start, Catherine knew that Sam Wilson was not what she was looking for, and right from the start, he challenged that conviction. Although he seemed not just different but wrong, it was Sam's notable difference from what she'd have thought would be right that arrested her attention. Of course, it didn't hurt that he had beautiful eyes, a handsome face, and a vigorous physical presence, but more than anything else, it was the improbable combinations—rural simplicity and complex thought, virile energy and gentle concern— that had surprised, confused, and undermined her prudence. Devon had been right about this guy. He *was* dangerous; he thoroughly upset Catherine's balance. She liked to guide as much of her life as she could by thought, but her thoughts now seemed to be guided, or even imprisoned, by emotion. It was as if she were on a whirling merry-go-round—up and down, up and down—riding a whole herd of emotions. She was frightened, though she felt more alive than she'd ever felt before.

This hypersensitivity also made her alive to the fact that Sam, and her unfettered attraction to him, was only one cause of her emotional turmoil. She felt waves of shame, embarrassment, and fear about having made an offer to Ms. de Bonnair that Banter wouldn't be able to honor. In the heat of the moment, she'd gotten carried away and had impulsively rushed to win at all costs. Unfortunately, she realized that the actual cost of her impulse might be the loss of the book deal with Ms. de Bonnair and the loss of Sam's trust—and interest. She resolved to deal with this first and foremost when she saw Sam. She'd tell him the truth, then ask if he would, or even could, contact Loretta and see if she would take any less than what had been foolishly offered. Then she'd call Vito and find out what that wheeler-dealer could do: slow the advance until presales revenue started to come in, give de Bonnair an even larger royalty percentage... He was clever. Surely he'd be able to do something.

Even though getting a deal with de Bonnair had originally been the one and only focus, central to her life now was making sure her mistake wouldn't destroy the nascent relationship she had with Sam. Would he understand why she'd exaggerated things, and could he forgive her purposeful exuberance, or would he be unrelentingly offended by her lie? Up and down, up and down she went with fear, shame, lust, embarrassment, love, excitement, and a whole lot of nervous anticipation, all of which she brought to the Black Barn at precisely 8 p.m.

In a booth in the far corner, Sam was already there and waiting. He was dressed in an attractive white Western shirt, clean and pressed Wranglers, and his favorite beige hat. When he saw her, he jumped up from the table to greet her, offer her a seat, and remove his hat.

"Hello, Sam," she said as she approached the table. "You're early."

"Got impatient."

"No problems with the calves or the cows or—no, no, wait—the 'culling'?"

"Nope, everything's fine, except, well"—he leaned back and lifted her Marc Jabobs heels from his seat—"I found these somewhat outa place in our tack room, and now I'm most anxious to find the woman whose feet they fit." He gently inclined them toward her on one finger.

"Mr. Charming, I can prove right here and now that those shoes fit my feet, but"—she slipped the shoes from Sam's finger and set them down by her seat—"I have to admit that I forgot your lovely ranch boots back at Violet's. I'll get them to you as soon as I can."

"There's, well, there's… no rush." Sam sounded both giddy and a little nervous. He paused and watched her slide into her seat, then said, "That's a mighty beautiful dress, Catherine. From New York?"

"Yes, though when I wore it to breakfast this morning, someone said it looked like I was going to a funeral, so I went out and bought something with a little more local life and color. I didn't want Loretta to think I was in mourning. And the funny thing is, she never saw me in it."

"No, but I did—and it was very nice. But so's this one. And if you think that makes you look like you're going to a funeral, then I'd be willing to lie in a coffin just to be able to see you in it."

Catherine laughed. "Please," she said, "you don't have to go that far, at least not for the dress. And, well, speaking of death and all, I was thinking about Ms. de Bonnair—not *her* death, but maybe *mine*." Catherine was determined to forge ahead and deal as quickly and completely as possible with the exuberant "misrepresentation" she'd made by promising Ms. de Bonnair a lot more money than Banter could pay. She hated lies under any circumstances, and here she was, the author of one that sat in the middle of everything—an obstacle to a good and honest relationship with Loretta de Bonnair and an obstacle to a good and honest relationship with Sam Wilson. "I have to talk to her about my offer."

"To be honest, it's not going to matter. Loretta's dying. In fact, she is about to die."

"She's about to die? But—"

"Don't worry. It's not what you think. But before I get into all of that, I think we should have a glass of wine or something. It'll make all of this a little easier for me to talk about. What would you like?"

"I… I don't know…" Catherine said, confused and concerned by what Sam had just said. But since he didn't seem too concerned and Loretta was his friend, she tried not to seem too concerned. "Honestly, I can only tell the difference between red and white, and only with my eyes open. I'll let you pick."

"I'll do my best." So saying, Sam lifted himself out of his seat and walked up to the bar.

Walt saw him coming and motioned for him to come to the empty end of the bar. Smiling broadly, Walt leaned toward Sam and asked quietly, "How's it goin', Loretta?"

"Complicated."

"Oh, I'm sure you'll figure out how to spend that million soon enough."

"It's a million I don't deserve."

"You gonna tell me you're not writing Loretta's next book?"

"No, I'm writing it, all right, but Loretta isn't. I got this gal's interest with a pack of lies—from culling cattle in November, thank you very much, to everything else, and now I'm falling in love with her, and worse, she's falling in love with me."

"I'm sure it's not the first time an author's slept with his editor."

"This is not that sort of thing. And she's definitely not gonna wanta sleep with me, or do anything else with me, when she finds out *I'm* the author."

"So go back to New York, get the money for that poor, frail, big-footed Loretta, and then tell her the truth."

"No, I can't let this lie go on—not with her." Sam shook his head and glanced back at Catherine. "Not with her..." he repeated softly.

Walt stared at his friend for a moment, then said, almost exasperated, "Man, I hope you don't blow it. You and me both, we've played it perfect—well, close to perfect. You've got what you wanted and now, right when you're about to have it all, you're going to blow your cover because you just might be in love?"

"It's not 'might be.' It *is*! She's smart, funny, kind, gutsy, and so lovely. This is not how I thought it would happen, and she's not who I thought it'd happen with, but it did. So give me a couple of glasses of the best Santa Rita Hills pinot you've got in this two-bit bar, then stand back and watch the fireworks."

"I think you're making a big mistake, but..." Walt shrugged, turned, and did as he was asked. After handing over the glasses, he leaned against the thick shelf behind the counter and watched Sam return to his table to light the fuse to his future.

That fuse, however, never got the chance to spark. Instead, the fuse that set everything off walked in the front door as Sam was handing Catherine her glass of wine.

"Don't look now," Catherine said, taking the glass from Sam and glancing at the door, "but Sharie and Devon just walked in together."

"Really? Maybe they won't see us. I have nothing to say to them, and a whole lot to say to you, alone," he said, sliding as inconspicuously as he could into the booth to face Catherine.

With her glass stopped in midair, Catherine asked with a combination of genuine concern and playful incredulity, "You aren't married, are you, Sam?"

"No. Never have been, and only will be when I find the right person. And there's no one else in my life. Well, that's not exactly true, in a weird literary way." He took a deep breath and launched into his confession. "Listen, Catherine, I need to tell you about something I did, for a semi-good reason, and it's even kinda funny." He took a gulp of wine, then raised his glass to Catherine and began what he hoped would be a quick, ice-breaking toast about telling the truth. "Here's to—"

He was interrupted, however, by a loud voice from behind him.

"To you, Catherine, the woman with the winning offer," Sharie said with a strange laugh. She walked to the side of the booth and turned to Sam. "And to you, too, Sam, the author's business agent. What a lovely couple the two of you make. I hope for your sake," she said to Catherine with mock concern, "he shares some of the spoils, if he ever gets any of those spoils from your bankrupt company."

"We are not bankrupt."

"Maybe not yet, but you will be when you pay this fellow."

"We are paying Loretta de Bonnair, not Sam Wilson."

"Oh, really?" Devon asked tartly. "You *think* you talked to Loretta de Bonnair, but the Loretta de Bonnair you talked to was a large man in a wig. For all intents and purposes—Loretta is dead," he concluded with a theatrical flourish.

There was a pause that Catherine was sure Sam would interrupt. When he didn't, she broke the uncomfortable silence. "What do you mean, 'she's dead'?"

"I was about to tell you that—" Sam began.

Sharie jumped in with a malicious smile. "Let me tell her instead. I won't leave out any details. Y'all left with your knight in shining cowboy boots to fight a fire, but Devon and I stayed behind to wrap things up with Loretta, and boy did we."

Catherine shot Sam a worried glance, then turned back to Sharie and Devon, who continued the tag-team barrage.

"You never looked in that big, comfy chair," Devon continued, "but as soon as you left the ranch, we saw a man who looked very much like that guy tending bar right over there jump out of the window right next to where Loretta was sitting, so we decided to take a look in that chair, you know, to see if Loretta was all right."

"She wasn't," said Sharie.

"She… wasn't?" Catherine asked, now even more profoundly worried. "What do you mean?"

"She wasn't there at all," Sharie replied. "Our dear Loretta was that guy"—she added, pointing to Walt at the bar—"in a wig, a robe, and seriously oversized slippers. Loretta de Bonnair doesn't exist."

"And *if* she ever existed at all, she's almost undoubtedly dead, possibly, just possibly, because she was killed," Devon said, lowering his voice to emphasize the point—and its target, though he was careful to avoid looking anywhere close to Sam. He certainly didn't want to inspire this particular man to a rash response, though at the same time, he hoped to impress his new female partner with his fearless candor.

"Killed?!" Catherine said, more loudly than she'd wanted to.

"We're really not sure about anything," Sharie clarified, "but whatever happened, it seems this cowboy's taken advantage of Loretta's stubborn 'absence.'"

At this, Sam finally spoke up. "Look, I can explain," but that was as far as he got before Devon interrupted him.

"Yes, you do have some explaining to do, and we, Sharie and I, need to see some physical proof that Loretta de Bonnair is alive and well. No more games, please, just the truth."

"And certainly no more bidding wars to attract the interest of someone who isn't there," Sharie added.

"Loretta is either alive—or she's dead."

"And a whole lot of people want to know which it is." Sharie then turned to Catherine with a smile. "You, dear, despite your brilliant literary sophistication, have promised to pay this cowboy, or, actually, his bartender friend, one million dollars for a new book that probably hasn't been written by an author who's no longer alive. Quite a coup." She turned and gave Walt a hearty wave and a bow.

Unsure what was going on, but sure it wasn't good, Walt responded with a confused smile and a quick, barely visible nod.

As Catherine's listened to all of this, her jaw dropped then snapped shut as she turned to Sam, stared at him for a moment, and fired, "Is this true?!"

"Not the killing part, that's for damn sure." He shot Devon a cold glance, then continued with halting difficulty, "but, well, I, well, I..."

As Sam was having such a hard time answering the question, Catherine impatiently answered for him. "You took advantage of an unclear situation in the hopes of getting money you most certainly didn't deserve."

"No, Catherine," Sam said with conviction, "not for the money, not really, but I admit—"

"You lied to me," she concluded for him with pain in every word.

Sam raised his hands in a gesture of frustrated apology. To say anything less than yes would have been a lie, and yet to say yes would have proved he'd lied. The quandary silenced him for a moment.

"Oh, Sam." Catherine choked with disappointment as she slid awkwardly out of the booth. Fighting back tears, she spun around and said, "I don't need to know the details, I don't *want* to know the details, I don't want to hear anything anymore. You've been lying to me since the moment I met you. No, that's not true. The first time I met you, you were flying out of those saloon doors backward because you were in some barroom brawl and you were truly and honestly happy about going back to it. I'd intended to find out about that peculiar habit of yours tonight, but clearly, that is the least of your flaws." She ran out of words and started to walk out.

Sam quickly pushed himself out of his seat and announced to Catherine's back, "Loretta de Bonnair *is* alive and—"

"Oh is she?" intoned Devon with delighted, if subdued, doubt.

Sam paused to solidify a spur-of-the-moment and absolutely necessary plan. "...and I swear on my life, you will be able to see her as a—as a surprise guest at the Fans of Romance Convention first thing tomorrow. Please don't judge me until you've heard Loretta *in person* in front of hundreds of people. Please, Catherine," he pleaded. "Please."

It was impossible for him to know if she'd heard him since, as soon as she'd said what she'd said, she'd started to walk past the now almost silent and thoroughly curious patrons and out of the restaurant. Sam's final "please" was said just as Catherine burst through the saloon doors. It was a noisy and violent exit.

Catherine did, however, hear every word, though this fact didn't mean much. She was angrier than she had been in years, and never had she been so demonstrably angry in public. Devon had been right all along. Sam had played a very clever game. He'd gotten her attention by being upsettingly offensive, then he'd convinced her he wasn't what she thought he was. "Persimmons for the sweet librarian, indeed! And that insane letter—'Suspend your disbelief,' my foot," Catherine spat out loud as she turned the corner toward Violet's. And he seemed to be so daring and decisive too. Well, Catherine reflected, he didn't just *seem* to be those things. He actually was daring and decisive, but, of course, those were qualities more important to a murderer than a minister. He was also distractingly handsome and spoke well and said he read books and—well, how could she resist? Assaulted by his insistent charm, she'd finally opened like a stagecoach safe, the door blown off its hinges and the loot spread out for the taking.

"He trapped me," she mumbled angrily as she marched down the deserted street, "and he tricked me so he could try to get some lovestruck New York editor to offer him an astronomical amount of money because he was..." She fell silent and slowed her pace. What, she wondered, did he really think he could get from his twisted scheme? He couldn't get royalties from a book that had already been sold for a flat fee, even though, cleverly, he had gotten Blushing Dove to offer more as compensation for their paltry prize money—but he couldn't have anticipated that would be an item for negotiation... could he?

At this thought, Catherine walked right past Violet's and farther down the street. She needed to think these details through, and walking down a quiet street was a good place to do just that. "No," she said out loud, "unless dead Loretta has a book that she'd written *before* she'd died, and she'd handed the rights over to him, there'd be no possible basis for a contract." That's a detail Sam Smarty-pants hadn't thought of—or, she wondered on second thought, had he? But even if he had, it would be far from clear that Sam could negotiate legally for a legally dead person! "And to pretend she wasn't dead so we would throw money at her—it's fraud—and it's disgusting!" she announced loudly while standing in front of a modest house, the owner of which was standing in his front yard watering his dry grass. This sort of outspoken internal dialogue was not uncommon on the streets of New York, but in Sisquoc, it was a rare and frightening thing to witness. Seeing her temporary neighbor turn and stare at her warily, Catherine smiled politely and decided to retreat to the unquestioning gaze of her stuffed roommates.

# Chapter 32

Catherine had hoped to avoid all contact on her way to her room, but the proprietor of the B&B was an ever-busy woman. When Catherine slipped in the front door, Violet was in the midst of replacing the not-noticeably-fading flowers she'd bought the day before with some not-noticeably-fresher flowers she'd bought that afternoon.

"Oh," Violet exclaimed as she turned to see one of her two "New York girls" walk in. "You're back from dinner early. Or maybe you're just back to pick something up."

"How... how did you know I was at dinner?" Catherine asked, taken aback.

"Put social media in a small town, my dear, and there isn't much that isn't noticed and commented on by somebody. That Sam is quite a charming fellow, isn't he?"

"Somebody even saw who I was with?"

"Oh, yes. Sam is one of the most noticeable people we've got around here, even if he isn't a celebrity. There are quite a few ladies, young and not so young, who would like to get to know him better. You're quite lucky to have gotten him to sit down with you."

"Lucky? Oh, I don't think so. If I had any advice for those poor ladies, young and not so young, I'd say, 'Avoid him like the plague!'"

"Sam Wilson? Like the plague?"

"Yes. Well, no. The plague just kills you. Sam plays with you, then kills you."

"*Our* Sam Wilson?"

"You mean *our* Loretta de Bonnair."

Violet couldn't have looked more confused and curious if she'd tried, and Catherine indulged her nosy concern with a rich mix of anguish and the unexpected. "I was invited out to Sam's ranch this afternoon to meet the famous Loretta de Bonnair, and what Sam had done was to dress his buddy, the bartender at the Black Barn, in a robe and a wig so that one or both of your two *naïve* New York girls would make our inflated contract offers to him while he was hidden in a huge chair, and that way Sam could steal both our money and at least one of our hearts."

"Did this *really* happen?"

"Not six hours ago and discovered by my wiser rival while I was… let's just say, addled by his infectious charm."

"Hmpf!" Violet snorted as she turned to straighten her flowers. She just couldn't, she just *wouldn't*, believe there was any ill intent on Sam's part. She had to believe that the young woman had been hurt by her own romantic expectations and not by Sam's devious intentions. "I can't address the details but, if I were you, I'd believe the big picture instead. Sam may be playing some very strange game with this Loretta thing"—Violet paused to think about this for a moment—"but, if I'm right, there's more, much more, to this than meets the eye. I've known him for as long as he's been alive, and he's always been, well, a little wild but always good and honest to a fault."

"Good and honest fights at the Black Barn. Good and honest lies about who he is and who he knows. He's a handsome, charming liar, and that's all I have to say," Catherine snapped as she turned briskly and started out of the room.

"My dear," Violet said thoughtfully to Catherine's receding back, "I believe, truly, that he has not been good to you about all of this, but—he must have some good reason. I admit, Sam is too charming by half, too clever by half, and too handsome by half, but he's not a malicious liar, and he's not foolish enough to make something up about Loretta de Bonnair, not in this town. Still," Violet allowed in a voice trailing with wonder, "I just can't figure out what he's doing with all of this Loretta de Bonnair business."

"Well, you won't have to wonder for long," Catherine replied. "Sam says that all will be made clear when Loretta comes as a surprise guest to the convention tomorrow to explain herself."

"Loretta? Loretta de Bonnair is coming to the convention tomorrow?!"

"That's what he says, for what it's worth."

"Oh, this is unbelievable news!" Violet abandoned her flowers and clasped her hands in excitement.

"You don't really believe that, do you?"

"I've known Sam a bit longer than you have, my dear, and if he said something as... as unbelievable as that, then I am inclined to believe it. He would be an utter fool to lie about something like that in this town. Did he say this in front of other people?"

"Yes. Not ten minutes ago at the Black Barn in front of both Sharie and Devon. There were probably a lot of others who heard it, too, since the conversation was getting a little loud at that point."

"My, my"—Violet chortled—"this is interesting news—very interesting. And, if you'll excuse how blunt this sounds, I think you'd be foolish not to at least go and see for yourself what this is all about. Now," she added, almost jumping out of her skin with excitement, "I'd love to chat some more, but I've got a few phone calls to make and this *has* to go up on social media. The surprising possibility of Loretta's arrival at the convention is important news."

And with that, Violet bustled out of the room, presumably to find various communication devices by which she could startle Sisquoc with the exciting news.

Catherine walked back to her room quietly, opened her door, and closed it as silently as possible. She was feeling emotionally pummeled and didn't want anyone to know she even existed. She'd exhausted her anger on the streets of Sisquoc, had expressed her frustration, disbelief, and disappointment to Violet, and now all she wanted was to crawl into a hole and hibernate with shame and sadness for a year or two. She sat down on her bed in the dark and kept remembering various scenes in which she and Sam had played leading roles. At the end of each painful, inconclusive recollection, she said into the darkness, "How could I have been so stupid?" The one recollection she wanted most to avoid was, however, the one, in the end, she couldn't avoid: the scene on the Sedgwick Ranch after the fire had passed, after they'd watched the cow barn burn, after Sam had said he was sorry they hadn't been able to save that last heifer and calf, the scene where she was standing in a charred field looking at Sam and touching Sam and... but before she got to the memory of the kiss itself, Catherine started to cry silently, tears streaming down her cheeks. Unable to control it any longer, she started to sob while asking herself over and over and over again, "Why did I let this happen, why did I let this happen, why... why... why?"

She slid back onto the bed and cried into the covers. Eventually, she rolled onto her back, stopped crying, and just lay there softly panting. She was too exhausted to think anymore. Maybe... maybe she should call Vito, but she didn't have the energy and wouldn't know what to say. After all, she had nothing to show for her expensive business trip to California except a broken heart. Vito would not be particularly charmed or impressed. And he certainly wouldn't be sympathetic. She could maybe call her father. He would be sympathetic. But she checked that idea, knowing that he would be too sympathetic. Admitting to her father what had just happened would both sound and be pathetic. At age twenty-eight, she just couldn't admit such a complete romantic screwup to anyone in her family. Maybe she could call Rachel. She'd probably have some good advice, but she couldn't do anything that would change the situation, and just describing it to Rachel, who had flown through this emotional turbulence many times before, would be very embarrassing. How naïve could she have been? It was almost laughable. The wise, level-headed Catherine Doyle goes west and falls for a charming liar of a cowboy because—because he was some handsome, swaggering Svengali in a cowboy hat.

She sighed, wiped what was left of her tears from her face, then smiled with subdued satisfaction. Tomorrow she would be going home. Tomorrow she'd be going back to a place where she knew the game and knew the rules. The West was a silly place anyway. All of that space seemed to have given the people living in it the notion that they had no restraints, that they could do and say whatever they wanted: lie, cheat, kill. It was all part of some epic film that they had running in their heads, and as long as it was entertaining, it was all right.

Well it was not all right for her, and with that thought, she got up, turned on her light, and started to prepare to get out of town as soon as she could. She phoned the airline and found the earliest flight she was sure she could make, given how long her drive up from LA had taken. Then she packed. And then she read. She started with *The Rise of the Moron Nation*, one of the four books she'd brought from New York. It seemed appropriately cynical for the circumstances. After reading a few pages, however, she realized that what the book described was a little too stark, tragic, and true for her present mood. So she started an Updike book she'd also brought. It was refreshingly *not* about anything west of the Hudson River, but the story wasn't very gripping, and she found her mind wandering far more than she wanted it to. She actually found herself wishing that she hadn't finished reading *Rancho de Amor*; it would have been the perfect escape from this moment, after which thought, she began to wonder—shouldn't she at least see who or what this Loretta de Bonnair was that Sam promised would show up?

Violet and Laura Lee were silly old romantics who were obviously in love with love and well past the age when they'd actually have to pay for its passionate and painful consequences. Still, they had had interesting things to say about Sam. Could they have been so thoroughly blinded by his charm? Shouldn't she at least find out what all this was about, if not for herself, then at least for Vito? What if Loretta really was going to be there and Sharie stayed, met her, and, in so doing, got the deal—just like that? And what if Sam had had some reason for doing what he'd done—putting Walt in a wig, pretending to have Loretta at his house? It didn't make any sense at all, but it didn't make any sense for Loretta to show up in person in front of a large crowd of fans if she were dead. Sam was a liar all right, and couldn't be trusted, but so what? She wasn't out there to deal with Sam anyway. She was out there to deal with Loretta.

Catherine rolled off the bed, called the airline, and pushed her flight back a few hours. "To hell with Sam Wilson," she said, turning to her immovable field mouse, "I'm going to see Loretta de Bonnair, if Mr. Sam Wilson can pull off this last little trick."

# CHAPTER 33

In no mood for another one of those crystal-clear, absurdly warm days, Catherine kept her eyes closed as she woke up the next morning. To raise her spirits, she began to visualize in her mind's eye various things she missed back in New York—things she would soon be seeing—things like snow, lots of snow. Well, maybe not *lots* of it. In fact, maybe not snow at all but just a wonderfully chilly day with everyone wrapped in wool. Or maybe not *so* chilly—more like a beautiful, gentle fall day with leaves wagging on all the trees in bright yellows and oranges and reds, although that season with its leaves was now pretty much over. So she went indoors with her fantasies: into her nice, warm apartment—her nice, warm, somewhat cramped apartment—with her cat, with Emily, seated on the back of the couch, eyes half-closed, and the smell of green tea steeping in the kitchen. Yes, this she missed—Emily, comfort, her quiet routines— and she lay there thinking about all of this until she realized that the smell of that green tea steeping in her kitchen was not just a sentimental fantasy but was the smell of green tea actually steeping in Violet's kitchen.

Her eyes popped open and focused on the first thing she saw. It was Ezekiel's mountain lion snarling at her. Revolted, she got out of bed and quickly got herself ready for the day. The sooner she got through with the California part of things, the sooner she could get back to the New York part of things. She had decided not to show the least bit of distress or concern to anyone. Obligingly, she would smile at any residual and irrelevant advice Violet might offer. Coolly and collectedly, she would smile at any barbed comment Sharie might toss in her direction. No one and nothing would bother her. She had a bit of business to do, and then she was going home.

Luckily, Violet was too excited about the possibility of seeing the famous Loretta in the flesh to give anyone any further advice than to "get to the high school gymnasium as early as possible." Taking her own advice, she left Ezekiel in charge of breakfast before it was half over. Violet didn't just want a good seat. Now that she knew that Loretta de Bonnair would be there, she wanted to make sure she would have a place on stage with the VIP seating. After all, who had done more to promote Ms. de Bonnair's reputation in town than she? Surely a chair on stage would not be too much to ask in return.

Although Sharie didn't show up for breakfast, Catherine did cross paths with her at the front door. She was coming in as Catherine was going out.

"Can't wait to see the real Loretta and offer her a million?" Sharie said with a crooked smile as Catherine slipped past her out the door.

"Either that or to see if you can maybe have Sam arrested for storytelling," Catherine replied.

"Would you wait for him to get sprung?"

"Sharie, my disappointing romantic entanglements in this town are blessedly over, though," she said, noting Devon's car pulling away from the curb where he had obviously just stopped to let Sharie out, "it looks as if your entanglements continue to evolve. Good luck. His poetry is, as he says, 'beyond the zeitgeist,' as I'm sure you'll discover." She turned and continued out the door.

Catherine had no desire to have a front row seat. In fact, she hoped she could blend into a wall at the very back of the East Valley High School gym, home of the Mighty Cougars, where the main events would take place. She wanted simply to witness this final show—or no-show, as she expected it would be—from an unseen distance. Sam was bound to be somewhere near Loretta, if there was a Loretta, and she wanted to be as far from him as she could get.

Catherine milled around town for half an hour, then walked slowly to the high school on the outskirts of town. She had glanced at a schedule of events sitting on a side table at Violet's earlier that morning. The Fans of Romance Convention would apparently start with a soft opening at 9 a.m. featuring "seventeen booths of interest to the fan of Romance." One woman would be selling pillows she'd embroidered with "significant scenes from *Rancho de Amor*"; another would be selling tastes of a local pinot noir that some enterprising, though not very talented, local winemaker had decided would sell most effectively with the label *Pinot de Amor*; someone else would be selling handmade *Rancho de Amor* bookmarks, and the list of opportunistic entrepreneurs went on.

At 10 a.m. sharp, the ceremonies would begin in earnest. Ms. Penelope Trueblood, the local chairwoman of FORC, would deliver her opening remarks and give Ms. de Bonnair her award in absentia, if Loretta didn't surprise them all and show up herself. She would then be followed by a series of other speakers: a professor of women's studies at Cal Poly who would deliver her recent paper "Hay Bales, Heifers, and a Feminist Hermeneutic of the Heroine in de Bonnair's *Rancho de Amor*"; local journalist Paula Thistleton from the *Santa Barbara Barb* would be discussing her recent article about book contract issues, "Don't Sign in Ink Before You Think"; the East Valley High School valedictorian, Sarah Campbell, would talk about the inspiration she had received from romance novels, most particularly *Rancho de Amor*; and at noon, there would be a lunch catered by the Dos Caballeros Café of Tres Robles. The afternoon events would begin with a panel of local scholars and writers discussing the role of "romance" in the modern world. This would be followed by what was described as "a true innovation to the typical convention": an open mic at which anyone who so chose could come up and describe "the effects of *Rancho de Amor* on my life." The mistress of ceremonies for this emotional free-for-all would be local radio phenomenon Amy Lough, host of the popular early morning show *Wake Up to a Better You* on KGOO, 89.9 in Solvang.

Catherine didn't want to be seen milling around the "Pinot de Amor" table, or any other table for that matter, so she walked past the gym and onto the Cougars' football field. She took a seat in the middle of the sunny-side bleachers, and with still almost half an hour to kill, she decided to call Vito. She didn't want his or anybody else's sympathy. She'd made a mistake; she would pay with some pain for a while, but she would pay in private. She would heroically proceed with the practical, and the first practical thing she could think to do was to give Vito the disappointing update. He needed to know what was going on before he did anything crazy like sell his house to raise money either to bail out the sinking fortunes of Banter House or pay for an advance to a dead author.

"Hi, Vito. It's your errant editor," Catherine said when he

answered the phone.

"Yes, I can see. I was beginning to worry. I thought I'd get a text from you last night or, rather, this morning at one or so."

"Sorry. I decided to let you sleep."

"So what's the news?"

"Bizarre."

"Oh?" said Vito with a hint of concern. "What's going on?"

"You remember I told you that I was invited to go out to some cowboy's ranch and meet our famous author, me and the pushy editor from Dove? We were going to bid for her favor, right then and there. Loretta was, however, too frail to meet us face to face, so we, the woman from Blushing Dove and I, had to stand just outside the door and shout our bids to the back of the old woman's head."

"That sounds bizarre all right."

"And that's just the beginning. I got caught up in this crazy bidding thing. I wasn't going to let that... that *horrible* Blushing Dove woman beat me in a bidding war and destroy Banter House. And so, well, like I said, I got carried away and offered the frail, unseen, and husky-voiced Loretta an advance of... of a million dollars, which, needless to say, won the bid."

"A million dollars?! Were you insane?"

"Yes, but—"

"No, there's no 'but,' Catherine," Vito raved into his phone. "I just found out yesterday that my house, my grandfather's house, is only worth $1,200,000, and with the second mortgage I took out last year to keep the company going, I could get no more than $500,000 out of it, which means that's what I, and my company— which means you and everyone else on salary—will have to live on, and that won't last more than six to eight months. How could you offer a million dollars?"

"I got caught up, and I knew we needed to win, but—"

"That's insane! *Really* insane! I'll be living on the streets long before we see money from any sales—and so will you. And you say Loretta accepted it?"

"Yes, except that dear old Loretta de Bonnair wasn't really there."

"Anybody who can make a deal for a million-dollar advance for a romance novel, no matter how old and out of it she may be, is definitely *all* there."

"No, Vito. I mean she wasn't real. Things got crazy, I got distracted with some nearby brushfire and whatnot, and, long story short, the Blushing Dove editor discovered that Loretta wasn't and never had been there. We were shouting our bids to a man dressed up in a robe and a wig. It was all a setup by that conniving cowboy. Loretta, whoever she may have been, is gone and presumed dead."

"What?! This is even *more* insane. What are you saying?"

"I'm saying that Loretta was no more than the local bartender talking in a gravelly falsetto while wearing a wig. He's a friend of that cowboy who's trying to get as much out of a presumably dead author as he can."

"But..." Vito grunted and paused, trying to make sense of all of this. He couldn't, so he said, "I don't see how that would work."

"Neither do I, but I don't see how anything works out here. I'm flying back tonight after I check out one last weird event with that cowboy who promises to bring the real Loretta de Bonnair— hopefully as a living, breathing human being."

"Catherine," Vito said, suddenly sounding very serious, "do *not* offer a million dollars to anyone—especially a real person. Two hundred thousand, tops! And... I don't even know that you should do that. This whole thing sounds too bizarre and more than a little dangerous. A bunch of lying, thieving, gun-toting cowboys who take advantage of presumably dead authors—no, no, this does not sound good."

"Don't worry. I'm just going to the high school gym, where there are a few hundred romance fanatics waiting to see if Loretta de Bonnair actually shows up. I have to at least see what happens, and nothing, absolutely nothing's going to happen to me in a crowd like that. Unless she does miraculously appear, I'm out of here. I'm so sorry, Vito. I really did try."

"Yes, with a million dollars. Thank God she *wasn't* there. Anyway, you be careful, you hear? And come back to us. I don't know how long we'll have this business, but until the ship sinks completely, we'd all feel better seeing you on the deck."

"Aye, aye, Captain. I'll be there soon."

# CHAPTER 34

At ten o'clock, precisely, Penelope Trueblood came to the podium and addressed a crowd of well over five hundred people. In her hours outside of serving as chairwoman of FORC, she was the very efficient assistant manager of the Buellton Walmart. She was used to crowds, but not like this, and it took her some time to quiet the audience down. In that time, Catherine scanned the crowd from her perch at the top and far end of the bleachers. Overwhelmingly female, and overwhelmingly older. There was one detail, however, that seemed to divide the audience. Although the vast majority of the women in the audience either wore no hats or wore hats with some sort of floral flourish, roughly ten percent of the crowd, a group which included almost all of the attendant males, wore cowboy hats and angry faces, and they were there to confront Ms. de Bonnair with some very specific questions and concerns. In three of the four tightly packed patches of cowboy-hatted attendees, Catherine saw someone she recognized. In the midst of one group was the woman to whom she'd spoken at the feed store. If she were true to her word, she was there to give Loretta "a piece of her mind." In the middle of another all-male group of cowboys was the sheriff who would, if he were ever to meet her, ask her to "move to LA." In another group was the cowboy she'd met at the Black Barn bar who had said he knew plenty about Loretta and "didn't like much of it." Seated next to him was the glowering editor-in-chief of the *Sisquoc Patriot*. She even saw Devon and Sharie (in her pink cowboy hat) seated next to one another, confident sneers on both of their faces.

When Ms. Trueblood finally got the attention of her rambunctious audience, she cleared her throat and announced, "This is perhaps the most important moment in the history of Sisquoc and its surrounding territory since, well, since Michael Jackson moved into Neverland, and we all remember the hubbub that that caused. Though really, my dear friends, I think this is possibly even more momentous because our dear Loretta is homegrown and still growing in worldwide esteem. Her very first book, *Rancho de Amor*, is being translated into ten different languages as we speak, and I even hear there's talk of a movie deal. Stay tuned, Lorettians. As my granddaughter likes to say, this thing is going viral."

Nine-tenths of the crowd broke into warm and sustained applause. One-tenth didn't. Catherine even heard a "boo" or two. Penelope Trueblood must not have heard this, however, since, after she let the applause die down, she said, "Before we get to that moment we've all been waiting for—ever since we got the call last night from Violet and then confirmation from an anonymous source!—I just can't go on without acknowledging and welcoming the impressive number of romantic brothers in cowboy hats who have come out here today." Penelope pointed to the patches of cowboys, and a few women responded with spontaneous applause. "Yes, ladies, let's give a warm and welcoming round of applause to those brave boys who have the courage to be seen and counted at the celebration of romance writing in general and our local romance writer in particular. Stand up, boys, and take a bow." The audience not included in this group broke into loud applause.

The two local news cameras set up to film the speakers at the podium swung around to pan the audience. Although some of the men and cowboy-hatted women remained unmoved and frowning, most felt compelled to stand up and take their awkward bows. "That takes guts, girls. And that's what romance is all about—the courage to be sensitive, even in a cowboy hat. And if courage is, as I think it should be, revealed by how sensitive you allow yourself to be, I now have the distinct honor to introduce one of the world's most courageous souls—a woman who hates the crowds and the fame; who, I'm told, would rather sit in a warm room alone with her cat and her amazing imagination than do pretty much anything else; who, despite the fact that she is frail and sick and very busy on her next book, decided, at the very last minute, to delight us all with a most unexpected visit. This is truly a momentous moment when America's most popular writer of romance—an angel from the paradise of impassioned prose—graces us in person right here in the Sisquoc Cougars' high school gymnasium. Please join me in welcoming Ms. Loretta de Bonnair!"

As the cowboy hats awkwardly resumed their seats in silent protest, the rest of the audience exploded with cheers, cries, and loud applause as a large, elderly woman was wheeled out from the wings by a tall, paunchy man in a cowboy hat. Catherine squinted and was able to recognize the man in the hat and large boots. It was Walt, the bartender at the Black Barn and yesterday's Loretta. Then she squinted to see what the real Loretta looked like. For a woman whose excuse for not meeting people was her frailty, she looked surprisingly large, muscular, and robust. She also had a surprisingly strong chin and tight, tan skin. This did not look like a woman on the brink of death. In fact, but for her nicely coifed hair, her large dress, and her rhinestone-studded glasses, this did not look like a woman at all. Credulity, however, is often based less on confirming detail than on affirming sentiment, and the sentiment was high in the East Valley High gym for seeing in this tan, robust, and very manlike apparition the frail, pale, female-like appearance of Loretta de Bonnair.

While the rhythmic applause was sustained by an energy akin to rock-star hysteria, a microphone stand was produced and the podium mic affixed to it. With many up-and-down adjustments, the wheelchair-bound author was finally presented with a device that would amplify her frail voice.

The poor woman sounded, if not frail, at least very ill when she cleared her throat. In fact, the very first sound Loretta de Bonnair ever made in public sounded less like a dainty cough than a cranky old lawnmower coming to life, choking on an over-rich mixture of air and gas. When she finally stopped sputtering, she gave a discreet sniff and whispered huskily, "Hello, my lovely fans, I'm so honored by your... well, by your love. My greatest hope is that my work is worthy of such affection."

To this, the response was a patchy standing ovation. Catherine was thoroughly confused and yet oddly entertained. She didn't know what was going on, but it was a lot more interesting than she thought it would be. When the applause subsided, Loretta once again cleared her throat. Luckily, the engine of her voice barely turned over this time. When she was done clearing her throat, she sighed and said in a low and tremulous whisper, "I have been, perhaps, good to you as a writer, but not as a person. The reasons are many, and they were good at one time. But that time has changed, and, consequently, so must

I." So saying, Loretta took the microphone in her surprisingly large hand and slowly started to rise out of her wheelchair. "Oscar Wilde once suggested that if you'd give a man a mask, he'd show you who he is. Well," she said with a slowly deepening voice, "take a look at the other very real part of who I am behind the mask. I didn't expect and I sure didn't want it to happen this way." A number of people in the audience were beginning to whisper to one another in either delighted or horrified suspicion as Loretta de Bonnair paused, reached up with her large, tan left hand, and took hold of her beautiful gray hair. "But I can no longer live as two different people, and so, with this, Loretta de Bonnair dies"—slowly, carefully she pulled the wig from her head—"and Sam Wilson can finally face up to being who he really is, the author of *Rancho de Amor*."

There was a collective gasp in the audience, and then there was pandemonium. Some people were laughing, some were clapping, some were yelling in profound disappointment, others were yelling with a combination of anger and shock. Most people, however, sat in their seats in awed or amused silence. And Catherine? Catherine opened her mouth, took a quick breath, and held it... held it until she slowly exhaled in a whisper, "No..."

While the audience indulged in its conflicting responses, Sam quickly removed his glasses and the dress that had lumpily covered his cowboy duds, grabbed the hat that Walt, on cue, proffered, and took a speaking position behind the podium. The reaction of the VIPs seated next to him mirrored much of the reaction of the rest of the audience. Four of them jumped up and were clapping wildly (these included Violet Smith). Three of them sat frowning, their arms stubbornly folded, their mouths shut. Two applauded politely, their smiles stoically tight. One got up, shook her head in disgust, and walked out. Checking some of the most extreme reactions, particularly on the negative side, were the audience-panning TV cameras (Violet had done a very good job of getting the press there on very short notice), which captured a few loud "boos" amidst the generally delighted surprise.

Sam let the noisy chaos of his unmasking take its course. In Catherine, however, it took a unique turn. She was definitely the only one in the audience who sat staring at Sam with a violent combination of love and shame, relief and remorse. She realized with breath-tightening regret that she had not suspended her disbelief quite long enough and now... now, she didn't know what to think or do.

"Y'all deserve an explanation, and so I'll do the best I can to give it to you. For better or worse, I'm a country boy and love being out in the rough-and-tumble, tell-it-like-it-is country. I like the quiet, I like the space, and I like watching things happen that no man or woman has had anything to do with. It's one of the reasons I love ranching, which, for those of you who don't know me, is what I do. I'm the foreman of the Circle D up at the end of the valley. Ranching's my livelihood and a big, wonderful part of my life, but it also makes possible another big part of my life—reading and writing. 'Cause I don't like TV and radio all that much, I get plenty of time to read, think, imagine, and write. And when I started writing in college, I realized I could tell a story, maybe not real deep, but deeply real. But I never could have written *Rancho de Amor* without my good buddy, Walt."

Sam glanced at the patches of cowboy hats. "Y'all who are local know him, and because you've probably had too much to drink in front of him at the Black Barn, he knows way too much about you. Come on out here, Walt, and take a bow with Loretta de Bonnair." When Walt lumbered out to take a quick, embarrassed bow next to his friend, there was a mixed response. Those from out of town tended to clap just because it was what they'd been asked to do. The locals were more conflicted. Most of the women who weren't offended by this unmasking clapped, and the cowboys didn't know what to do. They loved Walt; he made sure their glasses were brimful of beer, not foam, and he put up with their language and most of their fights and even, occasionally, their need to run a tab. But to have been a part of this Loretta de Bonnair thing? It was very confusing.

"Walt showed me this five-hundred-dollar prize in a magazine for writing a romance, and I said to myself, why the hell not? Especially since I'd already written a short story with essentially the same characters and a lot of the plot, I figured it wouldn't be too hard to expand it into a novel, so I let the unrealistic goal of winning a prize and the very realistic goad of a deadline propel me to do something I'd wanted to do for a while, write a novel." Sam paused briefly. He was not interrupted by either applause or boos. No one seemed to know what to think. They simply let him tell his story, despite the fact that this particular story seemed less "deeply real" than deeply confounding and, at least for one member of that audience, deeply painful.

"The problem was, Loretta and her damn novel became famous. And then I was stuck. For one, the rules of the prize said the author had to be previously unpublished and—an older woman. Those were the rules. The unpublished part was easy. I hadn't published much of anything before *Rancho*. And all I had to do to prove that I was an older woman was to say I was an older woman on the contest entry form. Like I say, I was sure I wasn't gonna win, so I wasn't worried. Problem was, I *did* win. As soon as I saw that online, I wrote a nice letter to the publisher saying that I was too old and too much of a loner to be ambitious for any fame and that I didn't need the money. That way, my little secret could remain a secret. But I've also got to admit that once I got started writing as Loretta, I started to like the way Loretta was thinking. You can't write good fiction if you can't imagine what other kinds of people think and feel. I got to get to know the—well, the older woman in me. And I even have to admit that I got a little jealous, from time to time. I sometimes think she writes better than I do.

"But it was more than that. You see, I'd already written a lot of stories, poems, articles, letters to editors, and I was having a hard time getting much of it published. Most of the time, the problem was, frankly, that it wasn't very good writing. But when it came to the articles and such, I had a feeling that Sam Wilson, professional cattleman, was part of the problem. I didn't have a fancy college degree, didn't work for a highfalutin university or newspaper, so what could I, a country boy, know about anything other than corrals, cattle, and killing? Workin' up a sweat every day, not by jogging but by doing good, hard work; preferring the company of a tree-scented breeze to the company of most people; and being proud of our long history of taking care of business whatever way we've had to—these country values are at best ignored, and at worst made fun of by some who haven't worked a day in their lives outside of a city. I liked the idea of slipping this little story of mine, *Rancho de Amor*, past people who wouldn't have read it had it just come from a cowboy. And then there was dealing with my very own neighbors and friends. I wanted to explore a couple of things we just aren't supposed to think out here. We, too, have our share of narrow-minded presumptions or, should I say, prejudices.

"I honestly wonder, for example, when you own land in this great country of ours, does that mean you can do anything you like with it, on it, or to it? And yes, I sometimes wonder if we shouldn't be *growing* more beets and *grazing* less beef. Mostly, though, I wonder why we don't think more about what we are thinking—and *why* we're thinking it."

Sam paused. It was silent until the man to whom Catherine had spoken at the Black Barn two nights prior got up and yelled, "You want to take away our property rights, get rid of our cattle, and bring in a bunch of 'boo-tiques' and bookstores, don't you, Sam?" With some barely audible mumbling and grumbling, there was a stirring of support for this blast of questions.

Sam let the grumbling die down, then said, "Well, Timmy, I certainly wouldn't mind seeing a few more bookstores around here if they all sold scads of my book, but no, I do not want to change much around here at all. I got no interest in 'boo-tiques,' and I ain't for getting rid of cattle. It'd be kinda hard to be a cowboy without cows, and cowboying's what I love. I will tell you though that if I ever owned the Circle D, I wouldn't waste that good bottomland on raising flimsy annual grasses for once-in-a-year grazing. On the other hand, I sure as hell wouldn't put a subdivision of houses or another rich-guy vineyard on it either. Just 'cause I like to read and write doesn't mean I can't be a cowboy. And just because other people live in big cities and make their money sitting at a computer screen, doesn't mean they can't and shouldn't get out of town, pick up a ninety-pound bale of hay, buck it onto a flatbed, and feel what it feels like to do some good, hard physical work out in a place where there are a lot more trees and coyotes than cars."

Tim started a rebuttal, but a wave of applause effectively drowned him out.

When it diminished, Sam bowed his head for a few long seconds. No one seemed to know what to make of it, though no one, not even those there to heckle him, made a sound. After this uncomfortably dramatic pause, Sam looked back up and stretched into his full six-foot-one-inch height. He took a deep breath and said, "In the end, my book, *Rancho de Amor*, does not have many really important ideas. It asks some questions, but it doesn't really answer any of 'em. After all, it's just a romance novel.

"And yet, the more I wrote my little love story, the more I realized that except for death, there is nothing more important in our lives than love and romance. Death makes things stark and simple. You either face it well, or you don't. It's how you deal with it, whether it comes in a flash on a battlefield or slowly but surely in a hospital bed. Death defines character and the meaning of life. Which, when you think of it, is a whole lot like love. It's how you deal with that all-consuming challenge—in the moment and over time—that defines character and the meaning of life. They say romances aren't realistic 'cause they end happy. Well, of course they do, 'cause in real life that's not just what we *want* to have to happen, but what most of us do eventually find. We get a romance that ends—or at least continues, sometimes for a long while—happily. 'Unhappily ever after' ain't more real than 'happily ever after.' I've had plenty of unhappy in my life, and I'm sure I'll have plenty more comin' my way, but I'm not going to live my life in fear or resignation just because bad things happen. Good things happen too, and I feel no shame and make no apologies that I spend some of my time and a good part of my imagination in *that* part of reality.

"I do, however, feel ashamed and do have a very difficult apology to make about something I've done wrong—or not done right." He stopped speaking and took a few seconds to scan the audience.

With a chilling jolt, Catherine knew who he was looking for and what he was likely to say. One part of her wanted to jump up and down and shout, "I'm here, I forgive you, I'm yours..." But the greater part of her wanted either to flee in shame, fear, and confusion or sit inconspicuously still to witness yet one more bewildering performance by this very strange man. And this is what she did—too numb for movement or expression.

Not finding who he was looking for, Sam pressed on. "I may have been able to write a good romance novel, but I haven't been able to live it. I didn't understand that until just a few days ago when someone who unexpectedly came into my life made me realize that I've never let myself be both courageous and vulnerable enough for love. The woman I've fallen in love with—all she knows is that I've lied to her, and it's ruined everything." He sighed heavily. "You see, it seems to me that the very essence of romance is courageous, even daring, vulnerability. And until now, I hadn't had the courage, or

224

the *reason* to have the courage, to be daringly and vulnerably myself. Loretta de Bonnair would've known better, but Sam Wilson didn't. I hope it isn't too late for an honest and very public apology to this woman... though I suspect it is. She was completely honest and straightforward with me, and I blew it," he said with regret as he scanned the audience one more time for the woman he couldn't see.

The audience didn't know what to do. Some started to clap. Others uttered confused and annoyed comments. Most, however, craned their necks and looked around the gymnasium, trying to find the woman to whom Sam seemed to have just spoken. Who was this lucky lady? Where was this fool who didn't jump out of her seat and rush into the arms of this handsome, sensitive man?

She was out of her seat, all right, but she wasn't running to this man. She was silently and quickly making her way to the back door. She didn't want him to see her. She needed to breathe, needed to escape, needed to survive her own profound embarrassment and passionate confusion.

"Anyway, thank you, fans of Loretta de Bonnair. Please continue to be her fans. She—and I—will have another book out soon enough. And please continue to call her Loretta de Bonnair, not Sam Wilson. Loretta de Bonnair sounds so much nicer. And it is, after all, my name too. Now if y'all want me to sign something, or if you want to take a swing at me, I'll be..."

Catherine didn't hear the rest of what Sam said. She'd dashed out the back door and started to run. She could barely face herself, and she had no idea how she could ever face him. It wasn't that she didn't want to. If anything, it was that she wanted to far too much. And it frightened her. She didn't know this strange man well enough to open up to him as deeply and completely as she'd need to. And, feeling more attraction and affection than she'd ever felt before, she didn't trust that she'd do or say the right thing. Before saying anything, she'd need to think first and think carefully. He'd lied to her, and he loved her. She'd lied to him, and she loved him. It was all too confusing. She needed to calm down, she needed to breathe, she needed to get out of town and think.

When she got to Violet's, she heard Ezekiel busy in the kitchen washing dishes. Without disturbing him, she rummaged around the common room until she found some violet-hued stationery. She took it back to her room, went over to her field mouse, and looked down into his frozen eyes. "I blew it, completely. I lied to get Loretta, and I lost Sam. I didn't believe him, and I missed the truth." She paused and grimaced slightly. "Well, I mean, he did make it hard for me to believe him, but I shouldn't have been so defensive, so sure of everything when things weren't clear." She shook her head, then sat on the floor, put the stationery on her luggage, and wrote:

Dear Sam,
I was just in the gym. I heard your talk. I don't really know what to say now other than to say that I, too, have to apologize and declare something to you. You say I have been honest and straight, but that's not exactly true. I am ashamed to admit that my million-dollar offer to Loretta was as fake as Loretta. It was an impulsive exaggeration said in the heat of the moment, but I knew it wasn't true as soon as I said it, and I didn't take it back. I am incredibly embarrassed and apologize for the lie.

And I, too, have to declare that I'm falling in love with you. Unfortunately, I don't want to. Please, Sam, trust me, this would never work out between us, not in the long run and probably not even in the short run. I suppose I've been in love before, but I have never fallen in love until now. This is a new feeling for me, and I'm not sure how to act. By nature, I'm cautious, careful, and too stubbornly independent to give myself over to an overwhelming feeling, however wonderful it might feel for a while.

Now suddenly, with you, I'm not me. The most obvious, though by no means the only, example is that, in my desire to impress you and Loretta, I lost control of myself and I lied. I hate that, but that's only one problem. You know as well that we are very different from one another. You're country, and I'm city; you are brash, and I'm bookish; you seem ever confident and sure, and I am ever skeptical; you are open and occasionally quite theatrical, and I—well, I am more like Loretta.

I've rushed to the brink with you—willingly, willingly— but I can't go any further—not fully, not completely. Please,

Sam, don't ask me to go any further. I still have doubts about you and the truth, and I now have serious doubts about me and the truth. In fact, about the only thing I know for sure is that I am not yet courageous and vulnerable enough for love and probably never will be, not the kind of overwhelming love you deserve. You need someone who is more than I can be. There are others out there who are more courageously vulnerable than I will ever be, and some of them, I'm sure, are able both to read books and ride horses.

With unique and lovely memories, my best wishes,
Catherine Doyle

She folded the letter, put it in an envelope, and wrote *To Sam Wilson* with a shaky hand. A tear fell on the word *Wilson*. Quickly, she wiped it off. How ridiculously like a schmaltzy romance novel, she thought. Then she got up, collected her bags, gave a sympathetic nod to her mouse, and walked out of the room. She settled her bill with Ezekiel who, knowing precisely who her roommates had been, significantly reduced the price of her stay beyond the slight discount Violet had promised her. "I hope none of my furry friends, well, scared you too much," Ezekiel said as he handed her credit card back.

"At first all of them did, but we eventually became friends, and I've grown particularly fond of that field mouse who, on first glance, seemed to be reaching up to protect itself from some imminent danger, but now, I think, seems to be anxiously reaching for something that's caught its eye."

"Yes, I like that little fellow. One of my better, more interesting and, more, well, equivocal stagings. So often when I pick them up, there isn't enough, no, not enough flesh and fur to stretch them into a, well, into a dynamic pose, but that little field mouse came in almost completely intact."

This was a gruesome detail she could have done without, but it made sense. As she walked out, the thought crossed her mind that her whole experience here in California had taken on a taxidermic feel. Inside, she was dead, but outside, she had just enough flesh to pull over her wounds to present the convincing look of life. And definitely, she was frozen in the eternal act of reaching for something that had caught her eye, but which she would never be able to grasp.

Her final task in Sisquoc was to quickly swing by the library and drop off her letter. A new librarian greeted her as she rushed in the door. Both confused and concerned, Catherine asked the fifty-year-old man at the counter, "Is Laura Lee here?"

"She's supposed to be, but she called me early this morning and asked me to come in for her. She's feeling a little under the weather, a cold, she said, and we both felt that it would be better for her and our customers—is that what you call people who come into a library, 'customers'?"

"Ah, why not?" Before the man could answer her rhetorical question, Catherine rushed forward. She wanted to escape as quickly as she could. "So, if I give this letter to you, could you make sure it gets to Laura Lee?"

She handed the letter to the man. He looked at it carefully then said, "Yes, but it's addressed to Sam. Sam Wilson."

"I know. But"—Catherine began to adjust her request—"the important thing is to get it to Sam. If Laura Lee comes in before Sam does, give it to her, and if Sam comes in, say, today, that is to say, before Laura Lee, give it to him. He's the one who has to get this as soon as possible."

"Got it. Sam's the ASAP destination, but if Laura Lee comes in first, let her be the preliminary destination, right?"

"Preliminary destination," she repeated, considering. "Yes... as long as she gets the letter to Sam."

Catherine turned to leave, but the librarian didn't make it easy. "So," he started slowly, "you know Sam, huh? He and his daddy built my garage. Fine job it was. Still is. It's too bad about Sam's father though."

"Yes, yes it is. Look, I'm sorry, but I've got to catch a plane in LA."

"Okeydokey. I'll say hello to Sam for you. What'd you say your name was?"

"I didn't. He'll know when he reads my note. Just make sure it gets to Sam ASAP. It's important."

"It seems to be," he said, giving her a crooked smile and a raised eyebrow.

Catherine parried with a tight, noncommittal smile and left.

# CHAPTER 35

And, indeed, Sam did get the letter as soon as possible. He picked it up from the library on the following Thursday.

# Chapter 36

The drive back to LA was painfully easy. No wrong turns, no frightening signs—there was nothing to slow her down. Earlier that morning, she had been almost ecstatic at the thought of driving away from Sisquoc. It would mean that she was done with this thoroughly unsuccessful excursion. Now, even though the excursion was as thoroughly unsuccessful as ever, she was not very happy to be leaving. Had she not heard Sam unmask himself and profess his affection for her, she could have left with the reassuring feeling that she'd been the one who'd been cheated and wronged. Now, she left with the knowledge that she was contributing to her own emotional disaster. She wasn't leaving things that had been but, instead, was willfully tearing herself away from things that might have been.

Even the countryside gave her no relief. It was painfully beautiful, with mountains to the left and the Pacific Ocean to the right. She felt as if she were driving through one of those posters of the California coast, and she couldn't escape seeing how brutally attractive it was. The indigo of the ocean, the deep green of the oak- and chaparral-covered hillsides, the rows of incessantly moving waves, the soft clarity of the late morning, late November sun. Catherine prided herself on living her life without regrets, but she was now leaving California with a pile of them.

Her plane left LA on time and arrived in New York on time. On the cab ride into town, she texted Vito: More insanity. Found Loretta; she is the cowboy, or better, the cowboy is she. Everything got complicated in more ways than one, and everything fell apart. The Blushing Dove rep made an offer of five hundred thousand dollars. He's worth twice what Dove's promising, but I'm sure he'll go back to her now and take what she's offering. We'll commiserate Monday.

Almost immediately, he wrote back, WOW! You know I have a thousand questions but... fine, they can wait till Monday.

When she got home, her cat was already waiting and greeted her in a catlike sort of way. There was much purring and rubbing of her back against Catherine's legs until she opened a can of food for her and put the contents into Emily's dish. Then it was a quick return to priorities.

While her cat ate, Catherine checked her two e-mail accounts and her texts for messages, hoping Sam had kept her business card despite everything that had happened.

Seeing, however, that he hadn't made contact, she shut her phone case with a disappointed snap. Emily looked up from her dish, blinked twice, then went back to eating.

After quickly unpacking, Catherine got ready for bed and took the Updike she'd started the night before out to the couch for a cozy and distracting read. It was, indeed, cozy, but not distracting. She was too upset just under the surface of consciousness to be able to concentrate. After a few pages, she abandoned Updike and turned on the TV to watch the local news. Nothing had changed. The garbage workers were threatening to strike; department stores reported sluggish in-store sales just after Thanksgiving, though online sales were slightly better than last year's; two men were shot in a Brooklyn club, one died; and snow flurries were expected by dawn. After the news, she tried to find a movie, but nothing grabbed her attention. So she turned off the television and sat there, silently, for a while. Eventually, Emily roused herself just enough to slide down the back of the couch and place herself in Catherine's lap. She purred perfunctorily two or three times.

"I met a little furry fellow you'd have loved to chase, if he'd have been alive. We talked, but he didn't seem to listen as well as you." Emily shifted her position in search of maximum comfort, opened her eyes slightly, purred once, and fell asleep.

Catherine sat there for half an hour while indulging in various painful memories of her recent past. Then she wandered into thoughts about the present—specifically, Sam and what he might be doing at that moment. She imagined him at the Black Barn, a very crowded Black Barn, a Black Barn overflowing with fans of the newly discovered author of *Rancho de Amor*, the charming, handsome, single cowboy, Sam Wilson. They would all be women, they would all be flirting with him, and he would love it. Sharie, of course, would be there to remind him of her five-hundred-thousand-dollar offer and wave a wad of cash under his nose. And then there'd be all of the other offers—romantic, sensual, irresistible offers—forming a line extending out the door and into the warm Sisquoc sun, a line of beautiful women wearing nothing but cowboy boots and cowboy hats, each one in turn dancing, prancing, writhing past Sam's admiring blue eyes. Would he even remember her name in a day or two, so overwhelmed now with the names in this line of endless, ready temptations? After ten minutes in this inferno of fantasies, Catherine was frantically exhausted. She forced herself to take three deep breaths and shook herself out of it. She gently lifted her cat, put her in the abandoned warm spot on the couch, and trudged off to bed.

She rested on Sunday, silent and sullen. She read a bit, watched a bit of television, listlessly played with the cat, and, against her better judgment, couldn't stop checking texts and e-mails. She was well aware that she'd closed the door on her relationship with Sam, but, in her heart of hearts, she hoped that she hadn't locked that door. When she'd left California, she'd been sure she had clearly, if sadly, put an end to the beginning of the most bewildering relationship she'd ever had, but as she moved further from Sam both in time and space, the less sure she was that anything had really ended for her or that she even wanted it to end. The small hope that she'd suppressed as she drove away from Sisquoc was growing in inverse proportion to her distance from the object of that hope.

She could, of course, have tried to send him some note of her faltering resolve, but now, two days after she'd resolved to end the relationship before it even really began, she was far too confused and conflicted about what she really wanted and what she felt she should want. Stymied by a profusion of doubts and desires, she retreated into the protective thought that if there really were anything possible between them, Sam would have to do more than make a dramatic apology in a crowded high school gym and should, instead, reach out to her privately, intimately, and honestly. She knew, of course, that he wouldn't. As far as he knew, she hadn't even come to the gym as he'd begged her to do, and when he'd finally get her letter, he'd see that, though she actually had been there and had even accepted his apology, she was, nonetheless, ending things for other, more profound reasons. She was resigned to have to live with the finality of her decision. And to relieve some of the pain of that resignation, she rehearsed all the reasons a relationship with Sam would never work. Although she didn't believe half of what she conceived of, it was at least better than wallowing in unmitigated sorrow.

The next morning, Catherine woke up early, dressed for work, and went in to quit. As a longtime and much-trusted employee, she had her own pass to the front door of Banter House Books. And she was, as she'd hoped she'd be, the first person to arrive. As the first person through the door, she was expected to get the coffee going, which she was in the process of doing when Vito showed up.

"Well, well, the detective is back."

"Yes. I solved the case but blew the deal."

"So... what happened? The whole thing sounds absolutely insane."

"It was. Some of the gory details will be in the trades in a day—all of it in front of cameras, the press, and hundreds of fans. It was crazy, Vito. The upshot, my million-dollar offer was as fake as Loretta, and Blushing Dove's five-hundred-thousand-dollar offer being genuine, wins. In the end, there really was no contest. I made a few discoveries, personal and professional, but I've got nothing to show for it. I'm sorry, Vito. I really did try, but..."

Vito sighed loudly, then said, "It wasn't your fault. We don't have the resources to have given you enough ammunition for the kill. I'm sorry. So, welcome back to—what? The stoical last stand on the quarterdeck?"

"No, Vito. I'm here to tell you that I'm going to lighten your ballast, if that's the term, and jump ship."

Vito stared at her for a moment. Then, both angry and hurt, he said, "You can't do that. Well, I mean, you *can*, and maybe you should, but I don't want you to, not to another publisher, not now."

"I'm not going anywhere else. If I'm lucky, my dad will hire me to help him find and sell some of his lower-end books online. There is no one waiting for me—anywhere. I need some time to think about... everything, and in the meantime, I can lighten your financial load, which might help you stay afloat long enough to find the next *real* Loretta and this time get her to sign."

Vito said nothing but simply looked at Catherine, his expression now softened and pained. After a sigh, he said, "You've been the best, Catherine, and I wish I could convince you to stay, but all I'd really be doing would be convincing you to go under with us. Maybe it is best for all of us if you... well, if you find yourself elsewhere."

Catherine fought back tears as she gave Vito a hug. "Thanks, friend. I'm not going far—at least physically. Stay in touch, okay?"

He, too, blinked back tears, and with a high, constricted voice, said, "Will do." They hugged again.

Then Catherine turned and walked decisively to and through the Banter House door for what she was sure would be the last time.

That afternoon, her father did what Catherine had hoped he would; he offered her a job helping him look for and catalog the sellable used books that one could, with a good eye and a bit of luck, find in various second-hand stores in and around the boroughs. She asked him, however, if she could take a day to gather herself before starting. He was tempted, profoundly tempted, to ask her what had happened in California. He knew her job was gone, but that was no surprise with Banter on the financial ropes. He sensed, however, that something more troubling had happened to her out there. Based on the tone of her voice, her evasive answers, and the abruptness of the changes in her life, he suspected that things were not going well romantically. It was not an unknown source of pained introspection for her. But it was hard for her father to ask about such things, and even harder for his daughter to respond. And so he gave her the peace and quiet she needed, and she took it by going on a long walk in the city. The snow flurries of the two days before had, by Tuesday, congealed into a real snowstorm. It was the first big snowstorm of the season. Inconvenient as it was, it was that first burst of soft and all-encompassing weather, an inescapable presence from a world untouched by humans and just the sort of thing that took Catherine out of herself, at least for a while.

That evening, she called Rachel. To her, and to her alone, she related pretty much everything that had happened, although she did not fully describe the extent of her attraction and the depth of her disappointment. Not that Rachel needed to have it spelled out. She could hear in her friend's voice how very unhappy she was.

True to style, Rachel tried to make Catherine laugh. She could be very funny, but when all humor failed, she realized that Catherine was—and would for some time be—truly suffering. And so, after they hung up, Rachel rushed a huge bouquet of roses to her ailing friend. On Friday, another package arrived full of assorted dark chocolate, a postcard of Central Park with the handwritten message *Watch When Harry Met Sally. Love ya, Rachel,* a bar of lilac-scented French soap, and the self-help bestseller *Women Who Love Too Much.* Catherine devoured all the chocolates as soon as she opened the package. She very much enjoyed the transportingly foreign smell of the soap. She watched *When Harry Met Sally;* she'd seen it twice before, but on this third viewing, she found it amusing, though the romantic parts were more painful than the funny parts were funny. And she immediately cataloged *Women Who Love Too Much* and added it to her father's online bookstore. She didn't want advice about love. She wanted to forget everything about it.

# CHAPTER 37

Unfortunately, she couldn't. By that time, everyone in book group had, in one way or another, received the news—Loretta de Bonnair turned out to be a gorgeous, young, and very romantic-sounding cowboy, and, apparently, Banter House didn't get a book contract with him. What had happened? By Saturday, all the members of the group, except for Rachel, who already knew the details of Catherine's misadventure, had asked that question in text or e-mail. Catherine contemplated ignoring all of their queries, but to have remained silent would have fueled even more insistent concern and wild speculation. Although the circumstances were unique, the situation was anything but. She'd begun to fall in love but ended up falling on her face. It was an old story, and no one needed to know about this particular case, except that everyone did. So to all, she wrote the same terse response: I'll see you on Monday at the party with hummus and details.

That next Monday, details were, indeed, forthcoming, but not right away. When Catherine didn't mention anything about California or Loretta or Sam when she arrived at Rachel's apartment, it was clear that whatever had happened wasn't going to be a funny, lighthearted tale. Adding to the collective inference that the story would be more painful than playful was her expression, a sort of proud grace in response to some not-so-distant tumult. It said, *Don't ask—I'll tell you soon enough.*

The format of this annual year-end party was certainly conducive to unrestrained conversation. Each member was to talk about a favorite book—and why it was a favorite. Now in its third year, no one had ever picked a favorite that was anyone else's, which led to some enjoyably impassioned discussions. Consistent with her reserved demeanor, Catherine spoke last. She also spoke in a tone completely different from all the others. There was no passion at all in her voice, just subdued resolve.

"I'm going to read an excerpt from something I never thought I'd have chosen as one of my favorites, but, somewhat regrettably, it is...." So saying, she pulled a copy of *Rancho de Amor* out of her capacious purse. No one said a word. No one even made a sound. Catherine was, herself, capable of powerfully understated drama, and this was certainly an example of that. Unfazed by the silence, she carefully opened the book to the first of many marked pages and, after explaining where this passage was in the plot, slowly read:

Wanting not only to *be* but to *look* like the man who held another man's life in his hands, the newly appointed local magistrate, Don Domingues, tugged at the lapels of his borrowed robes and tried, unsuccessfully, to pull them together over his irreducible girth. The former magistrate, whose robes these had been, was a much smaller man, and the far more capacious robes Domingues had ordered from Madrid six months before had yet to arrive.

Giving up on distinguished appearance, Domingues leaned over the bar heavily and addressed the defendant in a supercilious tone, "And how do you plead... *Sir?*"

"Guilty of everything but malicious intent. I shot a man who'd shot at me—and he died. I ordered my men to ransack the Orlando house for any valuables we could sell for provisions. I am a traitor to Spain and a confrere of those who fight for an independent Mexico. And I am guilty of loving someone who is forbidden to love me. I am yours to do with as you will, Your Lordship... *Sir.*" To this, the audience in the overcrowded gallery reacted with a mix of jeers and cheers, gasps of disbelief, revulsion, pity, and even a tear or two.

The forbidden one, however, did not cry. She had done more than enough of that already. Stoically, she sat unmoved, though her heart and mind were racing.

It may not have been Pynchon, Didion, or Patchett, but it was certainly moving, and pretty much everyone wanted her to read more when she stopped. Instead, she put the book down and asked, "So, is this the right time to tell you what happened with Loretta de Bonnair?" Immediately, she heard a nervous and collective chuckle and "yes," "you bet," "finally."

To her rapt and sympathetic audience, she calmly related the relevant details: the funny, surprising, inspiring, and depressing. When she got to the end, with Sam's unmasking in the East Valley High School gym and her painful, embarrassed escape, she had to stop and re-discipline her demeanor. Her pain was beginning to leak out more than she wanted.

Into this pause, various friends poured their sage advice:

"He sounds a little confused."

"And confusing."

"He also lied."

"Which really isn't good."

"If he can wriggle off the hook that easily..."

"...He's obviously not worth the effort."

"So forget about him, honey," Rachel concluded. "Seriously, there are a lot more cowboys in the sea."

# CHAPTER 38

It might, in fact, be true that there are a lot of cowboys in the sea, but the more Catherine thought about Sam, the more convinced she was that only one of those cowboys could be right for her. She didn't want to believe this, and she resisted the idea with as many damning recollections of him as she could think of. But the strength of these thoughts was easily overwhelmed by her recollections of the things she liked—even loved—about him. And the more she thought about Sam, the more foolish she felt for having yanked her hook out of the water just as he was about to bite.

Even though her feelings tempted her to fly back to California and confront him, she knew this would be at least as foolish. That move would be way too bold, particularly given the fact that, as of yet, Sam had made no overture—not even the slightest hint—of his courageous, vulnerable, and continuing interest in her. Just an e-mail or a brief text would've done it, but neither came. She felt she was in the middle of an emotional showdown with Sam. They'd walked their transcontinental paces from one another and now stood, afraid to draw, afraid to show their potentially disastrous commitment. But if no one pulled the trigger, they'd never know what might've been. She was the one who'd left, and, in so doing, the one who'd said no. In her heart of hearts, she knew she was the one who'd have to make the first move, the one who'd have to pull the trigger and change "no" to "maybe." And so, the next morning, she penned a new note:

Dear Sam,
Honestly, I am not exhibiting courageous vulnerability, at least not yet, but I can't stop feeling a sort of courageous curiosity. Why have you moved me so deeply, and why can't I forget you? It's not just those beautiful eyes, not just that humble swagger, or your folksy erudition, nor is it what I

heard about what you'd done for your sister, or what I saw you do at the fire. It's not really any of that. Instead, it's that I can't stop wondering what you would think, what you would feel, what you would say about pretty much everything I see these days. I know, I know, we're probably all wrong for each other, city mouse/country mouse, etc., etc., but we do deserve one another. We are, if nothing else, equally capable liars. I'm thinking maybe we could share a lie or two over the phone.

I will certainly understand if you don't respond. I simply needed to tell you I was more final in my last note to you than I think I should have been.

Curiously,
Catherine

Not knowing his e-mail address and not wanting to have to speak or casually text this message, she decided that she would send it by regular mail the quickest way possible: priority express scheduled to arrive at the Circle D Ranch by noon the next day.

Later that afternoon, the phone rang while she was sitting at her computer cataloging books for her father. Stumblingly excited, she jumped up, then stopped herself, realizing that Sam couldn't possibly have received her letter yet. She took a deep breath and slowly walked over to the phone. It most certainly wasn't Sam; it was Ali, the receptionist at Banter House, calling to invite Catherine to come into the office on Friday morning. Ali would not tell her why, but from her tone, Catherine knew that it was going to be the sloppy, sad, but necessary toast to the memory of a fine New York publisher which, with the clink of a glass of champagne, would close its doors and be gone.

It was not something she wanted to be a part of, but when Ali told her that Vito had been especially concerned that she, Catherine, show up, Catherine could really do nothing but accept the gracious offer to "stand on the burning deck" as the ship sank and all of its fires went out. And anyway, the hours she worked for her father were, at the very least, flexible. She could swing by the funeral of her previous place of employment, then go out to the Bronx, where her father wanted her to check the new stock at a couple of usually fertile second-hand stores. The boroughs were good hunting grounds for resalable used cookbooks, coffee table books, popular modern firsts, and romances.

What had been a dull, though not hopeless, pain when she'd sent her last note to Sam became more acute when the only calls she received in the next two days were three unwanted solicitations: one from a recorded someone selling life insurance, one from a recorded someone offering her a romantic, all-expenses-paid vacation for two to Disney World if she would attend a weekend real-estate seminar in Queens, and one from a live someone who warned her that her computer was about to crash unless she immediately let this helpful man on the phone root out the problem, remotely—the man's accent underscoring just how remote that access would likely be.

On Friday morning, Catherine, in no rush to get to the indulgent last rites at Banter House, arrived ten minutes late. When she opened the door, Ali, who seemed to have been waiting for her, said, "Quick, quick, into Vito's office. Everyone is there and waiting for you."

"Me? Why me?"

"I don't know. Probably because you're the last to arrive."

Catherine allowed herself to be ushered by a nervous Ali past a table with thirty champagne flutes roughly equal to the number of people there and six cold-sweating champagne bottles. It was a display waiting for a toast. But at 9 a.m.? Catherine wished she'd saved a bit of her Venti Frappuccino so she could at least raise some sort of liquid at the appropriate moment. She disliked champagne at the best of times, and this was, on many levels, not the best of times.

Things went from odd to inexplicable when Catherine walked into Vito's large office and saw all twenty-seven of the assembled crew crowded in front of a large television screen on a wall.

"What's going on? Was Vito arrested last night?"

"I honestly don't know what it's about, Catherine. Vito won't say. All I know is that he's here, which I guess means he isn't in trouble."

"Not necessarily," Catherine returned. "It just means he's out on bail."

Because there were so many people in his office standing between her and the screen, she couldn't see a thing. When Vito craned his head around and saw her standing in the back, he shouted, "People in front, please sit down on the floor so that the people in the back can see." Then, more calmly, he added, "Hello, Catherine. I'm glad you could make it."

"Hi, Vito," she replied. "Are we watching you win the Super Lotto?"

"No. Not me. Just watch."

She did, and what she saw was even more bizarre. It wasn't the news at all, but one of those morning interview shows taped in Hollywood the day before. Catherine hated this sort of infotainment and had no idea which one it was or why it was on with the entire Banter House staff, past and present, watching it, until she heard the host announce that Loretta de Bonnair was the next guest.

"Loretta de Bonnair?" Catherine asked the space around her, more in surprise than in expectation of an answer. Her question was, however, answered almost immediately when Sam Wilson, in his cowboy hat and boots, walked onto the set and took a seat next to his two young, beautiful, and constantly smiling hosts.

For the next five minutes Catherine could not quite close her mouth as she listened, baffled by what Sam and his interviewers were saying. Even from three thousand miles away and viewed through the lens of a television screen, he was still a thoroughly unnerving presence. He said something about pretending to be a woman, an older woman, so that he'd be eligible for the prize, so that he could channel a woman's sensibility about romance, and so he could successfully hide a few controversial ideas behind a pseudonym. He said something about writing a new book under his own name—"a book," he added, "that will have plenty of romance in it." And he said something about how this whole wild experience had taught him to be more courageously vulnerable in life and in love.

And then it was over. He got up, shook hands with the hosts, and left the set.

Everyone else in Vito's office started to talk, but Catherine was stunned. She didn't know what to make of it. Why was she there, why were *all* of these people there, watching an interview with a man who had become one of the most painful failures both for Banter House and for her? This seemed to be another one of Vito's convivial gaffes. Throw a party to toast a collective failure...

...which, indeed, he began to do when he boomed over the

chatter of his assembled employees, "Here's a toast to our biggest and grandest disappointment..."

Vito was clearly going from embarrassing gaffe to mean-spirited regret, and it seemed to be directed right at Catherine. As she began to feel a rush of anger, Vito continued, "But sometimes the biggest disappointments lead to the biggest opportunities, isn't that right, Ms. de Bonnair?" Vito pointed toward the door behind Catherine.

Everyone, including Catherine, turned as Sam Wilson, also known as Loretta de Bonnair, slowly walked into the room. There was some clapping and a few cheers, but it was an essentially awkward, unresolved moment. Everyone had heard Catherine's story—at least that it affected their jobs—and it wasn't a happy story.

As soon as Sam saw Catherine, he looked at no one else. He stopped in front of her, took off his hat with one hand, and with the other hand delicately presented her heels, dangling from one finger. "I'm still lookin' for the woman who fits into these shoes. She seems to have left them in a restaurant in some small California town."

Catherine took a deep breath but said nothing.

Sam looked her in the eye and said, clearly and calmly, "If Vito wants my new book, he can have it. I waive my advance, though I'll take a little more than customary in royalties. What I do need is a good editor, and there's only one editor in the world I want to work with." He paused, smiled softly, then continued, "I got your letters, both of them, and both a little late. When I got the second one, I'd already talked to Vito. He tried to convince me to sign with Banter, but I said I had one condition that had to be met. Unfortunately, he said that that condition had quit, permanently. It didn't look good until we came up with a kinda theatrical last-ditch way to get what we both wanted. I don't know that you and I deserve each other, as you say in your last letter, but I do know that what began to grow a couple of weeks ago deserves to grow some more so we can see what's really possible. What do ya say?"

Catherine opened her mouth, but because she could barely breathe, she could only whisper, "Yes."

"So... will you come back to Banter House and edit my book?"

Catherine glanced back at Vito, who nodded encouragingly, then she turned back to Sam and said with more theatrical control, "Yes." She was on the verge of screaming, crying, and laughing, but she certainly wouldn't allow herself to indulge in that kind of show. The kind of courageous vulnerability she now allowed herself to feel had nothing to do with show and everything to do with feeling, and she was most definitely feeling.

"And will you consider, just consider, coming out to California, from time to time, to work with me there, mostly on the book, but sometimes to help around the ranch? I'll have some real culling to do soon."

"Yes."

"And, well, will you let me take you to lunch today wherever you'd like in this amazingly vibrant city, which, I must say, I would like to see a whole lot more of on a good and regular basis?"

"Yes."

"And... well, will you let me kiss you? It's been way too long since the last time."

Catherine broke into a huge smile, quickly took a breath, blinked, and rearranged her expression into a combination of hope and challenge. "Yes," she said. "Right here. Right now."

Which,
　　　of course,
　　　　　he did.

THE END

# ACKNOWLEDGMENTS

My thanks to:

Cowboys, lovers, and friends; Jane Austen and Zane Gray; New York City; the Cojo Ranch; Cary Grant, Billy Wilder, Nora Ephron, the Hepburns (Katherine and Audrey)...

and, to name the names of most vital importance:

My excellent editor—Kristen Tate; the smart and adventurous crew at West Margin Press—Jen Newens, Olivia Ngai, Angie Zbornik, and Rachel Metzger: cattleman and (formerly) foreman of the Bixby Ranches: the Cojo and Jalama—Brad Lundberg; executive film producer—Devorah Cutler-Rubenstein and entertainment lawyer—Paul J. Laurin who were the catalysts for the original film treatment of *Rancho* many years ago; the Santa Ynez Valley Historical Museum; the mind-engaging author—Vivian Gornick, whose book, *The End of the Novel of Love*, becomes the hot topic of conversation in Chapter 5; the perceptive, ever-ready reader and re-reader—Don McReynolds; and always first, foremost, and most enduringly inspiring, my bright, beautiful wife—Ora Schulman, and my sons—Joseph and Nathaniel———without all of you, this book wouldn't be.

DAN HARDER is an award-winning playwright, author, and poet, as well as ex-cowboy, truck driver, translator, sculptor, sailing instructor on the Mediterranean, ski instructor in Switzerland, restaurant owner, and teacher (English and Philosophy). His work has received several honors, including a Pulitzer Prize nomination and a James T. Irvine Grant. Dan lives with his wife, Ora Schulman, in San Francisco, California. Learn more at www.danharder.com.